Passion and honor collide in the wild and rugged American West, where one woman's love of adventure is matched by her desire for one man...

Victoria Harrison had no desire to marry to secure her position as heir to her family's lumber business. And she doesn't want to seek a man's help now. But with her prized Great Mountain Lumber Mill threatened by one of her father's old enemies, she needs an ally. She's found one in Wall Adair, the handsome new leader of the notorious gang of rivermen known as the Devil May Cares.

It takes a lot of guts to run the biggest mill this side of the Rocky Mountains, and Wall admires Victoria's determination to do it on her own terms. With each day they spend together, he uncovers a vulnerability hidden deep behind her strong façade. Wall has a duty to uphold—one that'll soon call him away from the freedom he loves and back to his family's ranch. Until then, he'll protect the boss lady with every ounce of his strength... knowing the devil himself can't keep him from losing his heart...

**The Montana Mountain Romance series
by Dawn Luedecke**

White Water Passion

Wild Passion

Fiery Passion

FIERY PASSION

A Montana Mountain Romance

Dawn Luedecke

LYRICAL PRESS
Kensington Publishing Corp.
www.kensingtonbooks.com

First Electronic Edition: September 2018
eISBN-13: 978-1-5161-0345-4
eISBN-10: 1-5161-0345-9

First Print Edition: September 2018
ISBN-13: 978-1-5161-0348-5
ISBN-10: 1-5161-0348-3

Printed in the United States of America

To Taylor Scott, owner of The Missoulian Angler. Thanks for helping me with my research on fish and the Montana rivers. I can't wait to have you as my river guide when I come back home.

Glossary

Bateau—A flat-bottomed boat used to assist the rivermen. Often the men would loosen a log 'nest' and then fling themselves into the bateau to avoid being sucked down into the dangerous white water beneath the logs.

Bib and tucker—Fine clothes

Big Bug—An important or official person. The boss.

Blowhard—Braggart, bully.

Chute—A makeshift sloping channel constructed of special treated wood to get the logs from the forest to the lake.

Dandy—City person.

Doxology works—Church

Faller—The logger actively chopping/sawing down the tree.

Fisticuffs—Fighting with fists, boxing.

Flume—An artificial channel, which uses a stream of water in the chute to transport logs.

Full Turn—Full load

Greenhorn—An unexperienced person.

Homeboy—Loggers from the local community.

Hoosegow—Prison, jail.

Knock his galley west—Beat senseless.

Lady of the First Water—Elegant woman.

Log jam—A crowded mass of logs blocking the river.

Pugilist—A boxer

Raft—A group of logs tied together to be taken down the river to the mill.

River Drive—The movement of the logs from the lumber camp, down the rivers and lakes, and to the mill.

Riverman—A logger who rides the logs down the rivers and lakes to bring them to the mill.

River Rat—A riverman who drifts from lumber camp, to lumber camp, working only as long as they want to stay in the area.

Shindig—A large party. A social event.

Shin out—Run away.

Soaked—Drunk

The Grove—The area where active logging is taking place.

Timber beast—A logger who works the timber.

Travois—A type of sled formerly used by North American Indians using two poles joined together, and typically dragged behind an animal.

Wannigan—A cook raft constructed with a crude building on top. Often the building would contain bunks for the river men to sleep if needed.

Widowmaker—A dead branch balancing precariously high in a tree, which could fall and kill a man without notice.

Chapter 1

Missoula, Montana Territory, Spring 1889

Wall Adair sat back to enjoy the scene as Victoria Harrison—the new owner of Great Mountain Lumber Mill—tiptoed with her dainty, silk-covered slippers through the ankle-high mud. Somewhere between the train depot and the stockyards, Victoria had parked her expensive buggy. Now she picked her way across a street even he didn't like to trudge through. The question was why?

Not that he didn't enjoy the show.

In all his years working for the daring woman's father, and now the woman herself, he'd only met her the year before when she'd visited the camp, thinking herself engaged to Garrett—the old leader of the rivermen known to all as the Devil May Cares. She'd flounced into camp, snubbing all but Garrett.

Now Wall would return to work and find out just what sort of woman could run the biggest lumber mill this side of the Rocky Mountains. Especially since she couldn't be much older than twenty-five, at most.

A viper, no doubt.

Curious, Wall leapt from his seat on the top rung of the fence just in time to splash mud on her full, dark blue skirt. He cringed, expecting to hear a screech similar to the ones his four sisters gave whenever he offended their wardrobes. Like his pa taught him, he swept his large brimmed cowboy hat off his head, and ducked his chin. "Sorry, ma'am. I didn't mean to—"

"It's fine. I needed to clean my dress anyway, and today is washday." She said the words with a quaver of encouragement, but he didn't believe it for even a moment. Not when she swiped at it furiously with her gloved hand, only to spread it along the fine fabric. He tipped half his mouth back in a grin at the sight. The top of her shoulders dropped, and she stared at him once more with a frown.

He smoothed the edge of his hat between the pinched fingers of his left hand. Every time her eyes met his, his stomach flipped like he'd just launched from a log into the deadly white water beneath a log jam. And he hated the listless feeling of falling into the unknown. "Can I help you with something?"

"I was looking for Garrett."

"At the stockyards?" He didn't bother to hide his shock. Garrett owned the local railroad company, but the train wasn't due to pick up the traded bulls at the stockyards for another day, and his friend wasn't always on it. Unless Victoria was shut away in her white tower for the last twenty-something years, she knew the train schedule. Everyone in Missoula did. "Is there something I can help you with?"

Victoria pursed her lips and flicked her gaze out past the train station building. Wall followed her line of sight, but the only thing he could pick out that the daft woman might possibly stare at was the train depot itself—a few hundred yards away, past sections of muck and the rail lines.

He propped one muddy foot on the bottom rung of the fence, and leaned on his knee. The Lord hadn't skimped on materials when he made Victoria Harrison, but she knew as much. With long, dark hair and eyes to match the most delicious chocolate dessert at a fancy table. She possessed beauty, brains, and a bit of sass, which made a woman like her irresistible. Too bad she was the boss, and dead set on being the man of whatever household she graced.

While one hand grasped a folded piece of paper, she reached up with the second to rub the sapphire stone in the silver necklace she wore, still staring off into the distance. Silence stretched between them until his gut twisted in concern. Not for the venomous woman before him, but because he knew that look. She'd gotten herself in some sort of trouble.

"Miz Victoria?" he questioned, and let his foot drop to the ground once more, hoping it would be enough to break into whatever thoughts caused her eyes to change from the color of well-oiled leather, to the hue of the filthy mud staining her dress.

"My apologies." She glanced around the stockyards with her brows drawn together and lips pinched tight. Whatever caused the wrinkle in her forehead didn't sit right. She may be a vixen hell-bent on getting her way, but the look in her eyes was like the one his troublemaking sister, Willa, got whenever she needed help. If there was one thing that could get his attention, it was a woman in need. Victoria threw back her shoulders. "Do you know where Garrett might be? There's a matter of some importance I need his help with."

"He and Beth took off up the mountain this morning to offload my steam pulley. He won't return until tomorrow night. He's gotta come back to pick up the loader, men, and supplies."

Victoria's shoulders dropped once more, and she glanced back at the spot as if she expected a bull to come charging around the corner.

Wall took a step closer to her. "What do you need? I can help until Garrett gets back."

"No. I'll be fine. Now, if you'll excuse me." She bowed her head slightly and turned to walk away. He studied the sway of her hips as she picked her way through the muck. The filthy hem of her skirts dragged in the mud like a child who didn't want to go to Sunday services. Where in the world is she going? Her fancy carriage was parked in the opposite direction from where she walked now, but she'd headed toward whatever spot she'd stared at while they spoke. Wall always listened to his gut, and his gut told him that something wasn't right.

"I swear on the Good Book," he mumbled out loud, "if she's headed toward something dangerous, I'll kill her myself."

"Who are you going to kill?" He recognized his brother's voice, and turned as Jax stopped next to him. The youngest of the Adair brood, and only other male in the family besides their father and grandpap, whom they called Pappy. The kid had grown significantly over the last season and now rivaled Wall in height. In another year or two he'd be looking up at his younger brother—who otherwise could have been his mirror image.

Wall motioned toward where Victoria finally managed to find a dry patch of land to walk on. "My boss lady." He slapped his brother on the shoulder. "You wouldn't mind taking care of the bulls, would you? I've got something I need to do before we head to the hotel."

"Pappy wants to meet us when were finished so we can eat."

"I'll find you at the hotel if I'm done on time. If not, then tell Pappy I had some business to attend to. He should be fine with it unless he wants us to tell Pa he left us to sell the bulls alone while he went and shopped for a new cowboy hat and boots like a woman."

"I ain't telling him that," his brother said with a frown. "But I will make an excuse for you as long as I don't have to come bail you out of the hoosegow for murderin' your boss."

"Murder isn't what I'd like to do with that woman." Wall gave a half-smile and glanced over his brother's shoulder to where the bulls they'd driven over that morning stomped restlessly in the holding pen. "Make certain they give you no less than a thousand for the lot. If they try to bulldoze you, then tell them no deal."

"But Pa told us not to come home with the bulls. He don't care how much they give us."

"You, me, and Pappy knows that, but the buyers don't. Keep a hard stare and you'll get what you asked for. Especially for these bulls."

His brother nodded, and Wall rushed past, studying the corner of the building where Victoria had disappeared moments before. His gut told him to hurry. Whatever the woman was into, and no matter how independent she fancied herself, she needed a man.

Wall rounded the building in time to see the flash of her blue dress swishing into an alley across the street, and his stomach tightened as his blood pumped hard through his veins. What in the Good Lord's name was she doing?

He searched the streets, but other than a few passersby oblivious to anyone not in their paths, no one appeared to give one wit about Victoria's business. Except him. With care to avoid the piles of manure dotting the streets, he followed her into the alley, and slid among the shadows as best he could.

Halfway down the line of buildings, Victoria stood partially turned away from him as she met with Luther, a man who had been fired from the mill last season. Wall pressed his back against the building to keep out of sight as he picked his way silently down the alley.

Victoria gasped as if needing extra air, and she crumbled the paper in her hands as Luther scowled and mumbled something low enough only she could hear.

Wall inched his way closer until Luther's words were clear enough to understand.

"If you don't, Miz Harrison," Luther said. "I can't guarantee you'll make it past this season."

Victoria lifted her chin. "I will not be blackmailed by a bunch of vagrants, and I certainly won't be bulldozed by their half-wit lackey. You can tell your friends that should they set foot near my camps, they will be shot on sight. And believe me when I say, my men don't miss. They may be a bunch of hardened loggers, but they are crackpot shots."

"I know all too well what sort of men you employ up there. I can stop this from happening, but not if you aren't willing to help yourself. Take the deal."

"No."

"You don't know what you're getting yourself into. It'd be best if you were back home worrying about how to find a man too blind to see you're flaws as a woman." Luther pressed his hand over his chest with fingers splayed across the frayed shirt fabric. "You're in over your head. You're going to fail. I'm just trying to help you out here. I wouldn't want you to grow old all alone."

Victoria opened her mouth to speak and took a step forward.

"There you are," Wall said, emerging from the shadow before she had a chance to respond. "I thought the meeting was in the alley behind the bank." Wall hurried to stand next to her, looped is arm around her waist, and tugged her protectively to his side. He didn't trust Luther not to hit a woman. The man was no better than a river rat.

Victoria's lashes fluttered as she peered up at him. Her lips puckered as though the words had frozen in her mouth, and brown eyes flashed somewhere between shock and gratitude. *Lordy* she was pretty. Even with her face stuck in a funny expression. Pretty and dangerous, judging by the earful he was going to receive for interfering.

He smiled down at her, and then turned his attention back to Luther. "I meant to be here before Miz Victoria so I could send you packing with a warning or two to remember."

Luther snarled. "You're not involved in this, Wall, stay out."

"Miz Victoria's safety is of utmost concern to me. I will not stay out of Great Mountain business as long as she's in danger."

"You mean Big Mountain business. It's the Big Mountain Lumber Mill." Luther's face twitched.

"Us homeboys like to call it Great Mountain 'cause that's what it is to the people of Bonner. Great. Great for the town, and great for the lives of the people within."

Luther curled his lips back. "You're all the same, you Devil boys. Sticking your nose where it shouldn't be, and actin' like the world belongs to you."

"This world does. See, I'm a sort of business partner now, and I believe she gave you her answer. If you ever threaten her, or any other woman at Great Mountain again then you can guarantee I'll snap every bone in your body before feeding you to the wolf pack that lives near the logging camp." Wall gave him a smile and tipped his hat before picking up Victoria's hand and entwining it through his arm to guide her out of the alley, leaving the sniveling little fool to stutter to himself.

They rounded the corner to the nearest building when Victoria regained her composure, and yanked her arm from his. "What did you do?"

"From what I saw, I saved your pretty little hide."

"You've ruined everything."

"I beg your pardon?"

"You went and lied about our partnership, and they certainly aren't going to take me seriously as a businesswoman now if they think I have a man calling the shots."

"I hate to break it to you, but they don't take you seriously...as a..." He stopped talking once her icy glare permeated his thoughts.

She halted, and crossed her arms. If it wasn't for the mud and dung bogging down her feet, he suspected she'd be tapping one impatient foot.

"Don't stop now," he urged, hoping she wasn't going to be the one to go to the hoosegow for murdering him. "You're standing in the middle of horse shit."

She jerked her gaze down and yanked up her skirts to view her feet, ankle deep in manure. Wall chuckled as her chin quivered. She tried valiantly to walk with dignity, but tripped.

He might find the whole situation amusing were the pathetic person in question anyone but Victoria Harrison. Without waiting for her to argue, he took her elbow and entwined her arm through his once more. As expected, she fought to yank her hand free.

"Don't get your back up. My ma taught me to always help a woman cross the street." He studied Victoria's raised chin, and chuckled. Even a woman as surly and vulnerable as the one by his side. "I would do the same for a big ol' barmaid named Gertrude were she the one to step in dung."

"Aren't you the charmer," Victoria quipped, as she leaned onto his arm for support.

"Gertrude has never complained." He smiled, and maneuvered so they walked along the less muddy sections of the stockyard as they progressed toward her pretty little buggy.

"I'm certain she hasn't." Victoria straightened her back and eased her arm away from him when she was once more on solid land. "Do you even know what you've entangled yourself in by interfering back there?"

"From what I gather, you're an easy target because you're a woman in a man's world, and should be back home finding a husband who will look past your advanced age and manly disposition."

She answered by growling at him and stepping hard into her buggy.

"What did I say? Is there more to it?"

"Stay out of my business, Mr. Adair. Else you might find yourself being nothing but a filthy cowboy for the rest of your life. You certainly won't work at Great Mountain if you irritate me further. I can always find another logger eager to fill your position with the Devil May Cares."

Without another word, she snapped the reins and sent her buggy rolling, barely missing his toes as he stepped back.

Wall shrugged, and turned to check for his brother among the cattle and cowboys, but he wasn't there. He headed toward his horse. Victoria was right about one thing—if he wasn't careful he could lose his job at the lumber camp. And it would make his pappy and pa damn happy to have him back home to help on the homestead.

He wasn't ready to settle down on the Lazy Heart Ranch. Not just yet.

Victoria's spirit reminded him of the bay mustang he'd tamed five years ago. Wild and unmanageable. The mare had bucked and kicked whenever anyone tried to approach her, even took one of their cowhand's fingers clean off with one good bite, but in the end, Wall had won the battle. It had taken him almost a year to gain the animal's trust, but by God he'd broken the beast with a strong hand and hard determination. Maybe what Victoria needed was to be tamed like the mare.

* * * *

Victoria lifted her skirts as she climbed the steps to her father's house. The muck from the stockyards had long since dried on her shoes and hem, and the extra weight made the fine lace aligning the bottom of her dress heavy against her shins with each step. The gown was ruined, but it couldn't be helped. She had to address the blackmailer who'd sent her the letter earlier that morning and, to her great disappointment, without Garrett there to stand by her side as partner.

And then Wall—with his irritating smile and patronizing comments— showed up out of nowhere to intervene just as she was gaining ground in her battle. Didn't he know the blackmailers wanted to see her fail because she was a woman? And his interference had done nothing but help to prove the blackmailers right in their assumptions. They knew she worked with Garrett, but Wall's interference gave the impression she'd taken on a man in her life. One to take care of business for her. It would make them think she was weak in matters of business, and maybe she was, but it wasn't because she was a woman.

It was because she wasn't cutthroat enough. She'd expanded her father's business into railroad logging by making an equally beneficial deal with Garrett. One where they'd agreed to work together based on her managing Great Mountain as she'd always wanted…only this deal gave her free rein to do so without having to share the responsibility with a husband. To her surprise, her father had accepted the business arrangement with only minimum argument.

She'd gambled by adding a few dozen more workers to the camps. And who was to say if the risk would pay off in the end? It had better, or else she chanced running her company into the ground the very first year she took it over from her father.

What she needed to do was show her authority not only to her workers, but her rivals as well. But how?

"Victoria, is that you?" her father called from his study as she walked through the ornate front door, and shut it behind her.

She dropped her head to the side to stretch the tight muscles in her neck, and yanked her gloves from her fingers. Tossing them on the side table next to the front door, she hurried into her father's study.

"Ah, it is you," he said from his favorite wing-backed chair next to the large fireplace. "Good. Have you seen this article in *The Missoulian* about Hartland, Montana?"

"No." She sat into the chair opposite him and settled her skirts in an attempt to hide the filth.

"It seems Hartland is a little nothing town up the road from the mill. The mountains around the town are belly full of Douglas fir," her father said, folded his newspaper to fit in one hand, and peered at her from over the top of his spectacles. "And you know who needs a mountain's worth of fir, don't you?"

Lordy, this is a test. Although the man claimed to have retired, he loved to whip the reins from the back of the wagon. Not that she wasn't grateful for his help. Over the last year he'd taken her to task over the workings of the mill so he could take her mother to visit her sister in Washington, and that time was fast approaching.

But she had no idea who needed a mountain's worth of Douglas fir. She shook her head and held her breath, hoping he wouldn't reprimand her like he was apt to do when disappointed.

Instead, he slapped his knee with the newspaper and lifted his head when he said, "The railroad company. With Garrett expanding the lines for the new logging operation, he's going to need those trees."

"I'd venture to guess he already has a supplier."

"Yes," her father said. "Us, and we're running low. We need to broaden our reach, and Garrett's given us the means to do so with his railroad logging contraptions."

"So you think I should get the rights to log up there? Move the company?"

"Well, not today, obviously, you have a season coming up and plenty of trees where you are. But it's something to think about."

"Garrett is away on business. When he returns I'll speak with him, and then talk to Gustav to get the land rights from the town of Hartman. He seems like a good enough lawyer."

"He is," her father agreed. "Gustav told me Laughlin Hartman, the owner of the biggest ranch around these parts, well, he brought some cattle in today. See if you can't track him down and feel him out." Her father pulled his pocket watch out by the chain, and flicked it open, squinting at the face through his spectacles. "I imagine he should be finding a good place to eat right about now."

Victoria tipped her head to the side. "Why would we need to talk to a rancher?"

Her father peered at her from over his spectacles again. "Because he owns the town and all of the land around it. You need to meet with him. Charm him. See if he's open to selling the rights, or even some land."

"I thought you were retired?" she asked, giving him a teasing grin. "And letting *me* take over the family business. After I so subtly convinced you I didn't need a husband to run the mill."

Her father chuckled at her jest, for the way in which she escaped a marriage with Garrett was far from subtle.

"I am letting you run the mill, my dear," he said. "With Paul watching your every move until he's certain you're ready to go at it alone."

"Yet here you are, orchestrating a new endeavor."

"Discovering, more like. All the logistics I'll leave to you." Her father reclined back in his chair, and snapped open his newspaper once more. Successfully bringing their conversation to a close. Which she was happy for. Her skirts were all but begging to be tossed into the wash bin.

Victoria rose from her chair, and then leaned over to kiss her father on the cheek.

"Give that dress to Ms. Bates to wash before your mother sees you. You'll send her into a tither if she sees you've been traipsing around a hog barn in your French lace."

"Is she upstairs?"

"In the kitchen," he answered, and then turned back to his reading.

Victoria tiptoed in her no doubt smelly slippers down the hallway and up the stairs, flinching when the middle step squeaked. She wanted to change and escape without her mother knowing she was even at their Missoula home.

Lately, Victoria had been living with a small staff at their Bonner home, and only came into town for necessary social events and when her mother called her back. Her parents, however, had opted to stay in town, much to her father's irritation. But whatever her mother wished, her father supplied. At least that's how their relationship had been ever since her father had decided to retire.

It was sweet really. After several decades of sacrifice and tears on her mother's part, she was rewarded with a newly retired, doting husband who did nothing but please his bride of twenty-five years.

If only Victoria could find a man who loved her as much as her father did her mother. She'd fancied herself above such frivolity until Garrett had pleaded to be released from their engagement because he was deeply in love with Elizabeth Sanders. She'd released him, and ever since then had envied the looks lovers shared, and not just her parents or Garrett and Elizabeth, but any couple who peered at each other with that certain look in their eyes. She dreamed that one day she could be so lucky.

But first she must concentrate on making the mill even more successful than her father did. Not to mention fight off a couple of blackmailers who wanted to see her fail. Who were these men, anyway? Whoever it was had to be a coward to send another man to talk for him. She preferred to do business in person.

Not bothering to ring for help from Ms. Bates, she struggled to change into a simple white, high-necked blouse and black walking skirt. Opting for the sturdier work boots she loved to wear at the mill. When she'd set out that morning to run errands, she hadn't anticipated getting a threatening letter or meeting a nefarious lackey in an alley across from the stockyards—or stepping in horse manure, for that matter—so she'd worn slippers and a dainty dress suitable for tea with bosom friends, not barn work.

Victoria laced her shoes, and stood back to look at herself in the mirror. Satisfied, she ran a quick hand over her hair to smooth the loose tendrils, and sniffed to ensure she no longer smelled like manure. How cowboys could stand to walk around reeking of sweaty horse, or worse, was beyond her comprehension. Of course, Wall did have a more pleasant smell. Like leather and musky soap. As if he were the odd sort of cowboy who bathed more than once a month.

But she much preferred the scent of fresh-cut lumber. Wood was clean. It was earthy and light. Sure you might get a little sawdust on your shoes, but sawdust didn't make you smell like you'd only just come back from lunch with a pig.

She scooped up her ruined dress and, with as much care as she could take to stifle her footsteps and avoid her mother and the servants, made her way downstairs and out the side door. She searched the yard for Ms. Bates, but to her relief she was nowhere to be seen. She deposited her dress in the wicker basket next to the wash bin. Ms. Bates wasn't going to be happy that she'd dropped the laundry in the basket without even a word as to her being at home, but that couldn't be helped. She had to find Laughlin Hartman and charm him. Luckily for her, she was just as charming as a businesswoman as she was in society.

An hour and one hefty bribe later, she slipped through the doors to the quaintest little café she'd failed to ever notice before, and immediately picked out the man she sought. A weathered man who, at one point in his life, had left hearts scattered around Montana, maybe even all the way to the Mississippi River—based on a surprisingly good description from the desk clerk at the Grande Hotel.

She took a deep breath and made her way to his table.

He glanced up as she neared, and smiled. The knot in her stomach eased a bit.

"Good evening, sir." She held out her hand to him. "I'm Victoria Harrison of Great Mountain Lumber Mill. I want to talk to you about a deal I believe would be beneficial to both of us. May I?" She pointed toward an empty seat across from him.

He shook her hand and nodded toward the seat. She took it.

"Now before you go assuming I'm here for scandalous reasons," she began, not giving him time to introduce himself. "I own the mill and am talking solely of a business arrangement."

The man chuckled. "I wouldn't have assumed any different, Miz Harrison. Not with the way you came up to my table. Name's Laughlin Hartman, by the way."

"Yes, I know who you are. You own Hartland and the land surrounding it."

"My family does, yes."

"I hear you've got more trees than you can imagine up there. I'd like to purchase the rights to log those trees."

"I'm sorry, miss, but I can't sell. We need that land for our cows."

"I can offer you one hundred dollars above the going price."

Her stomach dropped when he shook his head. "It ain't the money. The land and everything on it has been Hartman land for quite some time now."

"We wouldn't bother your operation, or impede on anything but what is contracted to us. The only thing you'll lose from it is the trees we take."

He sat back and stretched one arm along the back of the chair next to him. "Them trees is what makes the land what it is. Without them, it's just dirt." "Would you consider selling me a piece of the mountain? From what I understand you have thousands of acres up there under your name."

"That's true, but I can't. Sorry," he said, and then straightened in his seat as the waitress brought him a plate overflowing with food.

Victoria's teeth began to ache and she realized she'd clenched her jaw. "I understand." She stood. "I won't bother you during your meal, but you can be confident that I will bother you again on the subject."

"I look forward to it," he said with a smile. "We're the second road on the left once you go through Hartland. Follow that road until you can't anymore, and that's where we live."

Victoria nodded her goodbye and left.

She wasn't finished fighting for the trees in Hartland, but she was smart enough to know when she needed to bow out and reassess. At the least she'd planted a seed, so to speak. She would get the contract with Mr. Hartman. Even if she had to use her feminine charms. Which, by the looks of the older man she left in the café, was more than likely the way to his grove.

The bell above the café door jingled as she left. As it closed she moved to duck past two cowboys who entered.

"Miz Victoria?" a familiar voice said. She peered up into frighteningly blue eyes.

"Wall," she said breathlessly.

Wall swiped his hat off his head, and a young man with a striking resemblance to him did the same. Like he'd done before, he smoothed the brim of his hat between his rough, calloused fingers. "Are you having supper?"

"No. A meeting, but I'm finished."

"I notice you've changed. Is your dress ruined?" He ran his hand down the front of his pant leg.

"I don't know. I've left it with our maid."

"Again, I'm sorry I got mud on your skirts. I can replace the dress if you'd like. My sisters should be coming into town later this month to shop. I can dispatch them to find you a new gown."

"No. Thank you. Even if it's ruined, I have plenty of other dresses. And it was never one of my favorites."

The moment grew silent, but for some reason she didn't want to walk away. Even though the man before her still smelled of leather and sweat. Somehow, the scent wasn't as bad as she remembered, though.

"This is my brother Jax." Wall motioned toward the young man next to him. "We were about to meet our pappy for a bite to eat. Do you want to join us?"

"I'm expected at my parent's house for supper, but thank you."

"Every time we're late at home," the young man said, "our mother whups us with her spoon."

"Sounds dreadful," Victoria said with a smile. Up until recently she'd accompanied her mother almost everywhere, so she'd never had an issue with being tardy to the table at home. She had no idea how her mother would react.

"It don't hurt." The young man flicked a glance inside the window.

"I suppose we should let you go." Wall placed his hat back on his head.

His brother did the same, and then excused himself and walked into the café, leaving her alone with Wall, who watched the door until it shut, and then turned to her. "No one bothered you again today, did they?" The tone in his voice showed a concern she didn't quite expect.

"No. I went straight to my father's home, and then here."

"I want to apologize for earlier. I was out of line. You are my boss, and I will respect that in the future. I would like to help with whatever I can," he began, and then held out his hands to stop the argument she opened her mouth to give. "Before you get riled up, I'm not trying to step on your toes. I won't pretend to be your partner in the future, but I would like to help. I'll stay out of your business, as long as I can be there in case anything untoward happens. I don't trust Luther."

If Wall promised to remain silent and be nothing but her muscle, would it be so bad to have him help her overcome her blackmailer? After all, she was a woman, and physically no challenge for a man if he were inclined to attack her. "Will you stay quiet and not interfere?"

"Promise."

"Where should I send for you if I receive another summons?"

"I'm staying at the Grande Hotel for another two days. Until we leave for the lumber camp."

"I'll fetch you if something comes up."

Wall's head fell back a fraction and his lips parted, curving in a slight smile as if he'd won. The knot in her stomach tightened. Had she just made a mistake letting him into her life in such a way?

Chapter 2

Wall stood next to the wagon outside the Grande Hotel as his brother and pappy stowed their belongings in the back. He waited for his pappy to climb into the wagon, and then turned to Jax. "Keep the girls out of the Miller's pond. One of these days they're going to get shot for trespassing, and we have a perfectly good swimming hole on our own ranch."

"They don't listen to me," Jax said as he mounted and settled on the buckboard seat. "They say they're older and know better what's good for them."

"Georgiana is only a year older than you," Wall pointed out. Although only a year older than his brother, his sister did indeed treat Jax as though he was still a baby. Regardless of the fact that he was a good foot taller.

"It's up to you to watch over them while I'm gone. You know how much trouble they like to get into."

"He's right," his pappy interjected. "Your pa is busy with the herd, and with my hip acting up the way it is, I'm no longer young enough to chase around four spirited women."

"Why don't you quit lumberjacking and come home?" Jax gave him a pained look.

"'Cause you need to learn how to deal with women. They don't change the older you get. Only their problems do."

His brother's face remained with the same downcast frown. "I'll keep an eye on them."

"Thank you," Wall said, and stepped back from the wagon. "I'll come home for good in a year or two. Promise."

Jax didn't answer, but settled his attention on something across the street.

Pappy pulled on his leather gloves. "He'll get over it by the time you come home."

"I suspect he will," Wall said, knowing his brother had heard. Besides the rivermen he worked with, Jax was the one person on earth who he didn't want to disappoint.

"We're all anxious for you to quit that wood business and come home, Wallace. Your pa needs you."

"Soon." Wall knew it was only a matter of time before he'd have to leave logging behind, but he'd only just become leader of the Missoula crew river loggers, known to most as the Devil May Care boys. He needed another year or two, and then he'd settle down.

"What's the name of the company you work for?" Pappy asked.

"Great Mountain Lumber Mill. Why?"

"Curious is all." Pappy snapped the reins, and over his shoulder said, "We'll be seeing you."

Wall waited for a few seconds before walking back into the hotel. He'd intended to retire to his room to tidy up before leaving to the rail yards to tinker with the lumber machines that Garrett hadn't yet taken to the camp, but before he could leave the lobby, the desk clerk hailed him over. "A boy brought this for you a few minutes ago."

Wall took the letter, mumbled his thanks, and read the note. The beautiful scroll could only come from a woman, and the only woman he knew in town who would be writing him was Victoria.

He pocketed the missive, and pivoted toward where he left his horse tied to the post near the livery.

When Victoria had promised to let him help her, he didn't think she'd meant to make good on her word. If she was summoning him to her Missoula home, then something must have happened.

Victoria's father's home sat high against the small hill nestled beneath the large Montana town. By the time a quarter of an hour ticked by, Wall stopped his horse before the gate along the front. If there was a way to enter the yard with a mount, he couldn't see one. With no other options, he dismounted and tied the horse to the tall, black spikes that formed the gate, and headed up the walk.

He'd not more than rapped on the door twice before Victoria opened it, urging him to enter with a wave of her hand.

"Everything all right?" he asked.

"No."

He stared hard at her hand when she grabbed his and towed him into a nearby parlor. Her fingers were warm beneath his, and made his mind focus on nothing but the feel of her soft skin. She shut the door behind him. "It's much more than I thought."

"The blackmail?"

"Yes," she said and started to pace. "It's not just Luther, but Sanchez as well."

Wall shook his head. "Who's Sanchez?"

"The man with the cane. The one Beth overheard bribe my workers to destroy the river drive last year."

"I thought your father took care of him."

She nodded. "He did, but he's back."

"What does he want?"

She shook her head. "I don't know. I thought Luther was just trying to exact revenge with some meaningless threats. But Sanchez waited until Father took Mother on her morning walk, and then stopped by to deliver this."

She handed him the paper, and he read the memorandum. "They're looking to make the land the lumber camps are on into agriculture land? Did you show this to your father?"

"Of course." She began to pace before him. "I mentioned it when he got back, but he said the politicians over in Helena have been threatening to do this for years. No more logging permits unless they are government-run mills. He says there was nothing in the threat before, and there's nothing in it now."

"So why call me? You don't believe him?"

"No."

"Because of Sanchez?"

"Precisely. We own most of the land that the camps are on, but we also have a permit for just outside our boundaries. Sanchez delivering the memorandum in person was a threat. And then there's the fact that Representative Nichols has decided to grace Missoula with his presence. The two are connected in some way. Of that I am certain."

"So what would you like me to do?"

She spun around and faced him. Her skirts twisted around her feet at the movement. "The mayor is throwing a party tonight for the Montana Territory Representative. We're going."

He frowned at the words. Not because he hated gatherings—which he did—but because her logic proved difficult to decipher. "You want me to take you to tea at a mayor's house the night before we leave for camp?"

"Not tea. Dinner."

"You didn't want me to help you out before. Why are you so determined now?"

"Because you agreed, and you have knowledge of the agriculture business. I need that."

"Taking me to the party with you would mean you'd have to explain to the whole town why we're together at a social event. Are you going to say I'm courting you?"

"No." She gave him a look as if he were daft. "I'll say you're an acquaintance of mine looking to be introduced into Missoula society."

"That may work. I suppose. I'll see if I brought my best bib and tucker, but I'm fairly certain I left all of my party clothes at home." Wall lounged back in his chair and half smiled. She obviously didn't know who he was, or who he was connected with. Why would she? It wasn't as though his family owned Missoula.

"Buy some new clothes. I'll add twenty dollars to your paycheck to cover the expenses." Victoria's brown eyes flashed with fear and something akin to disdain. "Dress like you're a gentleman of means, and not some poor farmer at a barn raising. This is dinner with politicians, not Aunt June's table, nor beans by the campfire."

"I'm a rancher, not a farmer. And I can afford to buy my own clothes." He said the words with a little more bite than intended. Although she was as pretty as the mountains on a spring morning, she had a tendency to voice every opinion that passed by her pretty little coif in her hair. He glared. "You learnt a lot more than mathematics and reading in the fancy school of yours."

"I'm certain I don't know what you mean."

If she was going to bite like the viper he knew she was, he'd rattle right back at her. "They took away your country manners and gave you airs instead."

She adjusted the weight on her foot and the toe of one shoe peeked from beneath the hem of her skirt, drawing his attention. She tapped it and he smiled. He'd vexed her.

"They taught me how to be aggressive and not put up with bullying. That includes you, Mr. Adair. Just because I've let you help me doesn't mean we're friends. You don't get to judge my character."

"This may come as a surprise, Miz Harrison, but I'll form whatever opinion I want about you. I like watching you flutter about like a nervous squirrel. The movement makes your cheeks the same color as a barely ripened strawberry."

"I'd thank you to not compare any part of my body to fruit."

"Fine," he said, but kept his sly smile as she blew at a stray curl on her forehead. The same curl that had framed her face every time he'd seen her, but had never before been offensive. If he were any braver he'd flick the curl, just to see what she'd do in response. But he was only fearless enough to ride wild broncs and brave the treacherous waters beneath crashing logs. Not courageous enough to flick Miz Victoria Harrison's wayward curl. He pinched his fingers together to stay the urge. "What does this Representative Nichols have to do with Sanchez?"

"I believe he's the one who's leading the charge to kick us out of the forest."

"And why would you think that?"

"Because Sanchez isn't powerful enough to pull off something like this. If he thinks he can get away with this, then he has to be working with someone with more pull."

"Why is he so determined to take down Great Mountain?" The question was a solid one. The man had done everything he could to take down the mill the year before, and now turned his attentions to a more political approach. But why?

"Father won't tell me," Victoria responded. "He said he used to know Sanchez, but they had a falling out years ago."

"It's personal then." The answer didn't sit right with Wall. It may be due to the way he was raised, but in his experience a father should be a bit more worried about threats to his daughter from a man who he knew a long time ago. Whether Victoria liked it or not, he would be her shadow. She may have outlawed him from speaking or interfering, but that didn't mean he couldn't be there to protect her if need be.

But first he needed to get his work done. After all, he couldn't show up to work tomorrow for Miz Victoria and have the loader that he'd built not work on their first run. He had to take a final look at it, and then supervise getting it onto the train.

After Victoria outlined her plans for him for the evening, he finally broke free. Not only did he need to check on his invention, but now he needed to follow his pappy's example and visit the stores.

The only clothes he'd brought into town besides his cowboy hat and boots were his logger's spikes and heavy-duty work clothes. Nothing suitable enough to accompany a lady to a fine dinner.

By the time he rode into the train yards, the sun shone high overhead. He dismounted and tied his horse to the hitching post before the depot building, and then crossed the platform, and headed down the tracks next to a large steam engine and its rail cars.

Ten cars down, he reached the flatcar where a group of men heaved and pushed the machine onto the train. Dick and Blue, two of the Devil May Care crew members, stood leaning against the side of the train.

"Hope she works," Wall said when he approached, half to get the attention of his men, and half to voice his thoughts.

"She's as pretty as Miz Carrie," Blue said, stretching his head back to view the machine.

"Or Miz Victoria. When she ain't bossing Garrett around," Dick supplied, followed by a chuckle of agreement from both men.

Wall wasn't amused. Only three women had graced their camp the year before. Beth, who was now married to Garrett Jones, the old leader of the Devil May Care boys and new owner of the railroad logging side of the company, and then there was the new assistant cook, Carrie Sanders, and their boss, Victoria.

"Better watch your tongue about Miz Victoria. She ain't no camp cook," Wall defended, although he wasn't quite certain why. Fact was, even the camp cooks were ladies of the first water. Not like the women in most of the logging camps. Ever since last year, a whole passel of beautiful debutants had been causing mayhem for the Devil May Cares and timber beasts. Even Victoria had ridden the river in the cook boat last season, but he suspected that had more to do with overseeing how the company operates than wanting to work on the river.

Blue slapped Dick on the chest with the back of his hand. "Right, she's our boss now."

"Don't know how I feel about a woman boss, or some of the new river rats on our team," Dick said. "We've always been selective of who we ride the river with. Hell, ain't that the reason Luther never became a Devil boy?"

The railroad workers finished loading his machine, and Wall jumped onto the car to inspect it as they tied it down. "Luther was a sidewinder and deserved more than he got if you ask me."

"Did Garrett ever get a chance to knock his galley west after he left the mill?"

"Nah," Wall said. "Garrett's become a changed man after Miz Elizabeth got under his skin. He let the reprobate go and told him to skedaddle."

"Shame none of us got a chance to clean his plow before he shucked off," Blue said with true regret dripping from his words.

"You coming tonight, Wall?" Dick asked.

"I got something I need to take care of before we leave for camp." Wall checked on the cotter pins in his machine, and then stood tall and wiped the grease from his hands, onto his pants. "What do you boys have planned for tonight? The Angry Grizzly?"

"Nah. We're going to help Aunt June and Carrie," Dick said. "They wanna hogtie Simon and take him up to camp. Garrett and them are taking him up early soes he can get over himself before the job starts."

Blue gave a toothy grin. "We get to hogtie him and bring him to the train. I'm thinking of taking my buckboard. The springs are all worn out in the back."

Dick pointed to Blue. "We could always drag him behind a horse."

The two Devil May Cares laughed. "A good rock to the head would knock the sense back into him."

"Or kill him." Satisfied at his machine's condition, Wall leapt from the railcar.

"Nah," Dick said. "If a cougar couldn't kill him, a little ol' pebble wouldn't make a dent."

"If a cougar couldn't keep him down, my bet is he'd break out of your ropes, and beat you for kidnapping him."

Blue frowned and nodded. "Right. Best take him in my buckboard."

"When are you meeting up with the women?" he asked.

"Eight-thirty at Aunt June's house," Dick answered.

"I might be able to disappear for a bit and help you boys out."

"Better not shin out." Dick began to walk toward the train depot, so Wall followed.

"I'll be there." If his men could say anything about Wall, it was that he was reliable. He prided himself in being the one they could count on. After all, he was their leader. If the men needed him, he'd find a way to escape from the party to help, even if for only a few minutes. But how was he going to leave Victoria alone without it gnawing on his conscience? Regardless of her claims, the woman was as vulnerable as a newborn calf.

* * * *

Victoria adjusted her grandmother's necklace, smoothed the sapphire stone between her fingers, and then sat back to view herself in the mirror. The small gems always gave her confidence whenever she had none. As if she could call forth the strength her grandmother had possessed when she'd lost her husband as she trekked across the plains to settle in Montana alone with nothing but Victoria's mother, and the will to survive.

Victoria pursed her mouth, plumping her thin lips, and then stuck her tongue out at her reflection. She'd never be as fearless as her grandmother, but the least she could do was try.

She twisted the beloved curl near her eye around her finger, and moved it to sit where she liked it best, and then stood to give one final look at her reflection.

This would have to do. She only hoped Wall had found clothes suitable for the party they were attending. Although this was the West and not the English parties she was accustomed to after having lived there for years while attending school, they still maintained a certain level of sophistication she valued in a society.

Off in the distance, a gunshot rang so loud the sound penetrated through her walls and made her jump.

Well, *most of the time* the town was civilized.

The old grandfather clock in the hallway rang. She grabbed her wrap and spread it over her shoulders as she made her way downstairs. Wall had better be on time. She needed to keep a steady mind in order to deal with the representative and his errand boys. With Wall by her side, though, she wouldn't have a problem.

The other day, when he showed up out of nowhere, she'd been stunned, but his presence lent a steadiness she'd felt slipping away as she talked to Luther in the alley. When Wall's voice boomed from behind her it was as though God had sent down a pillar from heaven for her to lean on while she dealt with the simpleton errand boy.

A pillar who talked…and smelled like musky leather.

"Let's hope word of Wall's interference doesn't spread," she said aloud, with no one to talk to but the stairwell walls.

"What interference?" her father asked, coming into view at the bottom of the staircase.

Blast! He'd heard.

"Nothing, Father." She stepped off the bottom stair and stood on her tiptoes to kiss his cheek. "A silly social thing is all."

"Ah," he said, and pointed toward the door to his study. "Well, Wallace is waiting in there, so you may not want to talk to yourself too loud if you're going to say silly social things about a gentleman."

"Thank you." Victoria made her way around her father. "And he is no gentleman."

"Smart fellow. You could do worse."

Victoria chuckled. "Yes. Like a drifter."

"He's an Adair, is he not?"

"Yes." She stopped and turned to face him. "You ought to know, Father. You hired him."

"That was before I knew who he was, and the brains he's got hidden behind that wild streak of his. Else the boy would be working with Paul and me and not trying to kill himself at the river. You may want to consider bringing him into the mill."

"He makes fine contraptions, and will hopefully increase our profit by ten percent this year."

"Best not leave a man like that waiting."

With one last, lopsided grin for her father's sake, she entered the study to find Wall standing before the fireplace. His white cotton shirt beneath his black jacket was a vast improvement from the greasy, dirt-covered clothes he'd warn earlier in the day. The knot in her chest eased a fraction and she stepped next to him, and smiled.

"Well, now, Miz Victoria, you go smiling at a man like that, and you may end up charming Nichols into submitting to your every whim. You won't need my help."

"Nonsense. You've got something I need."

Wall cleared his throat and shifted the weight on his feet. She wasn't innocent enough to mistake the signs of a man's wayward thoughts. It happened quite often whenever she spoke to those of the opposite sex. Although, for the life of her, she didn't understand why. Rarely did she say inappropriate things. Harsh, perhaps. At times fickle, but never inappropriate.

"Calm yourself, Mr. Adair." She straightened his jacket lapel. "You have a working knowledge of the lumber camp operation, and cattle operation. Should I need you to discuss the inner workings of either of those, you have my permission to speak."

He bowed his head sarcastically. "And should I wait until you give the signal to answer questions directed towards me?"

She glared and tipped her head, letting her loose curls drop to her shoulder. If he was going to play verbal fisticuffs, she'd jump into the fray. She'd heard he was a pugilist, but she wasn't afraid. When it came to verbal battles, she was a fighter too. "Yes, that would be best."

"Whatever you wish."

"Hhmm," she said simply, and turned to walk toward the front door, assuming he'd follow. She was right. His newly cleaned boots echoed off the floorboards behind her.

Outside, she led the way down the walk and toward her buggy. She lifted her skirts to take the steps when Wall picked her up as though her weight held no offense to his strength. The heat from his palms warmed through her corset and dress.

By the time she'd gained her wits, he'd taken the seat next to her and snatched up the reins before she had the chance.

"Beg your pardon." She reached for the reins, but he pulled them away.

"Not used to letting the man be the boss, I see." Through the faint light of the streetlamp, she saw his grin. "You should try it once in a while. You might find you like it."

She dropped her hands in her lap hard enough he should get the point, and faced forward. "I find things work out the way I want if I am the one to take control."

Wall snapped the reins and set the buggy in motion. "That may be, but when you're the one driving you don't get to see the scenery around you. I'll bet it's been quite a while since you stopped to watch the elk graze on the mountain side, or even smell a damn flower."

"I smell my neighbor's rose bush every time my dress catches on the blasted thorns."

"Not what I was talking about." Wall turned the buggy down a street, and then straightened it out. "When's the last time you let your hair down? Took some time to discover who you are?"

"Is that what you're doing? Taking time from being a cowboy to discover who you are?"

"Could be," he said.

"And you've discovered your real identity is a logger?"

"Not just any logger. The leader of the Devil May Cares."

"That's a lot of pressure for such a position. Imagine if you weren't the leader. What would you do then?"

"Ah, I never said finding who I am was a permanent thing. Sometimes in life, who you are, and what your job is are two different things. I'm a Devil May Care, and one of those filthy cowboys you seem to despise so much."

"And you plan to remain this way your entire life?"

"If life goes my way. I wouldn't be averse to straddling two worlds." Something in his voice made her think the words he spoke weren't the ones he believed. The sadness in the way he said "my life." Or maybe the way he spoke of being a cowboy. Granted, she had thrown out an insult or two his way, but why would her opinion sway his love of riding fences?

She was one to talk, or rather think. Had the right man entered her life before she'd taken over the mill, would she have been so determined to carry on the family business? "But you don't think you'll be able to? Straddle two worlds, that is."

Wall pulled the buggy up before the mayor's house, and placed the break. "Do you think you'll be able to succeed as a woman in the timber business?"

"I suppose determination has a lot to do with whether we both will succeed in the end."

"I suppose you're right." He jumped to the ground and walked around the buggy. He reached out for her and all she could focus on were his hands—strong and steady. "Are you ready?"

"I'm ready for the season to start and to make money. What will these fools say then?"

"You don't have to listen to them. What does their opinion matter if you're doing what you love?"

"You're right. I shall ignore all ungracious comments tonight."

Wall tipped his head at her remark and ushered her inside the large house, Candles aligned the wall, lighting the way toward the sitting rooms.

She was familiar with the house, having been to many affairs in these very rooms. From teas to balls, and even a literature exhibition. This was the first time she'd brought a man with her, though. Even Garrett had met her at the parties, and not accompanied her in the buggy.

Victoria straightened her back, although with the corset taking off a good inch around her waist, she didn't see how she could straighten her posture any more. She'd much rather wear her work clothes, which even though were a blouse and skirt, didn't require her to wear the restricting undergarments social events dictated.

She placed her hand on the tight barrier over her stomach as she searched the crowd. "Over there is the mayor's wife, Annabel. A flighty little flirt of a woman. If rumors are correct, the mayor bought her from one of those mail-order bride flyers."

"A most convenient way to find a wife." Wall motioned with his head to where two men stood talking. "Representative Nichols is in the corner. Would you like to go straight to him and begin our campaign, or do a round of the room first?"

"I don't see why we shouldn't get right down to business."

Wall pulled a pocket watch from his jacket, checked it, and then nodded. "Agreed."

She stared at his hands while he stowed the watch. "Do you have somewhere else to be?"

He shook his head. "I'm all yours."

On those words, he gently tugged on her arm to make a wide berth around the room, headed slowly toward the back corner. She plastered on a false smile, and gave nods and greetings to acquaintances they passed until they reached Nichols.

With expert ease, Wall maneuvered her to the group.

To Victoria's surprise, Nichols greeted him by name. "Ah, Wallace."

"Representative Nichols," he greeted with a nod.

"How's your father? Healthy, I assume, or else you'd be home running that ol' bag of bones ranch of yours." Nichols chuckled at some inside joke, as Wallace gave the same smile he'd given Luther in the alley.

"He's holding up well. I'll tell him you send your regards." Wall pulled her forward a tad, and turned ever-so-slightly, drawing the group's attention toward her. "May I introduce Miz Victoria Harrison."

"Ah, yes. Abner's little girl," Nichols said. "I hope your father is enjoying retirement. Best thing he could have done at this point."

"Why's that?" she asked, giving her own version of the social smile. Mentally she bludgeoned the politician with the candelabra just over his shoulder.

"I have it on good authority that Montana is about to become a state."

"That's wonderful!" the (up until now) quiet man next to him exclaimed, and then excused himself to go spread the news.

"And how would Montana becoming a state be of benefit to my father? Or are you referring more to my company, Great Mountain Lumber Mill?"

"Ah, that's right. I heard you took over the mill." He shook his head. "Such a shame. The women's teas will be greatly affected without your talent."

"I hardly think drinking tea requires any skills, sir," Victoria responded. "I can assure you, I'm much more effective using my talents at the mill."

"Well, then. You might be interested to hear that once Montana becomes a state, I'm afraid you're going to have to close your doors. You may consider getting out while you are ahead."

She frowned. "Why's that?"

"I'm not supposed to be letting this out yet, but you being a woman and all, I feel it's my duty to warn you. Montana doesn't look kindly to timber thievery."

"I can assure you, we own most of the land we're on, and have permits for the rest."

"Once the statehood is secured, the permits will no longer be valid, and you'll be breaking the law. I can assure you, the state does not intend to allow private lumber companies to harvest the beautiful mountain trees on state land."

"And who might be allowed to harvest the mountains?" Wall asked with a bite behind his words. Unlike before, this time Wall's interruption didn't grate on her nerves. Instead, she lifted her head. It felt good to have support. Even if he did disobey her wishes to remain silent.

"That, son, is government business. You understand."

Victoria opened her mouth to respond when a servant came in to announce supper. Nichols stepped past her, and in the process, leaned in close. "I wouldn't want to put a woman such as yourself through a long, stressful trial. Best get out while you can."

She waited for him to leave before turning to face Wall. She didn't know what to say. All she could do was shake her head, but he understood. Or at least she thought he did since he gave her a pathetic smile and took her arm to escort her to supper.

She knew this whole mess was a lot more than Sanchez trying to take over her father's company. It was political. If she didn't play her cards right, it would be the ruin of Great Mountain Lumber Mill.

Wall checked his watch again as they walked, but she didn't care what his reasons were for his new-found obsession with time. All she wanted to do was slink back home and form a plan of defense. Or attack. First, she had to feign interest in meaningless prattle for the next few hours. She was just glad she had Wall there to keep her company. At least she wouldn't be alone in her misery.

Chapter 3

Victoria searched for Wall in the group of men headed toward the front of the house, as she followed the other women to the back sitting room. A small, flowery-decorated haven of a space where the mayor's wife usually entertained her friends for tea. Victoria herself had been there a time or two, although she wouldn't exactly call Annabel a friend.

What Victoria wanted was to find Wall and leave. After the information she'd received from Nichols earlier, she hadn't the mood to entertain the frivolous chatter of witless women, and needed to form a plan to counter the territories' bullying.

She needed to find Wall and get him to take her home, but before she could pivot and make her excuses to her host, Annabel looped her arm through Victoria's and dipped her head close in secrecy.

"Dreadfully boring, isn't it?" Annabel whispered.

"Not at all." Victoria tried to match the woman's quiet tone. "The night has been most stimulating and informative."

"Then you haven't been to enough of these sort of parties." Annabel guided her into the sitting room. "They're all the same—a bunch of blowhard men congratulating one another on their ideas and accomplishments."

Victoria didn't think the mayor's wife knew how accurate her statement really was. Especially if one of those ideas she talked about was to destroy Victoria and Great Mountain.

"I've never heard a more profound statement." Victoria ran her eyes over the women in the room as Carrie's mother waved her over to the corner. "Excuse me, Ms. Annabel. I believe Mrs. Kerr is calling me."

"Of course." Annabel dipped her chin in acquiesce, and then faced a guest nearby as Victoria made her way to Carrie's mother.

Mrs. Kerr sipped her tea as Victoria approached.

"Ma'am," she greeted.

"Ms. Harrison." Mrs. Kerr set her cup on the small plate in her hands. "I'm not going to waste time with chitter chatter, so I hope you'll excuse my lack of etiquette, but I believe my daughter is employed in your camp."

"She is," Victoria said slowly.

"I suspect she wants to become a permanent resident of the Missoula camp. When she asks you for a job at the end of this season, I need you to reject her."

"Reject her? Why? From what I saw from her performance last year, she is an excellent candidate for the cook position. And although I don't see Aunt June retiring anytime soon, I can afford to employ Carrie as an assistant cook. Why would I reject her request for a position at my spring camp?"

"Because she is a lady of the first water and needs to secure herself a future. Here at home. I adore Aunt June, but I don't want my daughter being like her. I want to see Carrie settled. Happily settled with a husband who can care for her."

"And you don't think she's happy as a cook?"

Carrie's mother ran her fingers over the intricate design on the side of the fragile teacup. "I think she fancies herself happy up there in the wild, but the charm of the mountains will wear off and leave her with nothing but calloused hands and no hope for a future. Please, help me help my daughter. She doesn't know what's best for her like I do."

The thought of intruding in Carrie's life made Victoria's stomach hollow, but the plead in Ms. Kerr's voice was one of desperation. She had to help as best she could, but she had the feeling Carrie wouldn't go down the mountain easily. "I'll tell her she can only stay as long as the end of the season, but I can't force her to come home and find a husband."

"I understand." Ms. Kerr's chest rose with a deep inhale, and the niggling fear in the back of Victoria's mind eased a bit. Even if Carrie hated her, at least she'd brought a concerned mother some peace.

A movement near the door caught Victoria's attention as Annabel beckoned her over. She wished it was Wall. Victoria turned and made her excuses with Ms. Kerr, and then hurried toward where her hostess inched closer to the door.

"Thank goodness. I thought Ms. Kerr would never let you go. I need your help."

"With?" Victoria stepped hesitantly next to Annabel as the latter led them from the room.

"I need you to warn me. Be my guardian."

"I beg your pardon?" A voice screamed in the back of her mind to run, but the woman was the mayor's wife, and had a fierce clutch on her arm.

Her hostess remained quiet as she all but dragged her down the hall, through the house, and toward the back of the mansion. When they reached a secluded hallway, Annabel finally faced her. "We've always been friends, correct?"

"I was under the impression you didn't want anything to do with me since I took over my father's business. How did you say it last year...'subjecting myself to a man's job?'"

"No, silly. You're the dearest of friends to me. I feel as though we can do anything for each other. Now, stay here and warn me if anyone comes. Also stop them from coming into the room." Not waiting for Victoria's response, Annabel slipped through the darkened doorway, leaving Victoria standing alone in the hallway.

On the other side of the wall, a man's voice murmured inaudibly, followed by Annabel's more feminine voice. Victoria could only hope it was the woman's husband, but somehow she doubted it.

She shuffled her feet and stared at the light at the end of the passageway. She should walk away. Leave Annabel to be discovered. But she wouldn't. She wasn't that sort of person.

For what seemed like half of an hour she stood, flinching at every sound emanating from where the light touched the hallway. She paced along the decorative rug covering the wooden floorboards until Wall's distinct drawl echoed from the other side of the door where Annabel had disappeared. "Beg your pardon."

Her chest tightened at the sound of Wall's voice. Had he been the man Annabel met in the dark, back room? Did she care?

Yes. For some reason she did care.

As though destiny had heard her question and wanted a good laugh at her expense, Wall stepped hurriedly from the room and closed the door.

She made a squeak, and Wall turned—his expression one of shock and guilt.

"It's not how it looks," Wall said defensively.

Victoria regained her composure and shook her head. "It's none of my business."

It really was none of her business, but all the same a hard pressure formed in her chest and spread.

He motioned toward the door. "I just—"

"I didn't take you for the type to be fooled by her charms," Victoria bit out, and stepped hard to stand in front of the door with her back facing the knob.

"I'm not," he said slowly, and his shoulders dropped in defeat. "I left the party. Just for a few minutes. I came in through the side door and happened upon a scandalous scene in there."

"Oh." Victoria sighed the word, and clutched her chest as the tense sensation of jealousy ebbed.

"What are you doing out here? Hasn't the party moved to another room?"

"Yes." Victoria motioned toward the room where he'd been mere moments ago. "But she asked me to stand guard."

"Is she a close friend of yours?"

"Not particularly." *Or not at all.* When she'd made the comment about them being friends, she was being generous. Annabel had never paid her any attention beyond what social etiquette dictated. "I'd call her more of a close acquaintance, but in my world, if the mayor's wife asks you to do something, you do it."

"Can you break away from playing guardian?"

"Why?"

"Something's come up. I need to leave for the logging camp tonight, and I would rather not leave you here to fight the wolves by yourself."

"How gallant of you, but I can assure you I can fight off the wolves just fine."

He answered with a disbelieving glare.

"I can," she said. "However, I do not care to stay here any longer, so I will join you." She bit the tip of her thumb. "Do you think it terribly bad of me to leave my post?"

"I think whatever happens to the mayor's wife should she be discovered with her new lover will be well deserved." He turned toward the door. "I'll summon the buggy if you make our excuses."

"I'd love to." Relief, and a small sense of wickedness, spread through her chest.

By the time she finished giving the mayor their excuses and emerged into the night, the buggy stood waiting in front of the mansion with a servant holding the reins. Wall helped her up, and then took the seat next to her and once again slipped the reins from her grip before she could set the buggy rolling. Blasted man. He really was honorable, and well-versed in etiquette, although she wouldn't let him know she thought as much.

After a few minutes, he turned the buggy and broke the silence. "Are you planning on coming up to camp again this year?"

"At the beginning, but I won't stay like last year. Running a mill isn't easy, you know."

"I can imagine."

"How do you know Nichols?"

"My father knows him."

"Oh," she said, and then sat back, defeated. If Wall's family was friends with Nichols, then she was doomed. Wall would certainly side with the territorial representative. "So then you think I ought to give in and close down the mill like Nichols suggested?"

"I said my father knows him." Wall slapped the reins to pick up the speed. "I personally think the guy is a sidewinder. All politicians are."

"So I should fight?"

"Is that what you want to do?"

"I've always been a fighter, and I don't want to lose the mill."

"But?"

"I don't know if I can win against the entire Montana territory."

"I've seen small farms take on the government and win." He pulled up before her house, set the brake, and turned to face her. "We'll find a way to keep your company. And legally."

He jumped from the buggy and hurried to help her down.

With a deep, calming breath, she wrapped her palms around his biceps as he eased her to the ground. Her chest rose with each struggled breath. Both because of the effects the man before her had on her tonight, and the thought of losing the one thing on earth she cherished. "I won't lose the mill."

He dropped his hands from her side and stepped back. "You won't."

His bravado was enough to make her nod. No matter what happened with the mill, he would fight with her. That promise was evident in his tone.

He would be her champion.

Wall tipped his head to the side, and dropped his gaze to her lips. She didn't move. He stepped back and handed the reins to her servant as he came running up to them.

"I'll see you at the lumber camp," Wall said, and turned to disappear into the night. In another time, with another man, she would have said something to make him stop. Flirted with him. But she was a business woman now, and this was Wall Adair. A logger. Her riverman.

* * * *

Wall waited in the meadow for the last train bringing men to the mountain to slam to a halt. The early morning sun turned to the bright light of midmorning as men jumped from the boxcars and ran toward the camps. Last night had been one hell of a time.

Simon had disappeared up the mountain, leaving Wall and the rest of the Devil May Cares to settle into their crude cabin for a few hours of shut-eye before the morning train, and Victoria, arrived.

He'd felt anxiety before. Hell, he'd felt lust before, but he'd never felt the two emotions at the same time until last night when he'd ached to touch Victoria. To comfort her as she struggled to come to grips with the information they'd learned the night before.

But like his ma always said, "A brighter view comes with the light of a new day."

He'd waited for the feelings to disappear throughout the night. To fade with the light of day, but it didn't. He wanted to help her. To be near her, and like she said, his knowledge of both worlds gave him a reason to insinuate himself in her business.

The sounds of the train echoed off the trees and slowly faded by the time Victoria emerged from a passenger car with Paul by her side.

She spotted him, and to his relief, headed his way. "Glad to see your train made it up here all right in the night." She started to walk toward camp where the men were beginning to gather for the pre-season orders. Victoria searched the people gathered around Aunt June's cook camp. "I have a message for Carrie. Have you seen her?"

"I have not." Wall copied her search of the people as Paul walked ahead and began to bark orders.

"How is the drive looking?"

Wall glanced up to the mountain peaks, barely covered in snow, and thought back to when he woke and took his coffee near the lake to assess the progress. "The logs harvested over the winter are ready to go down, but I'm worried about the rivers."

"Why?"

"The winter was short and dry. I'm worried the spring runoff isn't going to produce enough water to take a raft down. If we do get one, it'll have to be real soon."

"How bad do you think the rivers are? Should we risk running a drive within the next week?"

"I don't know." He frowned as he stared in the direction of the mouth of the river, obscured from sight by acres of trees.

"Take the Devil May Cares and do a quick run down to the mill to check the water levels. Block any tributaries you need to, and make the rivers as deep as you can."

"Riding without a raft, we should be able to float the river in a week or two."

"Are there any spots that Paul or I could meet you? I want as many updates as I can get, as fast as I can get them."

"There's the Lost Horse Creek Bridge. We should be there in two days, and then The Thirsty Woodsman, probably day four. I don't think you should wait for us at a saloon, though."

"I'll meet you at the Lost Horse Creek Bridge in three days. If I'm not there by the time you reach it, then wait for me, but Paul and I plan to stay at least tonight to check on the railroad logging. We'll probably take the train down tomorrow morning, and then I'll head up to meet you at the bridge."

"I'll let the boys know to get ready to go down the river. We'll time it so we can get to the bridge same as you. If you'll excuse me, I need to go get my men prepared." He leaned in, perhaps a bit closer than was necessary, but he wanted to take a deeper inhale of the sweet, flowery scent that drifted on the breeze. A scent he'd found helped his mind to focus whenever it assailed his senses.

In a demure fashion only a woman could pull off, Victoria cleared her throat and turned her face enough that a large curl grazed his cheek and sent heat to his stomach.

Two dimpled lines formed at the corners of her mouth in a cat-like smile. She must know the effect she had on men. And she used the charm to get whatever she wished in life. He straightened up and left, hoping no one witnessed his momentary lack of curtesy.

For the rest of the day he and his men worked through the logistics of a pre-drive run. The supper bell rang through the trees at the same time a chilling whistle sounded from higher up the hill.

"Already?" Blue asked, and stared toward the sound. "We haven't even started the season."

Fear slid through Wall's core at the sound, and Blues words. The whistle meant something bad had happened in the trees.

"Let's go," he said the words, but they didn't really need to be spoken.

Wall's lungs burned and his thick muscled legs ached by the time he and the Devil May Cares found the scene of the accident. Behind them, a logger carrying Aunt June's stretcher elbowed his way past them. "Who is it?"

"I don't know," Simon said.

"Has anyone seen him before?" the logger with the stretcher asked.

Dawn Luedecke

The crowd mumbled their answers, and most shook their heads.

Simon moved toward the man. "Let's get him down to camp."

The logger set the stretcher near the body, and Wall stepped next to him to help ease the dead man on the travois. Once he was secure, most of the men who'd come to view the accident followed as they hauled the man down the path.

Wall stood with Garrett and Beth, silent behind their new assistant cook, Carrie, as she cried. Garrett moved to where the body once lay, and crouched to examine the ground, so Wall picked up the branch, weighed it in his hands, and turned it to peer at the broken end. "Does this branch look odd to you?"

He held the object out and Simon took it. "It looks a bit fresh, but I don't see anything else to make it seem off. Why?"

Wall shook his head and tucked the widowmaker under his arms to take it with. This whole scene didn't sit right with him. "No reason."

"We'd best get back." Simon eased Carrie toward the trail.

Garrett walked next to his wife, and Wall stepped beside him as they started down the hill. "Is Victoria at the train?"

Garrett nodded. "She and Paul are taking their supper in the passenger car while they work through some plans."

"When do they leave?"

"Early morning," Beth answered. "Maybe as early as midnight. Depending on the load and the conductor. Why?"

Both Garrett and Beth shot him matching, curious looks.

Wall adjusted the tree branch under his arm. "I need to speak with her about the drive is all."

The rest of the trek off the mountain was spent in silence, which Wall was grateful for. Usually he loved a good conversation, but today provided so many reasons for him to remain silent and think.

Starting with the look of the widowmaker that'd killed the logger, and ending with the way his core warmed whenever he stood next to Victoria.

He'd known many women in his life, and had even courted a few. Hell, he'd visited Beth a few times before she and Garrett had worked out their problems. None of the women he'd known in his past had ever made him unable to think of anything but her by simply being nearby.

The train came into view, and he headed toward it, taking the steps and knocking before entering the passenger car. Inside, Victoria sat in the center, which hosted two bench seats facing each other with a table between them. Victoria studied a map as Paul stood next to her doing the same.

He stepped inside and pulled the widowmaker through the door. "Pardon, but what do you make of this?"

He lifted the end of the branch with what he thought looked like cut marks.

Paul frowned and approached, studying the branch. He shook his head. "What is this?"

"A widowmaker. I wanted to see if you saw anything odd with the way it looked. Something seemed off with the scene of the accident."

"I don't see anything wrong with it." Paul turned toward Victoria. "Do you?"

Victoria eased out of her chair, and Paul stepped back to let her past. She studied the branch. "Who's the deceased?"

"No idea." Wall pushed the branch out the door, balanced it in the corner of the rail on the back of the car, and then entered again.

"Have they brought him down?" Victoria asked.

"Yes," Wall answered. "To Aunt June's cabin for assessment, and then they'll load him on the train."

Victoria slid Paul a look, and the portly man nodded. "I'll go check it out."

Wall pressed his back to the window along the wall to allow Paul to pass. Once the man had stepped off the car, and headed toward camp, Wall faced Victoria. "I don't agree. Widowmakers happen, certainly, and we cut branches all of the time. But the man didn't look like he belonged in a logging camp. Perhaps that's why the scene felt off."

She frowned, and leaned against the back of a seat. "Are you certain we don't know who the man is?"

"No."

Victoria straightened. "Perhaps look again. I took on many new workers."

He stepped close to her as she stood strong in the center of the car. "We filthy cowboys may live in the mud, but we can spot a dandy when we see one. The man wore logger's clothes, but they were clean. Too clean."

"Hhmm," Victoria said, and played with her necklace. "I'm certain it's nothing. We'll see what Paul says when he returns."

Wall watched as she fiddled with the jewels, her hand against the high neck of her white-frilled shirt.

"Have you had your pre-season log rolls?" Victoria asked, changing the subject. "I'd like to see them someday. I hear you're quite good at it."

"Well, I'll be. Are you complimenting a filthy cowboy?"

She answered with a crick of her head, and playful smile. "I'm not a harsh person, Mr. Adair."

"I know that." He wanted to touch the stone the way she did, feel the smoothness of the gem. What would it take to tighten her nerves enough to caress the stone or her hair? A touch? A kiss?

Wall inwardly chuckled at the thought. She'd probably yank the damn thing off if he kissed her, and then step back and slap him. She wouldn't stand for a kiss from a cowboy. She'd made that perfectly clear with her ongoing insults toward his winter profession.

"I'm glad you came." Victoria played with a loose curl and brought his focus to her face. Was she as nervous as he was whenever they were alone? She certainly fiddled with her hair and necklace a lot." I need you to take over as leader of the timber beasts as well."

"Simon's the leader of the timber beasts, and he's good at his job."

"Yes, but you know what's going on, and I need you to be everywhere. The raft, the railroad operation, and even The Grove. Aren't you involved with the railroad logging, anyway? I know Garrett oversees it, but I need you there to study the men, and report to me if anyone seems standoffish. I can't have a repeat of last year. Not with everything going on over in Helena. This year must go down without a hitch."

"Garrett and Simon are good men and can be trusted to help."

"Wallace." She said his name with a warning in her tone.

"Wall," he corrected, and stepped closer to her until no more than a few inches separated them. "Only my family or people from older generations call me Wallace."

"Wall," she corrected.

She threw her head back until her gaze met his, and stared with a challenge, but her pupils grew large and the look in her eyes mirrored the feelings he had deep within his stomach.

He needed to touch her. He ached to feel the softness of her hair. He was a fool, but he couldn't control himself. He reached up to tug at a curl along the side of her neck, just to see if it would bounce back. It did.

The only thing he could hear was the sound of her breathing, but she didn't pull away. Didn't slap his face like she should have. He smiled.

But he didn't dare push his luck further.

The feel of her soft hair in his fingers imprinted on his senses. What did her lips taste like? He had to find out. Someday. But not now, and not here.

He cleared his throat, and her hand fluttered to smooth the curl he'd touched, and then rested on her necklace. Wall took a wider stance, and tried to hide the smile he couldn't help but give. She was affected by his touch. At least as much as he was. He rattled her.

"Don't do that again," she said.

"Do what?" he asked and, just for fun, tugged on the curl once more.

He leaned down until her lips were mere inches from his. "I'll see you in two days."

Before she could form the words needed to fire him, he turned and walked out of the railcar, taking the stairs with a smug grin plastered on his face, but inside he reeled.

He couldn't afford the disturbance she created. Not up here anyway. If something was going to happen, he needed to have a clear mind and strong arm to deal with the issue. The damn woman made him weak.

Chapter 4

"I can handle it." Victoria paced before her father in her own office, and he sat behind her desk. "You promised Mother you'd take her to see her sister in Seattle. That's what you're going to do."

"Are you certain? I don't want to leave you if you're not comfortable with running the mill."

"I'll be fine. I have Paul, Garrett, and even Wall Adair to help me out. You promised Mother years ago you'd take her to Washington, and now you have no excuses."

"Good, good." Her father stood and walked to the door. He placed his hand on the knob, but then stopped and turned back to her. "Wire me if you need anything. I'll be on the first train home."

"I will. We will be fine, though." She said the words, but her heart tightened and the food she'd eaten that morning settled hard in her stomach. She didn't tell her father of the man who'd died at the camp, or talk further of her concerns regarding Nichols. If she couldn't handle this on her own when her father had done so many years past, she wasn't fit to run the mill. Plus, she had Paul.

And Wall.

Although he was a rough cowboy, he did make her feel at ease whenever he was near. Helped her to focus and she took strength from his warm presence.

The memory of how he'd touched her hair caused her stomach to flip the way it had at that moment. Men often bounced her curls when charming her, but with Wall, it was different. She didn't know if it was the feel of the gentle tug on her scalp, or the heat from the back of his hand that had shot straight to her lower stomach, but she'd struggled like a fool to take in air. He was a dirty cowboy. He shouldn't affect her this much.

It was an odd feeling. Like standing on the back end of a caboose, with nothing between her and the harsh ground but a thin metal rail, as the train chugged up an exceptionally steep hill.

"Don't worry about the season. I've experienced this before. There's a pattern to these things, you know. One bad year, followed by two good ones. That's why I'm fine leaving you this year. Last year was as bad as any I've seen, and you've got a solid plan and Garrett's trains. This is set to be a bang-up year. I'll give your mother your goodbyes," her father said, bringing her out of her reverie.

Victoria nodded, and checked the clock as her father walked out. She needed to get going. Wall was due to be at the bridge late this afternoon, and she had to be there to speak with him. Assess the rivers and future of her log drives for the year.

Like most days at the mill, she'd left her corset and bustle at home, opting for more practical attire for riding up the mountain. Outside her window, a noise caught her attention, and she drifted to view the layout below.

At the tracks, her father boarded his railcar while a worker pulled a wagon up in front of the main mill building. Paul stepped near the horses, and held them steady as the man set the break and leapt down.

She snatched up her jacket and buttoned it, peering one last time at her reflection. Although not her everyday attire, she enjoyed wearing her split riding skirt more than the other gowns she owned. For the sheer simplicity, comfort, and ease of wear.

Outside, she stomped right to the awaiting wagon, holding a new-style bateau she'd discovered over the winter, as well as a few supplies for the rivermen. She mounted. With logging near the water and the railroad, they could get twice the load down to the mill. And twice the load meant new men and equipment. At least she could have the men test out the boat before she sent it up to the camp.

But first, they needed to see if the rivers were even high enough to take a log drive down. *Blast!* It seems even the earth was waiting for her to fail.

Today she'd let Paul drive without argument. Mostly because she had no idea where she was going. She knew the road leading up to the bridge was just outside the gates, but after that she was lost. Paul knew where to go, though.

He mounted and set the horses in motion.

"Is there any news about the man who died? Have you identified him?" Victoria held her breath, hoping it wasn't one of the new men she'd taken on. Not that she wanted it to be a homeboy, but the guilt she'd harbor at having a man die in her camps on the very day he began to work would be too much. What would she tell his family?

"I received word this morning." Paul maneuvered the wagon down the road leading up the mountain.

"And?" she prompted.

He shook his head. "His name was Brewer. He was a surveyor from the Montana Territorial office in Helena."

"What?" Her fingers grew numb. A government man, dead on her property, could do nothing but bring her trouble.

"The man was up there assessing the property and operation."

"What sort of assessment was he performing?"

"My guess? He was trying to find fault with the operation."

"What sort of fault? My father led me to believe we ran a clean logging camp up here."

"Aye, we do."

"But?"

"After last year's problems, we left a lot of debris up there."

"Why should that be an issue? It all goes back into the earth anyway."

"The government doesn't see it that way. They believe leaving the dead branches behind increases the chance of a forest fire."

"And what do you think?" Victoria pursed her lips together. The government was beginning to meddle to a disturbing degree. There was no way the man's appearance in her camp right after the governor showed up was a coincidence. Was there?

"I think it'll cost us a few months' pay to get it cleaned up to their satisfaction, and after all of those new hires and equipment you've been purchasing lately, we don't have the money to spend on cleaning it up."

"You thought the new railroad logging was as good of an idea as I did, if I recall correctly. Is the government going to become a bigger problem now that their man has died in my camp?"

"It's a fair chance. They're going to want to put Great Mountain under fierce scrutiny. If they can find any reason to shut us down, they will."

"And do you believe the man's death was an accident, or was he murdered?"

Paul shot her a silent look, and then snapped the reins to get the horses to speed up a hill. "I think your father should have stayed behind."

"You don't think I can take care of the company like my father? Why? Because I expanded with the railroad? Why didn't you say something to him?"

"That ain't it, Miz Victoria. Your father's been through trials and lawyer battles before. He's better equipped to handle the legal aspect of it all, and I did tell him. He doesn't think there's any threat, and your mother is determined to go on vacation."

"Well, I've got to learn sometime. Baptism by fire is the fastest way to become proficient, I suppose." Victoria placed a hand over her hat to keep it secured as a breeze mingled with the wind from the wagon's motion. "And I have you."

She smiled, hoping to ease the wrinkle in his forehead with compliments. It worked, for he returned the grin. "I'll help you out, Miz Victoria, don't worry about that."

"Thank you," she said to the older man who'd become like an uncle to her over the years. Although he wasn't connected to them by blood, he had been with Great Mountain since the beginning. She'd grown up watching Paul work next to her father, and keep the mill running. He was family. Great Mountain family.

A few hours later, Paul stopped the wagon on a small bridge and set the break. In the river below, Wall and his men stood from where they lounged, waiting, in the grass next to the river.

Wall dusted his pants with his hands as he walked up the steep incline to draw near the wagon. "What's this?"

"I've brought you a surprise," she said, and stepped off the wagon. Before she could put so much as a foot on the edge, Wall stood next to her and lifted her down.

Like before, her breath hitched and the air in the mountain grew even thinner. His strong hands heated her side where they touched and all she could do was focus on his eyes until he stepped back to admire the boat.

He motioned for his men to assist him, and then yanked on the boat as the other three Devil May Care boys took up positions next to him. They heaved the bateau out, and the Devil May Cares carried it to the water.

"How's the river?"

Wall shook his head as Paul walked down following the Devil May Cares.

"We've had to blast a few forks." It didn't escape her notice when he rubbed his hand along his pant leg. A sign she'd seen him give before when nervous.

"But you're worried."

"Yes."

"Why?"

"The river closer to the mill tends to have more rapids than up here. We're probably going to have to blast almost every fork to divert the water enough for a drive."

"*A* drive."

"Yep. One drive. I don't see us making more than one trip down this year." Victoria began to take the small trail beside the bridge, leading to the river banks.

Below, she found Dick, Clint, and Blue standing next to Paul.

She caught Blue's eyes and motioned toward the supply crate. "Would you two mind grabbing the supply crates and loading them into the wannigan before Paul leaves?"

"Paul leaves?" Wall asked, his brows drawn together in confusion.

"Yes. I will be accompanying you the rest of the way down the river."

"That's not a good idea, Miz Victoria," Paul said, walking up to her as the Devil May Cares did her bidding.

"I need to assess the rivers. You can handle the situation we discussed on the way here until I return in a few days, can't you?"

"Yes, but the rivers are low. It's no place for a lady," Paul argued.

"I have to agree." Wall stepped closer to her, dipped his head, and caught her attention. "I can report to you once we get back."

Victoria stepped onto the wannigan. "No need. I will be here. I rode the river last year, I know what to expect." She peeked into the small cabin on the rough raft. "However, I will be taking the cabin at night."

"We'll be fine near a fire," Wall said. "But that's not the point. You're not prepared for a float." He motioned toward her clothes.

"I appreciate the concern, but I can assure you, I am not worried about the details. We brought food enough for all of us, and that's all that matters on the subject. Paul will take the wagon down and meet us at the mill at the end of the week."

"What about your reputation, Miz Victoria?" The muscles on Paul's face remained tense.

"My reputation will be fine. I am the boss of these men, and I wish to see for myself the difficulties we will have in bringing down a drive."

Dick and Blue struggled down the small hill, and stowed the boxes in the wannigan.

"But, Miz Victoria—" Wall started, until she held up her hand.

"It's decided." She turned to climb into the wannigan. "Now if you will, gentlemen, we really should get going before we're forced to camp here for the night."

Paul grumbled, but Victoria ignored him until he climbed the hill by himself, and left in the wagon. She turned to Wall and the two Devil May Care boys. "Well, shall we?"

Dick, Clint, and Blue climbed into the new bateau, and shoved off as Wall stepped up beside her. The raft shook under his weight. "I don't like this one bit."

"Luckily for me, it's not your call."

"Victoria," he said her name in warning.

"I'll be fine, and so will my reputation. But my company won't be unless we get a substantial amount of logs to the mill this season." She took up an oar and shoved at the bottom of the river to dislodge them from the bank. Wall did the same, and the boat eased into the water. "Besides you'll be here to protect me. Isn't that what you swore to do?"

"Yes." He guided the boat in the center of the river. More to himself he mumbled, "I feel as though you're taking advantage of my protective oath."

She smiled. Even she thought she was taking his offer to assist her a little far. But it was nice to have him with her. To be taken care of by someone, and have them guide you simply by standing next to you. It was nice to have a man there as she took on the world. Especially a rough, but quite capable cowboy like Wallace Adair.

* * * *

Wall studied Victoria as she dipped the long wannigan oar into the river in the most pitiful way. He laughed and stepped close to her on the raft, reaching around to grasp the handle above her hands to show her the proper way to work the current.

A mistake.

The scent of her hair made him dizzy with the need to throw down his oar and let the current carry the wannigan until they were far away from the rest of the world. But that's not how the river worked. Not how he and Victoria worked.

"I've done this before, I swear," Victoria said, taking him out of his ridiculous thoughts, but her voice lacked the definitive bravado she usually sported.

"I believe you." He smiled in reassurance and stepped back as she picked up the rhythm of the river. Needing the distance. He took his position once more on the other side of the boat as they began to turn due to the lack of work on his side. He snuck a peek at her split skirt and conservative blouse. Odd how it seemed to suit her more than the tight stylish dresses she typically wore. "You're dressed for a ride, I see."

"Last year I positively died in all of those fancy dresses when I floated the river with Aunt June." She dropped one hand from the handle and plucked at the side of her split skirt, only to grab the oar with two hands again when it began to jerk. "This is a much more practical attire for anything adventurous."

"So you met us at the bridge knowing you were going to ride the river? And here I thought it was a spur of the moment decision."

"I had an inkling." She twisted her mouth in a suppressed smile. "Had hoped, I suppose. I quite enjoy riding in the wannigan. And knowing what is going on with my river drive is the perfect reason to indulge in my wildest desires."

Wall cleared his throat at the words, but the action was blessedly drowned out by the roar of a small rapid up ahead. Although Victoria had intended the remark to be completely innocent, truth was the woman caused his thoughts to run in all sorts of directions with the simplest of remarks. No woman had ever caused his thoughts to wander so much. He prided himself in his ability to remain focused and unaffected by distractions.

Victoria distracted him to an uncomfortable degree. Especially when dressed down as though she fit into his world. Which she didn't. Would never. Not with her—oh so vocalized—aversion to cowboys. He didn't like the fiery woman, so why did his mind keep wandering to her blasted clothes?

The wannigan came to the rapids and Victoria stiffened and adjusted her stance for the ride, and he did the same. It lasted a few exhilarating seconds before they slowed into an eddy and Wall relaxed and stood straight, focusing once more on the woman who seemed to capture every thought he possessed lately.

She smiled.

Not her forced social smile, and not even the few genuine grins he'd seen her give over the last few days, but this one brightened her eyes and mixed with the pink dust of exertion to color her skin and accentuate her dimples. This was genuine, but not for anyone but herself. How often had she smiled for no one but herself?

Not very often, guessing from the tense way he'd always seen her.

"Who's that?" Victoria's voice brought his mind off her smile and back to the moment.

He turned to where she pointed as a man on horseback walked along the river, following the riverman's trail down the bank. The path they walked every year to follow the river drive. Wall shook his head. "He's too far away to see his face clearly, but he seems familiar."

"Yes, he does." Victoria squinted and kept her eyes fixed on him until he turned and disappeared on a trail leading into the trees.

"Maybe a local man? There's a few houses sprinkled between the camp and The Thirsty Woodsman."

"Perhaps," Victoria said, but her voice proved she didn't fully trust his suggestion, and truth be told, neither did he. There was something about the man that seemed off. Victoria turned once more to rowing, and then glanced back up to catch his eye. "What do you think about the man who got hit by the widowmaker? Do you think it was an accident?"

"I can't be certain," Wall admitted. "The cut was clean, and I think the branch looked a bit too fresh to have been hanging up there in the trees, waiting for the right moment to fall and kill someone."

"But there are widowmakers everywhere up there. A fresh branch isn't a good clue."

"I suspect if we find out why he was up there we might be able to figure out what happened."

"He was surveying the land for the territorial office in Helena."

"That doesn't surprise me. Who all knew he was up there? Obviously you didn't."

"That I don't know."

Wall studied the way she plucked at her skirt. Much to his consternation, he had the urge to place his hand over hers to stop the nervous tell. He didn't know how long he could keep his hands to himself. Eventually he may just give up and touch her. Just to see if it lent any comfort to her tense thoughts.

Why did he care? He suspected it had something to do with the vulnerability he could spot within her movements, her glances. A tell only a man constantly surrounded by women could decipher. Perhaps that's why he loved being in the logging camp so much. Up there it's men. And men are cut and dry. They tell it like it is, voice their strife, use their fists to settle arguments, and get over their problems easily. Women are vulnerable, but they bottle their issues up inside, secret it away, and make a man search for it. Victoria was no different from any other woman he'd met. Luckily, he was well versed in dealing with women. "Do you think the man's death was an accident?" He asked her the same question she did him.

"No. And Paul doesn't either."

"What does Paul say?" Wall dug his oar in deep to straighten out the wannigan as they floated.

"He didn't say it outright, but it was deeply implied that he was worried the government would come after us. He's also upset because my father left for Seattle."

"Why should he care about that?"

"Because I may just run the mill into the ground if I'm not careful, and if my father were here to check me, the mill would be fine I suppose. I think Paul is beginning to doubt my business skills. As am I."

"You shouldn't. I've never seen a woman more determined to make something work." He chuckled at the memory of his youngest sister, Georgiana's, determined face whenever she threw a rope—not one of her best talents, but one she never failed to accomplish nonetheless. He often saw that same sparkle in Victoria's eye whenever she took on a difficult task. "Even the devil steps aside for a determined woman. The railroad logging is going to open up more places to harvest, and you'll start doubling your loads. You'll see."

"If we can harvest after the government gets their noose around us."

"What was the man surveying? Your land?"

Victoria shook her head so hard that the charmingly loose curls at the nape of her neck flipped back and forth. "Paul says he was probably looking for things they can get us on. Things we're doing wrong."

Wall pinched his lips together. "Like the debris."

"You know about that? Why hasn't anyone said anything earlier, or cleaned it up?"

"I suppose the year-round team was too busy implementing the new rail system to worry about cleaning up the scrap trees."

"Oh great." Victoria jerked like she wanted to throw down the oar and pace like a queen but, to his relief, she held steady to rowing. "Now I'm going to lose the entire operation because the year-round camp couldn't take a few weeks to clean up what they left behind?"

"It's worse than that," Wall said. "There's widowmakers everywhere up there. It's downright dangerous to walk past the old Grove. I'd venture to guess we'll see more deaths this year."

Her chin vibrated as though she struggled to stop herself from crying, or out of anger, he wasn't quite certain which she was more prone to displaying at this point. Over the years he'd learned—with the way her chest rose and fell—that particular rhythmic heave meant one of two things. A woman was about to let loose desperate tears, or a man had damn-well better run for his life. He'd yet to be able to figure out how to tell which one. Jax always ran.

Wall continued. "It's normal to have a few deaths on a difficult year. You shouldn't fret. We know what danger we're getting into when we signed on, and each year gives us different difficulties. We adapt."

"Yes, well, I'm responsible for these men, and I will not accept their deaths as readily as you who live with the danger. We have to come up with something. Some way to prevent anything else from happening." She turned a pleading glance his way and made his inside hollow out. "You're the man with ideas in this company. Help me, please? Help me figure out how to prevent future deaths, and how to get the government from shutting down the company when they discover their man's death was not an accident, and more importantly, help me find out who killed him, and why."

What it must have taken her to swallow her pride enough to ask for his help. "Do you have any suggestions?"

"No." She frowned, and rowed hard enough the water began to tug at his oar, threatening to pivot the boat if he didn't keep a steady pace with her. He adjusted his stroke to match hers.

"We can think on it for the next few days, and figure it out by the time we get to the mill," he suggested. "The river has a funny way of letting a man think."

"I suppose it does," she said wistfully.

They rounded a bend in the river as Blue, Clint, and Dick pulled the bateau onto the bank near a blockage to the main fork. Wall angled the wannigan toward where the bateau sat. "That's not good."

"What's wrong?" Victoria squinted.

"That fork is never blocked off, and it wasn't a beaver who did it."

"Someone intentionally blocked it?"

"Could be. We need to check it out to tell for certain." In a few quiet minutes, Wall eased the boat up the bank and secured it to the base of a sturdy bush near the river's edge. He raised his head in greeting to his friends. "How's it looking?"

"See for yourself." Blue motioned with his head toward the blockage.

Wall caught Victoria's eye and then turned to walk toward where Blue had indicated. He followed the trail for a few seconds before the evidence of dynamite blasts eroded the banks, opening the fork to lead to a lesser used river, and closing off the main river from the water.

"What do we do?" Victoria's lips pinched tight, and she glared at the blockage.

"We'll blast it back open, and hope this is the only one, but my guess is that someone's come along and diverted all of the water."

"That man we saw riding?" Victoria asked, and glanced back up the river, even though the man was long gone by now.

"Perhaps, but we'd best concentrate on getting the water flowing again, and deal with whoever did this when we get the river open. We may want to get up the camp and get a load down as soon as we can after this float, just in case," Wall suggested.

Victoria nodded, and then bent to tug at a stick near the bank to pull it free and toss it into the brush behind her back.

"I wouldn't worry about yanking it stick by stick. We'll blast it open again," he said, and motioned for Dick to go get the dynamite.

Victoria stood back and wiped her hands on her skirt.

Wall continued, "I don't think whoever did this counted on us coming down early to check the flow. I think they thought the drive would get hung up pretty bad, which is why I think we'll find more."

"I just hope we have enough dynamite," Blue said.

Dick trotted up to them and began to hand out the explosives.

Wall took his bundles. "Come with me, Miz Victoria. We'll set ours over in the smaller fork. I'll show you how to stop the flow, while the boys open up the main river."

On her nod, he led the way to the other side of the brush to where the creek fork roared to life with water not normally housed on that side of the tributary.

Within a few minutes, he set three bundles of dynamite, and then directed Victoria where to stand as he lit the first bundle, and then ran to join her. The blast exploded through the air, causing Victoria to jump next to him. Instinctively, he reached out and pulled her into his embrace.

She tucked her head into his chest as the second blast sounded, and a few seconds later the third. The scent of her hair filled the dusty air around them and all he could concentrate on was the way she grounded him to the moment. To the importance of getting the creek fixed right so he could please her with a full turn to the mill.

Dirt filled the air as, in the distance, Blue, Clint, and Dick's dynamite blasted along the river. Victoria glanced up into his face, her eyes shining with something he'd never seen before. Was it desire? He couldn't be certain. Not with the way she jumped to her feet and stalked toward the main river like it owed her money.

More like she was mad at him for overstepping his role by taking her in his arms. But he couldn't be sorry. Not for the way she'd felt with her head on his chest. At the very least, he could say he'd seen the softer side of the viper's belly.

Chapter 5

Victoria settled down for the evening next to the fire, her arms dusted with grime from the last few days of the river float. She'd never been so exhausted, or thrilled, in her life. She felt free. Unrestrained from everything that held her back in life. The men had been more than hospitable, allowing her the privacy of the cabin on the wannigan while they took up beds on the cold, hard ground next to a fire outside.

And Wall. He was determined to keep his promise to protect her and had never left her side when the possibility of danger may have arose. They'd removed four more man-made blockages, all aimed at slowing down her drive. Whoever had set out to halt the river flow had only needed to wait another month or so and the mountains would have done the job for him, and the lower they got down the mountain, the lower the rivers seemed to get. It worried her. If they didn't get a load down soon, they may lose whatever logs they'd already put into the lake for a raft. Months of winter work wasted.

Wall always seemed to be there to calm her fears with his mere presence as she thought of what might be. He was the one constant in all of this. The solid foundation.

Her heart began to beat rapidly in her chest the way it did that day when she'd instinctively took comfort in his embrace at the sound of the dynamite. Since then, she'd checked herself. Lived through each boom like a normal person was apt to do when faced with such a situation.

She liked the deep earthy musk that scented the front of his shirt though. It made her focus. She'd read somewhere that fragrances had the ability to lend a certain ambiance to a moment. Could make one focus, or even take away someone's ability to think and put them to sleep. Perhaps that's why the dirty cowboy she'd grown to at least like throughout the last few weeks seemed to lend her enough wits to react to situations properly. As he had when meeting Nichols. She didn't think she could have done it with so much ease without Wall by her side.

His smell.

Not the man himself, of course. A hardened cowboy turned logger, while he has his burly uses, is not one to take home to father to help run the company. Even if said cowboy has the uncanny ability to invent odd contraptions.

Wall Adair was a man she needed to get out of her thoughts, steal whatever shirt smells the most of him, and then send back up the mountain before she lost her mind completely. As it was, she could barely keep it away from the man, and on the river.

The blasted man in question plopped his perfect backside down beside her and gave her that disarming grin. His irritatingly blue eyes sparkled as if he harbored a secret. "What?"

He gave a sideways nod toward the river. "There's a little pool upstream, kinda hidden from the rest of the river."

"And?"

He shared a knowing look with the rest of the Devil May Cares. "We like to use it to bathe."

Uncaring as to how rude her behavior was, she let her mouth drop open. Did she smell so bad as to catch the attention of the loggers? "Are you saying I need a bath? I know I—"

Wall held up his hand to stop her words, and chuckled. "No, no."

The Devil May Cares all quietly laughed as well, but graciously turned their attention down to the fire.

Wall continued, "I'm saying, if you would like to bathe, you can have the first turn. We'll stay by the fire until you return. Promise. This is a favorite spot of ours because it's sort of protected. Mind you it's a bit low this year."

Victoria searched the river for this treasured bathing hole. Still not quite believing him. After all, she did smell. A bit. "I wasn't aware that filthy cowboys bathed."

Wall shrugged, and stood. "We do when the right watering hole comes around."

He motioned up river in a silent question, and she nodded, standing to follow as he began to lead the way.

"At home we have the best little creek that runs right through the valley from the range. There's a tree next to it which sort of arches out over the water. My brother loves to disappear and hide out over there when my sisters get to be too much."

"You come from a big family it sounds like." She lengthened her stride and drew even with him, glancing up into his face as he smiled down on her. His scent drifting on the breeze to tease her senses, and ground her once more. "It's only me at home, I'm afraid. If my mother had another child…a boy…I'm certain he would be running the family business."

"And you would be unhappy at home?" Wall's eyebrows raised at the question.

"Who knows? I may have been happy."

"But you weren't knowing that your father was going to give the company over to whoever you married."

"Because it's a family business, and I am his only child. It's my duty to run it. Not a husband's."

"So you'd be fine being a wife somewhere if you had a brother to run your business?"

"Like I said, who knows. We certainly never will."

Wall answered with a simple smile, but it was a pity smile. One she felt down to her toes. She'd always wanted a sibling. She had Garrett, of course, but he wasn't a real brother. He was a family friend who treated her like a sister. Not the same. What she wouldn't give to have a big family.

Perhaps someday.

The trees opened up to a small cove in the river, allowing for the perfect bathing spot, just as Wall had claimed. Excitement bubbled in Victoria's chest. She didn't have soap, but even a dip in the water would wash off the grime of a few days enough to make her feel like a woman again.

She stopped on the bank and turned with a genuine smile.

"I like that one," he said, and mimicked the grin. His eye sparked with something that made her stomach flip.

"I rarely give it."

"I know." His voice was husky now. Low and almost primal, and the sound made her heart kick up.

He reached into his pocket and pulled out a bar of soap, wrapped in a cloth. "It's not new. It's mine. I figure if you can stand it, maybe you can give it a few swishes in the water to wash the filthy cowboy off."

Something deep inside her flickered to life. Warmed the inner chambers of her core and made her want to reach out to touch him. To have the feel of his skin mix with the heat within her, and imprint on her memory. Instead, she clutched the threadbare cloth. "I think I can manage. Thank you."

"I figure I'd like to see if my soap can make this curl bounce again." He lifted his hand to the nape of her neck and tweaked her curl, sending her mind swirling. Unlike her, he took a deep breath. "It's been a little limp since all that dynamite dust got in it."

She forced herself to breathe, only to take in the scent of him. However, at this moment it did nothing to ground her to earth. Instead, it sent her reeling even more as he bent down with the scent, and pressed his lips to hers.

Her knees buckled, but he caught her before she lost all balance. He deepened the kiss and her riotous body leaned into him. She returned his kiss as any woman would to a man like Wall.

A few dizzying moments later, he stepped back and simply stared down at her. His chest rose and fell in rhythm with hers. He slid his gaze to her lips once more, and she reached up to touch them. Needed to feel the effects he'd had on her mouth with the pads of her fingers.

Without another word, Wall turned and left her to her bath. Her body fiery with passion and knees weak. If she wasn't careful, even the gentle flow of the pool would take her down river in her weakened state.

Once her legs would carry her, she eased her boots from her feet and set them along the bank. She waded into the river, fully clothed. First, taking the soap to her shirt, skirt, and then intimates. She undressed underwater, and then chanced leaning out of the surface enough to hang them on a long branch extending over the river.

She turned her back where her clothes would hopefully dry enough for her not to be too chilled when she put them back on. If not, she'd sit by the fire to accomplish the task.

What had happened on the bank? Wall—the leader of her rivermen, and a cowboy—had kissed her. She'd been kissed before, of course, but never like that. Not once had it made her melt into a man's arms. Forget all thought but the sensation of his lips on hers. How did she feel about it? Confused. Thrilled. Violated? No not violated. Which surprised her. She'd never wanted to be kissed by a cowboy.

She took her time washing her hair and body, and was about to turn around to grab her clothes when a crack sounded from behind her. She spun around as her clothes fell into the water with the broken tree branch where they had hung.

Her heart pounded and she tried to run toward them as they picked up speed and headed toward the river current.

"No!" she yelled.

The force of water pushed against her, slowing her speed. She tried hard to run, but slipped, so she began to swim toward them, but it was too late. The clothes hit the current and drifted away faster than any log she'd ever seen take the river.

Tears began to fall down her cheeks. She never cried, fancied herself above such a weak emotion, but this moment warranted the action.

"My clothes," she said the words aloud to no one but herself. As if saying it would bring them back. She slid back into the water until it covered her breasts, and let her tears mix with the river water, and the crunch of vegetation sounded from the trail Wall had brought her down.

"Victoria," he called from behind the brush and trees hiding the bathing hole.

As fast as she could, she crossed her legs and covered her breasts with her arms.

"Don't come any closer." She knew her voice shook with her tears, but she couldn't hide the tremor.

"What's wrong? I heard you yell."

"My clothes went down the river." Although she cried, she managed to say the last with enough anger to overcome the weakness.

Silence sounded louder than anything Wall could have said, but she waited for his response. After a moment, he spoke, his voice now tinged with both humor and concern. "Are they retrievable?"

"No. They're gone."

She heard a chuckle, followed by, "Hold on. I'll fetch you some of my clothes. I have to warn you, though, I was going to do laundry today so the only thing I have is filthy cowboy trousers, but I think I have a clean shirt."

"How filthy?"

"Do you really want to know?"

"I suppose not. I don't really have a choice. It's either wear your filthy cowboy clothes, or go naked."

"Stay in the water. I'll lay the clothes in the thicket over here by your boots."

"Thank you," she said the words in a weak voice.

A few minutes later she heard the now familiar crunch of Wall's boots on the pine needle riddled ground. "Give me a minute to get down the path. I'll stand guard to make certain none of the men come up."

"Again, thank you."

She stayed until his footsteps receded, and then waded out to where he'd laid the clothes. To his credit, on top of the pile sat a threadbare towel, but the consideration was more than she could take. She broke down in tears once more as she dressed in the overly large shirt and pants, and then slipped on her boots.

Struggling to keep the shirt closed, and pants up, she straggled down the path like a child trying on their parents' clothes. Tears still streaming down her face when Wall came into view.

He laughed. The blasted man.

"Stop right there," he ordered, and took off toward the night's camp. A minute later he returned with a line of rope and approached her as he smoothed the lanyard out in his hands. "We'll make a belt. Figure out how to keep this up."

"I can't show up at the mill like this. I'll be ruined." She cried.

He laughed.

"You were never even on this trip. So I don't see why you would be ruined."

She swiped at her tears with the sleeve of the overly large blue cotton shirt she wore. "I don't understand."

"I'll talk to the men. You talk to Paul. We'll smuggle you in at night, and no one will know you were even here. My men won't say anything. We may be hardened rivermen, and I may be a filthy cowboy, but we're the most trustworthy bunch of roughnecks you'll ever find in Montana. As long as you can trust Paul, your reputation will be safe. I promise."

"I can trust Paul with my life," she said, her spirits boosted.

Wall took her hand and towed her toward the camp. "Come on, let's go give the men a good laugh at your expense. In a few hours, you'll be laughing too, I promise."

She doubted she'd ever laugh at this nightmare of a bath, but Wall's easy attitude toward her situation lent a sort of calm to the moment. Plus, his scent drifted on the breeze to tickle her nose, and she took a deep breath to clear the emotion from her chest. She would get through this, follow Wall's guidance, and come out on top. She always did.

* * * *

Wall didn't bother to hold back his chuckle as Victoria picked at the stain on the trousers she wore while Wall slid a large branch into the small stream to redirect the flow back to the main river. To give Victoria credit, she'd worn the dang things without complaint ever since the day before. As he'd promised her, his men swore not to tell a soul she was even on the river run with them. And they would keep their word.

Truth be told, he felt bad that he didn't have a cleaner pair of pants to give her. He wasn't as uncaring as she believed all cowboys to be.

"This area seems familiar," she said, and wandered around the clearing.

Wall searched the banks. "Downstream is where we usually have a major blockage. Up the trail about a quarter of a mile is The Thirsty Woodsman. I believe we camped here last year. Although with the back flow the banks were a bit flooded then."

"Yes, I remember." She picked up a long stick and tossed it onto his growing pile, only to have it catch the water and flow downstream. Wall pinched his lips to hold back a smile and shoved another branch onto his man-made dam. Victoria frowned at the stick. "How long until we sneak me back into my house by the mill?"

Wall stood tall and studied the river, although he didn't need to. He knew the float better than he knew his bedroom back home. "Without a load to take we can make it by tomorrow night. You'll be sleeping in your feathered bed in no time, princess."

"How many princesses do you know who wear men's britches covered in what I hope is moss and not cow dung."

Wall stepped next to her, hoping to knock her slightly off balance by standing closer than was necessary, just to tease her. "I'm a filthy cowboy. You've said it yourself. What do you think it is?"

She slowly lifted her gaze from his chest to catch his eyes. To his delight she wasn't breathless like she'd been in days past, but her eyes shined with challenge, but not the hateful kind. The kind that might get them both in trouble. The kind of fire he liked to see in a woman's eyes.

"If you tell anyone I masqueraded around here dressed like this I will fire you, and then find whatever poor farmer it is who employs you in the winter, and force him to fire you as well."

"My father employs me in the winter. I doubt he will oblige you since he's always trying to get me to stay home." Wall stepped back, but kept his smug grin plastered on his face. "I'm surprised you don't know that. Aren't you the one who hired me?"

"No. My father was. And I know you work on a ranch, but I like teasing you. I haven't been privy to company business until I started to take over, and I haven't gone through all of our employee's records as of yet, but I intend to when we get back."

"You definitely should. You might find some useful information in there."

"Like the fact that you're actually educated, and that's why you can design ingenious contraptions to revolutionize Montana logging?"

"Nope. I was taught by my mother at home so I could help my pa and pappy on the ranch."

"Too bad. I could use an educated man at the mill."

Wall plucked the top off a dried-out asparagus vine from last year, and tossed it down onto the ground. "You hold a lot of stock in education, don't you?"

"An educated man can go far in this world."

"Whereas we filthy cowboys can only go as far as the barn?"

"I didn't say that."

"But you think it."

She didn't respond, so he picked up the last branch he'd cut for the dam, and shoved it hard into the creek, and turned away from Victoria just as Luther came stumbling from the trail leading to The Thirsty Woodsman, clearly soaked. Wall sniffed. Cheap whisky, by the smell of it.

"What are you doing here?" Victoria asked, placing her hands on her hips, but ducking behind him before Luther could spot her attire.

"Good to see you too, sister dear." Luther stumbled, but caught himself before he fell. "Got the dams open, I see."

"What do you know about it?" Wall blocked Victoria even more from Luther's sight as he glared maliciously at her.

"Oh, it was me, of course." Luther laughed. "Hadn't planned on you coming down the river before the drive, but you're all-knowing, ain't you, Wallace." Luther fell against Wall's chest. "Wallace Adair, smartest jackass in Montana. Not so smart, though, are you?"

"You're soaked, Luther. Go back to The Thirsty Woodsmen and get one of their cabins. Sleep it off."

Luther stood, yanked a stick of dynamite from his back pocket, and handed it to Wall. "You're right. I've got to get to town. Got a big court date."

Wall clenched the delicate explosive in one hand, and spun Luther around with the other. "Best get a cup of coffee on your way out."

"Don't you know why you aren't the smartest jackass?" Luther stepped around him as though he had a solid foot about him and stopped directly in front of Victoria. Dipping his head low until his nose came within inches of hers.

She glared.

The pride Wall felt for her gumption was outweighed by the focus he had on every twitch of Luther's muscles. If the man so much as leaned toward her, he'd show him why the Devil May Cares called Wall a pugilist.

"Cause he ain't even smart enough to figure out that were related, you and I." Luther stumbled a step back, and Wall stepped closer, putting himself between Victoria and Luther once more.

Luther gave a drunk chuckle. In a dramatic tone, he said, "Sister mine. Gets everything while I get banned from Montana. You should be home being someone's wife. That's all women are good for anyway." He reached his hands out to his side. "Well, I didn't leave. I'm here. And I'm getting my half of the mill."

"We are not related," Victoria stated as if the man were daft.

"He's drunk," Wall said, and turned to try and usher Victoria toward the boat.

"I am. I am drunk, but I ain't lying." Luther began to saunter toward The Thirsty Woodsman, leaving his dynamite behind. "You'll see."

At that, he left.

Wall examined the explosive, once satisfied it was solid enough to store in their explosive box, he motioned for Victoria to follow him to the wannigan. "Don't mind him. Drunk men ramble all sorts of things when they've had a few too many."

"He seemed rather certain." Victoria rubbed her arms while she walked, and her face grew pale.

"You can't take anything a soaked man says seriously."

Her dimples showed, but not with a smile, as she tensed her mouth. She pointed toward the explosives. "What do you think he was coming out to do with that?"

"Probably one last effort to delay us getting down the river." Wall stuck the dynamite in the wooden box outside the cabin and took up his oar as Victoria did the same on her side. Ever since she'd started to float with them, the Devil May Cares had transferred the box of explosives they'd bought to redirect the water flow, to the bateau. "Let's go find Dick and the boys, and give them this."

On Victoria's nod, Wall untied the wannigan and shoved them free of the bank, leaping on board to take up his oar. They rowed for half an hour before the bateau drifted into view with all three Devil May Care boys piled inside. Blue saw them and waved.

Once they drew close enough, Clint lifted something into the air. "Miz Victoria!" he called. "Found your skirt tangled in a willow downstream about half a mile. Thought you might want to see if you can save it."

The bateau drifted close enough for Clint to reach out. Victoria dropped her oar next to her feet, and snatched up the skirt like a starving child to a piece of bread. Wall pulled in his oar and set it next to Victoria's and watched her examine the piece.

"It's not torn. Thankfully," she said, and turned it over. "A bit dirty, but I can rinse most of this out right now, hang it to dry, and be wearing it by sundown. I won't have to sneak into the mill yard in the middle of the night like some thief."

Wall picked up his oar and dipped it in the water to steady them as they began to turn. "Go ahead. I'll wait while you wash it." She rushed to the edge, and he grabbed the dynamite and then turned toward the bateau to hand it to Dick. "Did you boys find anymore blockages?"

"Nah," Dick answered. "Seems to have stopped. We were planning on riding for another few hours and then stopping for the night. Getting to the mill tomorrow by noon. Maybe there will be a train we can catch to get back up the mountain and get this load down before the river runs dry."

Wall nodded and searched the mountain peaks, almost shed of their yearly snowcaps. The lifeline to the spring runoff and log drives. "I say we get to town and turn around and take whatever logs are lakeside down within a day."

"Sounds good to me," Victoria said from behind him. He turned as she rang out her skirt, and hung it over a beam jutting from the corner of the crude cabin.

"We'll see you at camp then." Dick lifted his head in goodbye, and pushed the bateau away from their boat.

Lighter, the smaller vessel took the water at a faster speed than the wannigan, leaving Victoria and Wall once again alone. The memory of Luther standing threateningly over her tore a hole through his insides. He couldn't let the blowhard get close to Victoria again. He'd been close to beating the man, and in his inebriated state, Wall would have had an easy time blundering him to death if he so wished. Which at that moment, he'd wanted nothing more. Victoria, in all her charming yet dangerous state, ensnared his attention to an alarming degree.

She would end up hating him once she learned who he really was, and that his father wasn't the penniless farmer she believed him to be.

Chapter 6

Victoria stomped up the steps to the mill. They'd been back for over an hour and the only thing she'd managed to do was bathe and change into one of her fancy, uncomfortable dresses. She needed to speak to Paul, and then check on the operations.

One question that niggled at the back of her mind since they tied the wannigan to the dock was why hadn't the train moved? The same logging train that had been in the yards when she left, still remained in the same spot when she returned. Not a good sign.

She let her heels click loudly down the hallway as she walked, hoping the sound would do its job and alert Paul to her presence, and she wasn't disappointed. He peeked his head out of his office.

"Ah, you're back," he said as she entered, and shut the door. "I was beginning to worry that I'd have to send a search party up the river for you."

"We had some issues." She sat on his couch, perched at the edge as was the only position her corset would allow. "Let's just say I learned how to set dynamite to change a river flow."

Paul frowned and adjusted in his seat. The springs beneath his chair squeaked at the movement, lending to the tense moment. "That bad?"

"There's enough water to do one drive down soon, but Luther had blocked the flow down the main river."

"Luther?" Paul eased his shoulders, and the lines on his face turned back into their usual wrinkles. "He shucked outta here last year."

"He hasn't. And what do you know about his claim that he is my brother?" Paul remained silent. His face like stone.

Victoria's heart began to beat faster, and she had to force back the panic that bubbled deep within her chest. Paul always avoided topics where he had to tell the truth when he didn't want to.

"Tell me," she said the words in the most authoritative voice she could manage. She had no time for ridiculous secrets. "He's threatened the mill and I need to know how to fight him. Does he, or does he not have a claim on the mill?"

"He does not."

Relief moved through her, starting at her fingertips and spreading through her chest, and then slid all the way to her toes. It lasted only a second.

"He is, however, your half-brother. A family skeleton, if you will."

"What?"

Victoria stared at the polished knot on the wood floor plank. All but that spot grew blurry. Paul had never lied to her before. He'd left truths out, avoided them if he didn't want her to know, but never lied. If he said Luther was her brother, then chances were, it was true. But how?

She glanced up into his face, questioning him with a simple look.

Paul shook his head. "It's not my story to tell. You need to contact your mother and father. Maybe ask them to come home."

All she could manage to say as she stared at the floor again was, "Yes."

"And, Vicki," Paul said, drawing her attention once more. "The lawyer left something on your desk. He waited here for three days for you, but you didn't show on time, so he had to leave."

A tingle started in Victoria's chest as she stood and, without another word, walked into her office. She closed the door behind her, and settled in her chair, picking up the paper with the mill lawyers familiar scroll across the front. She ran a critical eye over the contents as a knock sounded.

"Enter," she called out.

Wall slipped into her office and then shut the door, enclosing them in privacy. She held up the paper. "From my lawyer. Apparently, Luther is fighting for half of the mill, and the courts have given me a month to get the logs down the rivers and to the mill, otherwise they will stop the drive and confiscate the wood."

"How do they plan to do that?"

"I have no idea, but now I have to go fight a brother I never knew I had apparently."

"So it's true?"

Victoria gave a curt nod. "Yes. Paul confirmed it, although he won't tell me the whole of it." She stood and started to pace in front of the large window overlooking the mill yard. How did she feel about it all? She'd always wanted a brother or sister, but not like this. Not one who shows up only to take everything she's worked for from her the moment she got it.

Family should be close. Loving. They spend holidays together and tease each other out of love. They don't sneak around with threats, and then try to break the other one down.

"I'm afraid I don't come bearing any better news."

She spun around. "Why? What?"

"They haven't gotten a load down the mountain on the railroad system yet. The train can't go up because it can't get back down unless the one up there moves. No one knows yet what's going on, but it's certainly not normal operations. The boys and I need to get up there to figure out what's wrong but—"

"But we don't have a train." She stated the obvious.

"We can ride up, but we'll be taking the rest of your mill horses. And we'll need to bring the wannigan and bateau up as soon as we can. Either with a wagon or train."

"Go up and get the blasted train moving. Send someone down with my horses, and then get a load down the river as soon as you can. I'll send the wannigan and bateau on the first train up. Maybe I can get a second engine from Garrett's father to stick on the other side of this train." She motioned toward the one standing still outside her window. "But if the new boat and wannigan aren't back by the time a load is ready to go, take the drive down anyway and have Aunt June take minimum food supplies in a bateau. We don't have time to wait for anything." She massaged her forehead. The small pressure helped ease the tension behind her eyes enough to give her a small bit of relief. "I need to go into town and wire my father. He needs to come home. Paul was right. He shouldn't have left." Tears burned behind her eyes. "I was a fool to think I could run a business. I suppose Luther's right and I'm not good for anything other than being a wife to someone."

Before she could even spin around, Wall rounded the desk, closed most of the distance between them, and then reached out to tug her to him, just out of sight from the window. "Don't ever let anyone tell you that you are only good for one thing. And certainly don't believe it if they do."

With those words echoing through her mind, he pressed his lips to hers again. Like before, her knees buckled. She didn't fight. Why, she had no idea. She should. A proper woman—whom she'd been groomed to be— would push him away and slap him for taking what wasn't his.

She didn't.

Instead, she leaned into him and entwined her arms around his neck. She needed this. Needed to feel the freeing sensations that swirled through her body whenever Wall touched her. Kissed her. Wanted to see what other freedoms he could give her with his calloused hands.

She wanted him. Shouldn't, but didn't care.

Spirits boosted, she pushed him until his back was against the wall, and leaned up onto her tiptoes to deepen the kiss, taking control. He groaned, broke the kiss to stare in her eyes, and spun around until she was against the wall instead.

She smiled seductively at his assertiveness, as she struggled to take in enough air to circulate through her body. As if her lungs grew, but the damn corset wouldn't allow her to take in the air needed to satisfy their needs. Why did she put on the blasted thing?

Wall's concentration moved from her eyes to her breasts. He reached up and traced one calloused hand across the collar of her dress. Every sensation in her body followed his finger as it moved across the sensitive skin on her breasts.

His other hand encircled one side of her waist and he squeezed enough that she could feel gentle pressure through the tight fabric, which seemed to do nothing more than shoot twinges down to her most intimate of places.

"I want to take my knife and cut this damn thing from your body. I want to see what perfection God has created underneath all of this finery." He flipped the lace between her breasts.

She opened her mouth to say something, but her mind ran blank. He let out a desperate chuckle, and then gave her a quick kiss, which helped force air back into her mouth. She swallowed hard.

Would it be so bad to give herself to a man like Wall? She had security in life. She had wealth. If life were to strip her of love as it appeared to have done already, would it be so bad to have one moment with a man like Wall Adair to carry her through? "Don't cut it. It ties in the front."

With those words Wall pressed his body against hers and groaned. "Don't say that, princess. A man can only resist so much before the devil takes over and makes his decisions for him. It's the way we were made."

"Then it's a good thing I hired you to be my protector. And a Devil May Care," she crooned. "Word has it they're as wild as the devil himself."

"Woman, you have no idea what you just did," he said, and then leaned down to crush her in a kiss that she felt to her toes.

Her insides shined.

Delighted in the response she got from Wall as she teased him beyond control. Knew she was flirting with a world she had no experience in, but didn't care. She wanted this. Wanted him.

* * * *

Whatever restraints Wall had before snapped at Victoria's words. She didn't truly know what she'd asked for. Not with him. He'd courted his fair share of women, even paid for a few back in his younger days, but he wasn't a young buck anymore.

He was a leader of men. A Devil May Care. A cowboy. And regardless of what Victoria might think, all of those meant he was honorable enough to know when to dance with the devil, and when to walk away with the angels.

Except, as Victoria's chest heaved beneath his palm, all he could envision was her hair twisted as it was on the top of her head like a halo, while he tore the blasted bodice from her body. Fine. He'd untie it like she requested, but either way the angel before him would stand blessedly naked if she didn't tell him to stop.

Yet she urged him to continue.

No. She wasn't an angel. She was a princess. Commanding him to do her bidding. Take her to a place she'd never gone before, and he was helpless to disobey her command.

She pouted her lips, and he bent to kiss her as he unbuttoned her bodice, and then began to tug at the lace of her corset.

He fumbled, and she reached up and began to undo it herself. He stepped back and watched as she undressed with expert hands, needing only minimal help from him.

She dropped the last of her clothes in a pool around her feet, and stood before him as breathtaking as he knew she'd be. Back at the river, when she'd lost her clothes, he'd been more than tempted to peek through the brush, but he'd managed to keep his eyes to himself. Now all he could think about was what he missed out on by not charming her earlier.

He couldn't tear his eyes off her form. Her curves so soft and perfect a man could run his hands up and down them for days and still not grow tired of how they felt against his overly worked hands.

"Your turn," she said, her voice like silk.

He shook his head. She may be the boss, but he was the master. At least in games of passion. "Not yet."

He stepped toward her, and lifted her until her legs wrapped around his hips. Her warmth pressed tight, uncomfortable against his manhood. "I'm going to show you what it's like to not be in charge for once."

He licked the dip between her clavicle and neck, and then kissed the moisture. Her heartbeat began to beat hard beneath his mouth.

"I already feel vulnerable," she rasped. "No clothes. Unlocked door." She leaned her head back and extended her neck to draw his attention, but he didn't take the offering. Instead, he walked to the side table, moved a stack of books aside, and set her atop the sturdy surface.

In three steps, he clicked the lock into place, walked behind her desk and pulled the curtains to the large window shut, and then returned to stand before her. "There. Now you're vulnerable only to me."

She bit the corner of her bottom lip and drew his attention. He leaned down, but instead of kissing her, he licked her teeth and mouth. She let go of her bite and he plundered her mouth, mimicking the way he wanted to ravish her body.

He smoothed his hands over the contours of her curves the way he'd envisioned when he watched her mere seconds ago. The feel of her skin was even more intoxicating than he'd anticipated. The way her nipples pressed into his palms, the heat from her womanhood against his hips, he suspected he'd remember the feel of her for years to come.

She tugged at his shirt, and he obliged, ripping it from his waistband, and tossing it over his shoulder. She stopped, her face frozen and eyes fixed on his chest as she reached up tentatively and traced his muscles. "I didn't know cowboys looked like this."

"There's a lot about me you don't know," he rasped out, and tugged her hips closer to his.

She gasped at the movement. "Your pants."

He tilted his head to one side

"Please?" she pleaded.

He answered by lifting her from the side table, bringing her to the couch along the edge of her room. He laid her down and began to strip as she'd requested.

His manhood sprang free as he dropped his trousers around his feet, and stepped out of them.

Her eyes widened, but she reached her arms up, beckoning him. He had to oblige. Couldn't resist. He struggled to keep his mind steady as he leaned over, kissing her as the heat from her body entwined with his.

They were perfection together. Without the ability to defend themselves, from each other or outside forces, but something about the way her body heated against his made him feel as though nothing could stop them.

Maybe it was the way her hips heaved against him, begging with a force he didn't know the small woman possessed. No longer able to deny her, he positioned himself inside her.

For the barest of seconds she tensed, but then relaxed. He'd forgotten she was a virgin, but the moment didn't seem to bother her much, so he retracted, and pushed again. Repeating the motion until she quivered.

She began to cry out, and he covered her mouth with his hand. "Bite down on my hand if you must, but don't let us be known."

"I can't help it," she said, her voice muffled under his hand. He let her mouth free, but her abdomen still quivered. So he kissed her. Hoping he could muffle her moans as he started again.

She grew frantic, and he hardened his kisses, occasionally urging her to keep quiet.

In one whirling moment, she exploded around him at the same time he did deep inside her.

He lightened his kisses until he figured she needed to breathe, and then drew back to watch her face. Her emotions. Did she feel the same as he did? Was she regretting the moment? Because he didn't. Couldn't.

He balanced on his elbow and scooted half off her, and smoothed back the wet tendrils of hair from her forehead as she worked to control her breathing. She stared at the ceiling.

They laid like that until the room began to chill.

Victoria licked her lips. "That was…" She turned to stare at him, her eyes still dazed.

He smiled. What man wouldn't? "Princess, that was only a taste."

She squinted. "What do you mean?"

Wall chuckled, and stood, plucking her discarded dress from the floor, and spreading it over her in case she was as chilled as he thought she might be.

"I'm a cowboy. We're known for working, fighting, and loving."

She sat up, holding her skirt against her breasts. "You're also a logger. What are they known for?"

Wall stared at the ceiling, searching for an answer, but everything he came up with was inappropriate to say in front of a woman. Luckily, he didn't have to speak because Victoria answered for him. "I suppose they're known for their stamina."

"Yes. Stamina," he agreed with a chuckle, and lay back down next to her.

"Does that mean you're going to show me what both a logger and cowboy are known for?"

Good Lord, this woman was intoxicating. "Do you want me to?"

With a giggle, she nodded, so he kissed her again.

Hell-bent on showing her whatever she wanted until she begged him to stop.

Chapter 7

Wall stood with the Devil May Care boys and waited for Victoria to walk out into the misty morning air, so ripe with fresh beginnings. Her full skirts dusted the ground around her, but if he hadn't clutched the sides of her corset the night before only to experience her beauty without it, he'd have missed the fact that today she'd forgone the item. Much to his delight.

Unbeknownst to him the day before, it was well after dark before Victoria had finally been satiated enough to leave her office. Innocent that she was before the event, it surprised him to no end that she could stand on her own this morning, let alone walk the dimpled dirt in the boots that peeked from beneath her hem with every step.

Had he met his match in the woman before him?

Victoria stopped next to him and sucked in a deep breath, with a shutter so slight one might have missed it if they weren't in tune to her nuances. Which he was. Especially after last night. She was still affected by him as he was her.

If he didn't need to get going, he might have made some excuse to retreat into her office once more. He didn't feel bad about taking her innocence. She was a woman. Strongest he'd ever met. She knew her mind. Knew what she wanted, and had sought it with vigor.

He hadn't counted on the way her body would become a drug he craved, though.

The jingle of bells sounded in the distance, just outside the mill gates, and interrupted his wayward thoughts as Victoria opened her mouth to ask whatever question she'd had on the tip of her tongue.

They all watched as a traveling merchant maneuvered his wagon into the mill yard.

"Who's that?" Victoria asked.

"Bud," Wall answered. "He visits the camps some years."

Bud pulled his wagon to a stop and saluted as he leapt down. "Is Mr. Harrison here?"

Victoria stepped forward. "I'm his daughter. I've taken over for him."

"S'that so?" he asked, and Victoria raised her chin in challenge. Wall hid a smile. She didn't know the old man the way the loggers did. His question was merely a question. "I suppose you're the woman I need to speak with, then. Wanted to go up to your camps and help keep your men well supplied." He patted his wagon.

Victoria's tense shoulders eased. "Only if you got room for my men here. They were just headed up that way and could use a ride."

"Aye. I got plenty of room in the back."

"Splendid." She turned as if to go into the mill, but stopped. "We're in a hurry, so if you wouldn't mind waiting for my accountant, I'll pay you to make haste."

"No need for that, miss. I got a box of fruit here for Miz June. I wouldn't want it to go bad."

"Obliged," she said, as Bud and the Devil May Cares tossed their belongings in the back, and then jumped onboard the wagon themselves.

Wall faced Victoria as Bud turned the wagon back toward the gate.

"I'll come back as soon as I can." He hoped the promise showed in his voice, and it must have for the finest of pink dusted her cheeks, and she suddenly grew interested in the tip of her shoe.

This coy side of her was quite charming.

"I'll be waiting." With those words she gave a smile. Different from all the rest. Different from even the one she reserved for herself. This smile was for him alone.

He didn't know if she meant the look to carry him back to her quicker than he normally would have, but that's what it did to him. Made him not want to leave, but at the least, return with all haste.

He would.

He'd go up, and bring a drive right back down as soon as he could.

If they weren't in the center of everything, he'd take another kiss. One to take with him, but he couldn't. Instead, he tipped his cowboy hat, scooped up his bag, and ran to toss the bags in and leap on the back of the wagon, feet dangling, as Bud set the wheels in motion and rounded the fence.

He rode like this for a few hours in comfortable conversation with his men, until Bud took the first water break for the horses.

The wagon sat underneath the shade of a tall pine, and Wall jumped from the back to stretch. They stayed only long enough to refresh the horses, and then Bud motioned toward the buckseat next to him. "I got a spot up here for one of you if you care."

Wall watched as the Devil May Cares settled in the back, and then inclined his head. "I'll take it."

"You the river boys?" Bud asked as Wall climbed up beside him.

"Yep." Wall settled, and the wagon jerked into motion.

"Lookin' dry this year."

"We're going to be taking a drive down as soon as we get back."

"Aunt June going on the drive?"

Wall turned a smile on the man. It wasn't a secret that Bud was sweet on their camp cook. "She always does. We'd starve without her I think."

Bud chuckled. After a few silent minutes, he continued. "How's Great Mountain fairing?"

"Fairing?"

Bud waved in the general direction of the center of the state. "With all of the hubbub from the government big bugs? Had a couple o'mills out Helena way who had to shut their doors. Weren't interested in working for the big bugs instead of themselves I suppose."

"We are surviving."

"Good to know. That cattle business is where the money is for the state, and them officials can't seem to find room for both loggers and cattlemen."

"I'm both, so I'm sort of torn between two worlds."

Bud whistled. "Are you, now? And how's that working out for you?"

Wall laughed, more to himself than anyone else. "Not very well. My hearts here with the river and timber, but my roots are over there with the cattle and my family." He pointed toward the far-off mountain range where his father kept their herd in the summer, just visible over the peaks of the Mission Mountain Range.

"I don't envy you that fight." Bud maneuvered the wagon across the bridge where Victoria had met them almost two weeks before. "I'm a firm believer that a man's gotta follow his heart. That's why I got myself this wagon. It's my dream." At Wall's bewildered look, Bud smiled. "Don't be so surprised. I ain't rich or nothing, but my family has a small little apple farm outside of Spokane. My brother runs it, and I'm free to travel as I wish. So I, too, know the importance of family and roots."

"It's a bit more difficult than that for me, I'm afraid." Wall didn't know if he should divulge the information he was about to share, but Bud had always proved to be trustworthy, and there was something about working out the issues plaguing his mind since the dinner with Victoria. "My father is Representative Nichols's biggest supporter. Especially when it comes to keeping the forest land for agriculture use. Victoria only just learned about the government's plans to make milling more difficult once Montana becomes a state."

"And you're sweet on the girl?"

Wall answered by tipping his head to the side.

Bud snapped the reins. "I saw the way you watched her when she was being the big bug. Ain't no hiding love I'm afraid."

"I wouldn't say love," Wall said, but paused. He'd never been in love. Last year when Garrett had asked him if he'd sacrifice honor for love, he didn't think much on the topic. Didn't think love could actually exist for a man like him. One searching for meaning in the middle of the woods, away from most of the opposite sex. Love was as fluid as the white water he rode every year.

"Well, let's hope Montana don't become a state. You and I wouldn't be able to follow our hearts no longer, and would be forced back to our roots."

Wall huffed his agreement and concentrated on the road. In truth, he didn't know what he wanted in life. He loved both the timber and the cattle, but it didn't matter. He knew it was only a matter of time before he'd be needed at the ranch and could no longer chase his dreams. How would Victoria fit into his life then?

She wouldn't. He'd never see her after he left for home once and for all.

The rest of the trip he spent in both silent thought, interrupted by occasional small talk. By nightfall they stopped and slept, only to wake up with the sun and continue on the trail. Shortly after noon chow the following day, they finally rattled into camp, and Wall leapt from his perch, as the loggers at camp surrounded the wagon.

He'd forgotten it was Sunday. The one day a week the men could relax and take care of their personal business. *Damn.* That meant he'd have to wait until Tuesday to get a drive started. He'd needed to tell Garrett so he could get the word out to the Bonner boys.

He didn't have far to look for the man came sauntering into the meadow with his wife on his arm, both of their faces shining with love. Is that how he'd looked at Victoria? Somehow, he doubted it. Garrett and Beth's love was deep. Smooth and easy.

Not primal like the way he felt when near Victoria.

He wasn't in love, but he had found a common interest with the intoxicating woman.

He beckoned Garrett over once his wife disappeared into conversation with Carrie. "We'll be heading out by Tuesday on the drive. If you'll pass the word along."

"Good to see you again too, friend." Garrett extended his hand and Wall shook it. "And I'll let them know as soon as Beth gets a peek at what Bud's got inside there."

"Thanks," he said. "I've got to get my gear stowed. I'll meet up with you later to let you know what's been going on at the mill."

Garrett nodded. "Sounds good."

As his friend left, Wall yanked his bag from the back of Bud's wagon, and retired to his bunk. Relieved to be home. His summer home, anyway. By the time he'd organized his gear, and cleaned off the road grime, the sun began to lean toward the western mountain range. He headed toward Aunt June's camp. The best place to find a hungry logger near supper time on a Sunday. True to the men's habits, Garrett stood with his wife next to Aunt June. With a whistle, Wall beckoned him over to a spot far enough away from the crowd of loggers to talk in private.

"Simon," Wall called, and waved him over as well.

Wall waited until Simon stopped next to them. His friend raised his head in greeting. "How's the river?"

"Low," Wall answered. "We're only going to get one drive down before we run out of river. We had to block some forks, and unblock others in order to get a direct route. The boys and I are going to have to take the drive down in no more than two days or else the raft will have to stay here until next spring. By then the logs will be no good to the mill."

"That's where we have a problem," Garrett said. "The steam pulley you designed over the winter is busted, and we have no idea how to fix it. If we're gonna get a load down the mountain, we need to get it repaired."

"Blast! The machinist who helped me make it shucked out to California last month. I have a friend near Frenchtown who might be able to help if we need any parts, though." Wall kicked at a pebble. "If I stay behind to fix it, then the boys will only have five on our team, three who know the waters and what they're doing. My two greenhorns did a run over in Wisconsin, but this is their first experience with Montana white water. I'm going to need someone experienced to go down."

"I'd go, but I have to stay with the train," Garrett responded.

"What about Beth?" At this point Wall was desperate. Victoria counted on him to get a load down, but she also needed him to get the loader fixed. They didn't have time for him to do both. He needed someone to take his place on the drive.

Simon opened his mouth to respond when Garrett shook his head. "No one tells Beth. She'd go whether I wanted her too or not, and I'd go mad up here wondering if she's gone and gotten herself killed."

"I second, Garrett," Simon said. "Beth stays behind, and no one says anything to her."

"Well, then, that leaves you." Wall stared at Simon. He knew his face showed his desperation, but it couldn't be helped. That's how he felt.

"I'll go," Simon offered.

Relief spread through Wall's chest at the words. Although Simon had been off this year, one thing was certain, he could count on the timber beast to get the load down. And fast. "You're one to ride the river with." He slapped his friend's shoulder in thanks.

"I'll remember you said that next time you need me to take your place. Can't ride the river with me if you're staying behind." Simon gave a crooked smile.

Wall chuckled and studied the chute. "I think the big bugs at the mill will be happy with the drive. Happier if we can get two down before the river runs low."

"Or get the train to start running loads." Garrett's eyebrows drew together, mimicking Wall's own concerned frown. He suspected they all knew the importance of this year's harvest, but they didn't know just how important it was to Victoria.

"I'll go talk to Aunt June, and get the men ready to head out in two days," Wall said, and rushed past, leaving Garrett and Simon alone.

At least now he had a plan to get a drive down. Now he just needed to figure out what was wrong with the loader so he could get the train going again. Not only for Victoria's sake, but for the river men, and the entire Great Mountain Lumber Company.

* * * *

Victoria dropped her chin to her chest hoping the stretch it gave on the back of her neck would be enough to ease the knot. The buggy jerked as it rolled over a rut in the road while she reread Wall's note. Making a mental note of the part he needed. She handed Paul the note with the address Wall sent to her. "When we're done at the courthouse we need to stop by this address."

"Looks like it's up Frenchtown way." Paul handed the paper back to her. "A little out of our way."

"Yes, but necessary for the railroad logging to get going again."

Paul answered with a nod, and yanked hard on the reins to stop the horses before the telegraph office. "Let's hope your father responded to my wire."

He jumped off and rounded the buggy to help her down, but she managed to leap off before he'd even approached her side. She entered the building behind Paul.

"Anything for Great Mountain?" Paul asked before the clerk even had the chance to great them.

The man shook his head. "'Fraid not. Not since Mr. Harrison first got to Seattle."

The familiar way the clerk spoke to Paul wasn't lost on Victoria.

"Do you send a lot of messages?" she teased.

"I have lately, I'm afraid."

"Whatever for? To my father?"

"Now, Miz Victoria," Paul began, and let all of his weight rest on one foot. "You're a fine boss. Just making certain we're keeping your father updated is all."

"Yet you haven't gotten a response in a while?"

She glanced between him and the clerk, the second of whom turned a bright shade of red, and suddenly found his paperwork interesting.

"I'd like to send a telegraph to my father," she said once confident the men weren't going to answer.

She took the paper from the clerk, wrote the message, and waited for him to type it out. Once he was finished, she lifted her hand holding her wrist pouch, took out the necessary money needed for the note, and handed it to the man, and then added a little extra. "When he responds, send someone to the mill with all haste."

The clerk dipped his head in agreement, and took the money to deposit it in a pouch as Paul turned to usher her outside. "Now to the courthouse. Gustav will meet us there."

Victoria's heart sped up at the thought of their next stop. "What do you think is going to happen? Do you think he has a chance of taking the company from me?"

Paul frowned. "It'd be a whole lot easier if your father was here. I told him it was a bad move to go away so soon after turning the company over, but he refused to listen."

"If he would have known something like this was going to happen, I'm certain he would have stayed."

Paul grunted his agreement, and the conversation fell silent as the courthouse came into view. Paul brought the rig to the bottom of the staircase to drop her off, and then left. Leaving her to stand alone at the bottom of a building so dominating in appearance it left her feeling as intended. About an inch tall to a grasshopper.

"Well, well." A voice she didn't quite recognize sounded behind her. She spun around as Luther and the man with the cane—she recognized as being Sanchez by his description—walked up beside her. Luther sneered. "Glad you could tear yourself away from your tower to join us."

Their family resemblance obvious with each wave of their slicked black hair, and tanned skin. Today the younger man—the one she knew to wear logger's spikes—sported a tailored suit cut similar to that of the man who was obviously his father.

Which meant her mother was Luther's mother. If they were, in fact, half brother and sister. At the thought, her throat closed all the way to the knot in her stomach. When he'd made the claim a week before, she'd honestly believed her father was behind the debacle.

But there was no doubting Luther and Sanchez resemblance.

Victoria struggled to gain control of her breath long enough to speak, but before she could, her lawyer stepped up next to her. "Harassing my client, I see."

"No, sir," Luther said, and took one step back. "Just greeting my sister is all."

"We'll see if that can even be proved." Her lawyer, Gustav, slid his arm behind her back and ushered her up the stairs. His hand at her back guided her in the right direction, but it didn't feel right. Didn't calm her like it did when Wall touched her in the same fashion. What she wouldn't give to have him here beside her for this.

If he were here, then she could speak when confronted with something that knocked her off her mental horse.

At least he was taking care of Great Mountain for her. He'd sent Simon down with a load while he worked hard to start up the railroad logging once more. If she could just get through these next few hours, get his part, and get up the mountain to give it to him then all would be well. She could smell his scent, be next to him, and find her calm.

Gustav ushered her into a seat behind a table, and shortly after Paul joined her on her right side while the lawyer sat on the left. A few minutes later, the judge appeared, and she stiffened her spine.

With a tap of his gavel, the room grew silent and the judge began to speak, but all Victoria could hear was the rush of the blood past her ears. At this point she had no choice but to trust in Paul and her lawyer.

Lord, I wish father were here. Or Wall. Even Wall would know what to do. How to make it right. Or at least that's how it felt when he was near. But they weren't. The only thing she could do was straighten her skirts, throw back her shoulders, and attack her problem head on.

A few minutes ticked by with more people saying things she couldn't quite comprehend, and her lawyer stood. Paul was right. This was out of her realm of understanding. She could balance books, barter sales, and even start a new logging system, but she had no idea what was happening in this courtroom.

Her lawyer paced before the judge, and she chanced a glance at Paul's face. He smiled and her heart eased the slightest of bit. She leaned over to him, and whispered, "What's going on?"

"He's just pointed out that the mill belongs to your father."

"And Luther is my mother's son," she managed enough sass behind her words to get her point across.

Paul jerked his head back a fraction. "I suppose you saw the resemblance and figured it out."

"You could have told me earlier and spared me the distress of such a shocking revelation."

The judge slid them a glare, and Paul answered her with a simple shake of his head while keeping his gaze on the judge. She'd have to wait to address her concerns with him later. For now, she needed to try to get her head in the proceeding.

Was that a bill of sale her lawyer had in his hand? Victoria squinted to see, and straightened to listen to what he said. "...As you can see it was sold back in '81. Everything was legal..."

Okay so a bill of sale, but for what? Blast! She'd missed that part by talking to Paul. And what did that have to do with her now, and Luther's claim on the mill? She was only twelve in eighteen-eighty-one. Which would make Luther...What would it make him? Was he her older or younger brother?

She focused once more as her lawyer sat, and Luther's stood, holding out what looked to be a birth certificate. Was he an older brother, or younger? If she'd known him growing up, would they have been friends, or enemies as they were today?

Unfortunately, she would never have an answer to her questions.

After what seemed like an hour of Luther's lawyer talking, while Luther and his father sat there looking quite satisfied with themselves, their lawyer finally sat.

"I've heard from both sides today," the Judge began as the room grew deathly quiet. "Unfortunately, I don't feel as though I have enough information to make a decision. I want to see Mrs. Harrison in this courtroom, and I believe Miz Harrison's lawyer. Since the company belongs to Mr. Harrison, he too should be here for these proceedings. Miz Victoria

Harrison, you have one month to locate and bring home your parents, or the court will rule in favor of Mr. Sanchez. In addition, I will be sending up three men to assess the property value of both the mill and the lumber camps. We will convene again in one month."

The judge slammed his gavel on the pulpit and a mumble erupted in the room.

"What just happened?" Victoria asked as she stood.

"We were granted time to get your father home," her lawyer answered.

"But if they don't come home by the next court date then Luther wins? Everything?" Had she heard that right? Could she lose everything over a technicality?

"I'll go to Seattle to fetch him myself if I have to," Paul offered. "We'll get him home."

"I'll organize a tour with the judge's assessors," she said.

"I'll be heading up to camp day after tomorrow to bring a part to my crew. I would prefer to be with them while they are traipsing around up there. We've already had one government official death this year, best not make it two."

"That was mentioned by Luther's lawyer. Weren't you listening?" Paul said.

"I—" Victoria blinked rapidly. "It was? I couldn't quite understand what was going on. It all happened so fast."

"They mentioned the death, and the report they received from the man before he died about the debris. That's why the judge wants an assessment."

"Not just because he wants to divide the company in half?" Victoria slouched her shoulders. What else had she missed? She'd let her thoughts keep her focus simply because she was out of her element in that room. She'd needed something to ground her to the moment.

"It'll be all right, miss," her lawyer said. And patted her shoulder. "We'll get your father here, and get it all sorted out. We've got a month. The judge granted us that much."

Victoria nodded, and followed as her lawyer and Paul walked out of the room. Numb from the whirl of confusion around the last few hours, and raw emotions running through her core. She needed to see Wall. Talk things over with him. Maybe even find a way out of this mess.

"I'll go get the carriage," Paul offered. "You wait here."

"No. I'll come with. I don't want to wait."

Victoria pinched her lips tight to stop her chin from quivering before all to see as she took the steps to the courthouse, and followed Paul to the back alley and the awaiting buggy. She mounted, not waiting for him to help her up. "Let's get Wall's part, and get home. I want to focus on getting up the mountain as soon as I can."

Especially if this was going to be the last few times she saw her beloved operation. She prayed her wire would reach her father, and that he'd return with all haste. Even before she'd gone to the trial, she'd known he needed to be home, and told him as such. If only he'd read the note, and return, then all would be well. He would fix everything. If not, she didn't know what she was going to do.

On the other hand, had her father known Luther was his wife's bastard child when he'd hired him on to work with the timber beasts years before? He must have. Right? And why hadn't her mother fought to keep her son? Those were all questions for another time. For when her father, and more importantly, mother, returned.

She just prayed they made it back to Missoula in time.

Chapter 8

Off in the distance, three loud train blasts sounded through the trees, but Wall didn't pay much mind. Not with the headache forming behind his skull at the thought that he'd not yet figured out how to get the machine working for Victoria without the part. He balanced on one leg and stretched to reach the gear deep in the belly of the loader when the sounds of feet crunching the dried-up grass in the Railroad Grove reached his ears. He stood, and ducked his head out of the machine as the cook's boy from the Bonner camp trotted up to him. "She's here."

"Who?"

"The boss lady. She came up on a train. They parked way down the tracks behind the timber car. They're walking up the rest of the way."

"Who's they? Who's she with?"

"Dunno. Some old guys with stuffy chests, but they got two engines on either side of the train. Weirdest train I've ever seen."

"Thanks." Wall frowned, and turned his attention to the path leading down the hill, beside the tracks. If Victoria had come alone he'd have only given half a thought as to why, but why bring others up the mountain?

After the assessor's death, she certainly wouldn't wish to have dandies traipsing about the Groves.

He started down the tracks and had reached the edge of the meadow when Victoria's prim form—regal in a flowing skirt that must have been tedious to carry through all this vegetation—led three men up the thin trail next to the tracks.

He waited until they neared, and then tipped his hat. "Miz Victoria."

"Oh, Wall." She said his name in a breathless plea. At least that's what he heard in the word. "These gentlemen are representing the judge who oversaw our little family dispute. They are here to place a value on Great Mountain. Would you be so kind as to help me show them the camp?"

"Of course." He motioned for her to proceed him up the trail.

To others, her voice would have sounded straightforward. Perhaps even sincere, but to Wall she sounded desperate. She'd needed him in town. If for nothing else than support. And he'd failed her by doing what an Adair does best. Work.

Except she needed him up here too, and on the river. Being Victoria's champion was a taxing business. But the rewards are well worth the effort. He slid his gaze over her backside as she stepped past him and led the way toward Aunt June's camp, and the way her hips felt in his hands dominated his thoughts. She was a woman well worth the struggle. Worth fighting with, and for.

They entered into camp, startling a frazzled Carrie who'd taken over cook duty since Aunt June left with the rivermen.

"Working alone?" Victoria said to Carrie. "If I remember correctly, even Aunt June has an assistant cook."

"Beth helps," Carrie answered.

"Hhmm," Victoria responded.

Wall knew the tense way Victoria carried her shoulders and squinted at Carrie as she worked. He'd seen it on more than one occasion since the dinner party. She needed to talk with her. About what, he hadn't a clue, but at least he could afford her a bit of privacy.

"Hhmm," Victoria muttered again, and Wall turned to the men, drawing them a few steps away with his movements.

"We've yet to be introduced. I'm Wall Adair." He extended his hand to the men.

"Churchill."

"Peters."

"Smith."

Each man introduced themselves as they shook his hand.

"I trust your train ride up here was pleasant enough."

"Beautiful scenery," Churchill spoke up. "The lakes up this way are breathtaking."

"Ah, yes. You've yet to see Seeley Lake, though. It's not as grand as the Flathead, but the Salish and Kootenai got claims over that one."

"How's the fishing in Seeley?" Churchill, whom Wall was beginning to think had been designated to speak for the group, asked. And funny enough, Wall hadn't pegged the stuffy man for a fisherman. Never could tell in Montana, though.

"Good, if you know the right spots. Our river operation starts on the banks of the lake so we get a good peek at what's in the lake."

"Ah, good, good. Have you seen anything odd this year up here? Like how the fish look?"

"To be honest, I haven't paid much mind to the catch this year. Far as I know there mainly bull trout."

"No, no." Churchill looped his thumbs through his pants. "A group of us have introduced a new species into the Madison River. There's brown trout now. Can't wait to see if they've made it to the lakes. It's going to change everything in the waters."

"Have you? Is it a group of you or government operation?"

"Sort of a collaboration of both, I guess you could say." Churchill took a few steps toward the direction of the lake. "I'm curious about the river logging. Specifically, how it's had an effect on the fish. I read that piece in the Missoulian a while back about a group called The Devil May Care boys. Been quite curious to see what sort of man takes on a job like that. I love all things to do with the water around here."

Wall chuckled. "I read the article. They called us 'touched in the head', I think. And in my experience, the rivers are as ripe with tails as any year before."

"You're a Devil May Care?" Peters asked in awe, finally breaking his silence.

"I'm their leader. Although this year I had to send them down the river without me so I could fix the loader." Which, come to think of it, didn't make him much of a leader now, did it? What sort of captain stayed on shore and sent his ship out with the first mate?

Not much of a captain. He was turning out to be less of a leader than Garrett. Of that, he had no doubt. "So you boys are from the city?"

"I'm from the city," Churchill said, and nodded sideways toward the other two men. "These two are from Helena."

"Ah" was the only response Wall could give and not let his hand be known. He knew what that meant. They were here under order of Nichols' office, and not the judge. Two separate matters entirely. At least they should be separate.

A movement near where the women sat at the cook table caught his attention as Victoria beckoned him over. Should he tell her? She more than likely already knew.

In a few strides, he stood before her. "Could you distract them for a moment? I feel I'm going to be a few more minutes."

"I'll take them to see the chute." Wall wanted to reach out and caress the lines from between her brows, but held back. "Is everything okay?"

She sighed. "Yes. When we were at the mayor's dinner, her mother asked me to fire her after this summer. It seems she is needed at home, but her mother fears she intends to hide away up here and become and old maid like Aunt June."

"And you're siding with her mother?"

Victoria shrugged. "She's right. I can't in good conscience keep her employed knowing I aided in destroying a woman's future."

"Don't you think that's her choice to make?"

"She can choose, just not at Great Mountain."

"I suppose you have a tough choice to make, and it is your decision." Although it isn't the one Wall would have made, in truth it wasn't his to make. For now, at least, Victoria was owner of the lumber mill.

With a curt nod, Wall turned to the men and motioned toward the lake. "Gentlemen, if you'll follow me, the river operation is this way."

"Ah, splendid," Churchill said like a boy who was about to get a peek at a new foal.

"Victoria mentioned you were here to price out the operation. Did you get a chance to talk to Nichols's people? From what I hear they sent a man out earlier this year."

"Can't talk business with you, but I wouldn't mind talking trout."

"Ah." Wall raised his head in understanding. The men weren't going to give so much as a hint as to what their intentions were up there. For all Wall knew, the judge was working with Nichols. He wouldn't put it past the man to have given into the strong thumb of the state official. After all, his father already had.

Wall emerged next to Seeley Lake and waved toward the open water. "We usually have our bateaus and wannigan here, but they've all been taken downriver. Over there is the chute, and below that is where we house the raft. Which is also downriver."

"How many logs do you take down in a raft?" One of the, until now, silent men asked.

"As many as a thousand. As few as a hundred. Depending on the haul the winter crew got to the water's edge, and spring runoff. This year was smaller than normal, what with the railroad logging and dry winter."

Wall let the men go as they broke off, meandering around the bank, checking things out. He stood watching them survey the surrounding land, chute, and—in Churchill's case—lake, until Victoria's dainty footsteps sounded behind him.

He turned as she approached.

"I'm going to lose it all." She stared at the lake.

"The trial didn't go well I take it?"

"Not as well as I would have liked. They want father here. Gave me a month to get him back. Problem is, he hasn't been heard from since he first got to Seattle. It's like he disappeared."

"Let's hope not if they need him to make a decision." Wall faced her, turning his back on the wandering men. "What about Luther?"

Her dainty eyelashes fluttered to her cheeks, but when she glanced back up the bottom of her eyelids held tears on the verge of escape. "He's my brother. My mother's child apparently."

Wall frowned. "So what happened in the past to make your parents give up their only son?"

"My mother's son. Not my fathers. I never knew it before because I've never met Sanchez, the man with the cane, who everyone talked about last year, but he and Luther bear a striking resemblance. There's no doubt to me that they are father and son."

"And they believe they deserve half of the company?"

She waved her hand before her face. "There was something about bill of sales, birth certificates. It was all fast and confusing. I need to get back to running the mill already. To get these men down the mountain and my father home. I just want to feel peace again like I did when I first took over the mill."

"We could steal away to Mother Goose's Cottage? Everyone finds peace up there. You could think. I'll even leave you be once we get there. Promise." He held up his hands in surrender, but dipped his head close to hers. "Although, I wouldn't fight you if you were to order me to unlace your corset again."

"What makes you think I'm wearing one?"

At her words, and the image it invoked, his body responded the way she no doubt intended. "You've certainly become a brazen, wicked woman since you became the boss."

"Yes, but you promised to be the boss in other aspects of my life, and I've decided I like bending to your...instruction."

"You've decided that, have you?"

She tossed him a sly, sideways glance followed by a crooked smile he'd never seen her give before. He could spend a lifetime discovering all the different smiles she kept hidden from most of the world. "I'll hand the men over to Garrett after supper. He's offered to entertain them in his railcar.

I'm assuming with cards to talk of railroad business. Whatever it is that keeps you men occupied will be the way for me to escape."

Wall tipped his hat. "I'll be fixing your loader so you'll have more money to report to the judge. Meet me at the foot of the trail?"

Her smile faded. "If I'm going to be forced to share this land, I'm not going to let the deal include the railroad or your inventions. I promise. And if I'm kicked out of my own company then I'm taking everything I can with me."

"Best not worry about that right now." He motioned toward where the men now gathered in a small, secretive circle. "Take it one moment at a time, and get those men down the hill."

"After supper," Victoria crooned with a sparkle in her eye, and then turned an expressionless stare on the men as she glided their way like a queen.

Wall headed toward the train to get the part for his loader. Now that he could get the machine fixed, he could get the train moving to help Victoria. At least he'd be able to help her there. What he wouldn't do to be able to take the weight from her shoulders, and help her carry it.

* * * *

"Gentlemen." Victoria directed the three men toward where Garrett waited by the train. "If you'll excuse me for the evening, I find myself rather piqued. Garrett has agreed to entertain you for the remainder of the night." She made a show of searching the sky for light. "Although, by the looks of the clouds, I think the sun may set a bit earlier than expected."

The men said their goodbyes in their customary manners, and she waited until Garrett shut the door behind him before ducking on the other side of the train.

In the distance, across the clear-cut area around the train tracks, Wall stood waiting for her. Her heart sped up at the same time her feet did. She wanted to disappear up the mountain. Needed to. Even if just for a few hours.

The sun faded into night, but she didn't care. She'd chance the trails during the night as long as Wall was there to guide her.

He smiled when she neared, and stood taller.

She returned the grin as he grabbed her hand and towed her up the hill. They disappeared over the ledge, and successfully shut off the world at their backs.

"The men are gone for the day so no one will see us, but we need to hurry before it gets dark."

"Shouldn't we place markers or something for when we come back?"

Wall chuckled. "Oh, no, princess. We're not coming back until daylight. We'll chance the early morning sun, but I'm not traipsing around these woods in the middle of the night."

He pointed to the graveyard of widowmakers, high up in the trees as they passed by last year's Grove. "Too many dangers."

The sight brought to mind the claim some had made of her company leaving debris, and she searched the brush. While some evidence of their previous year's operation remained, the scraps were not what they'd been the first time she came up the mountain. "What happened to the debris?"

"You said you were worried about it, so I talked to the Bull. He had his men clean it up when they weren't busy falling."

He grabbed her hand to tow her, forcing her to take longer strides. "You did that for me?"

"You've a lot going on, and it's our job to ensure the operation up here runs as smooth as you expect it too."

Victoria struggled to breathe evenly as she walked. The exertion of the hike causing emotions to swirl through her chest and curl in to bring chaos to her lungs.

The only other man who had ever taken consideration for her in such a way was her father. Even Garrett, during those brief weeks when they'd been unofficially engaged, failed in the little things. Yet here Wall, who maintained no connection to her family save working for her, gave her something so simple with an effect on her life beyond measure.

Sure, she'd given herself to him in her office, and in all honesty hoped it would happen again, but a moment of passion didn't make him obligated to ensure her happiness and well-being.

By the time they crested the top of the last hill to where the trail opened up to Mother Goose's Cottage, the sun had begun to stretch what light it could out onto the land, painting the greens of the meadow, and whites of the flowers in a golden light only seen in the high hills of the Rocky Mountains.

Halfway through the meadow, Mother Goose's Cottage sat empty. Beckoning her to enter into a fantasy of the now, and forget about the past.

In a perfect world, a man and woman could live in a cabin such as this, away from the world and all its troubles, and simply be. In a perfect world, she was the sort of woman brave enough to forget about everything down the hill—all the parties, money, and the business deals. What she wouldn't give to live in this ideal world.

But life wasn't perfect. It was flawed and full of injustices.

Wall began to lead her inside, and she pulled on his arm to stop him. "Let's stay out here until the sun completely disappears. The Mission Mountains are quite the sight."

Wall followed her line of sight to the blue peaks of the Mission Mountain Range, and nodded. "Be right back."

On those words, he hurried toward the cabin, and threw open the door. A few seconds later, he emerged with a single, crudely made log chair, and positioned it to watch the mountains, and then motioned for her to sit.

She let out a small, happy breath of air as she took the seat. Half for the comfort of knowing she'd left her damn corset at her house by the mill, and half for the serenity of the moment.

"You're different from most men," she said, keeping her gaze on the mountains. "Most would assert themselves in the mill. Try to take over for me. You don't."

"It's not my place."

"Yes, but it wouldn't be their place either."

"You're right. I'm not like most men. I grew up learning to respect women for who they are, and I don't believe that's something taught to boys at a young age. My four sisters are all fire and mischief. They ride with my father, and sew with my mother. Growing up, if I didn't treat them with the respect they expected out of a man, they'd whip me with their reins, and then I'd get put in line by my mother. Except my sister Layla. She's always followed my mother's advice of, 'kill them with kindness.'" Wall chuckled at some memory as he stared into the darkening grass. "So whenever she baked her famous cherry pies for a particular person, we knew she was mad."

"So you have a brother and four sisters?" She was truly impressed. How would she and Luther had been if they'd been given a chance to grow up together? Somehow she doubted their dynamic would have been the same. She certainly wouldn't have baked Luther a pie. "What it must have been like to grow up in such a family. Surrounded by people who love you so completely they wouldn't hesitate to beat the tar out of you, or turn around and bake you pie."

Wall gave a quiet laugh, the kind that doesn't even sound through his mouth, but one that speaks of truth and memory, and then motioned toward the open door to the cabin. Victoria peered again at the mountains, only to notice the sun had set. She stood and Wall gathered the chair and led the way.

Once inside, she stood quiet in the dark of the cabin as he felt his way around the blackness. To her surprise, she even enjoyed this. The eerie silence of nothingness in the middle of nowhere. Well, nothing but the sounds of Wall as he stacked wood somewhere in the cabin.

But in a few minutes, a flame licked the backside of the fireplace, and brought the cabin to life once more.

"What do we do in a cabin alone where no one knows we're here?" Wall frequently commented on her smiles, and she understood why. She rarely gave genuine ones, but for him, they came naturally. And right here, now, she let her smile show her true intention. What she wanted.

His eyes flared, but he shook his head. "No. Tonight is about you finding your calm."

She reached up and toyed with the curl Wall frequently tugged on. Why did he resist? She offered herself in what she thought were not-so-subtle terms.

He watched her hand at her neck, shook his head, and then stalked toward her. She let her own seductive grin slip on her face and dropped her hair when he stopped before her, his mouth so close their breaths mingled and her lungs began to struggle the way it always did when his body heat collided with hers.

"What we do has nothing to do with remaining calm." As she'd hoped, he reached up and tugged on her curl, keeping his gaze on it the entire time. "I'm not certain I am what you need tonight."

"You're a red-blooded man, aren't you? Don't you want this? Want me?"

"I'm as red-blooded as any man down the hill, but there are some things I learned as a cowboy. One is to recognize what a horse needs, and the last is to recognize what a woman needs."

"You certainly do learn a lot from being a cowboy." She reached up and began to unbutton his shirt. He grasped her wrists, but didn't tug them away, and she knew she'd won. "But what do you learn from being a riverman?"

She flattened her palm against his bare chest as she opened his shirt. His heart beat fast beneath her fingers. "That you can't tame something as fierce as the river rapids."

"Fierce is such a harsh word." She pulled his shirt from his waistband as he watched her. His blue eyes darkened to an almost black.

"Wild?"

She shook her head.

"Strong."

She tilted her head to the side, and let one dimple show. "Better."

"Spirited." He wrapped his arms around her and tugged her close.

"Passionate," she supplied, and reached onto her toes to kiss him.

He responded as she'd hoped, and scooped her into a crushing embrace. The heat from his body permeated through her clothes and caused instant warmth to pool between her thighs.

He kissed her, and began to ease the buttons free on her shirt, and skirt. Before long, she stood blessedly naked before him, while he stood shirtless but in trousers.

The flames roared in the fireplace and lent enough heat in the little cabin to stay off any chill the night might bring, but she didn't need it. Not with the heat scorching every inch of her body, flaming behind his hands as he roamed her skin. Concentrating on her hips.

He bit her lip, and stole what remained of her breath.

"These have to go," he said, and began to pluck out the pins holding her hair up. One-by-one, he flung them across the room and they landed on the table with a *ting*.

She felt the last of her pins go and her long hair fell heavy down her back to tickle the top of her bottom.

"Longer than I thought," he said as he smoothed the tendrils all the way down to the end. "Where are the curls?"

"It's too heavy when it's down. Only those that have broken away from the rest of the length curl up."

He didn't respond, but continued to run his hands through her hair. The gentle tug at the base of her skull added to the sensations swirling around the room, and she closed her eyes. These moments, the way his innocent admiration of her hair massaged her scalp and eased the tension from her head, neck, and shoulders was all new to her. She'd never been touched in such a way. When her maid did her hair at home it was always a tough tug, and jab with the pins. But Wall's gentle touch sent shivers down every inch of her skin and made her want to melt into the floor.

For a moment she simply sat and felt his hands until the briefest of kisses fluttered on her lips. When he pulled away, he pressed on her shoulders to turn her, guided her to the makeshift bed.

As he spread the bedroll down, she took that moment to fill her body with much-needed air. When finished, he stood and faced her. "Lay on your stomach."

She obeyed. Not knowing what was to come, but excitement bubbled in her chest at whatever he had planned.

Once she settled, his warmth enveloped her from the back of her knees to her head. His hand skimmed her neck as he moved her hair to lay off one shoulder, and he began to massage her muscles. The pressure enough to press her torso into the bedroll and push out a bit of air.

She tensed at the pressure.

"Relax," he commanded, and moved down her back with his hands. He massaged the knots from her muscles, but at the same time stirred something deep within her core.

She obeyed his command and tried to melt into the bed. A feeling she'd never had before. Not even at the moment right before sleep did she feel as she did now. As though she floated on nothing while rest tickled at every fiber of her being.

Darkness began to dominate the hot passion she'd felt seconds earlier.

From behind her, mere seconds before she drifted off, she heard him utter. "Sshh. We will. For now, you need to rest."

Chapter 9

Wall was a glutton for punishment. There was no other way to put it. Here he lay with the most glorious woman naked in his arms, a woman who'd once again begged him to take her, but instead he'd done what he thought she'd needed.

All he could do was hope he was right because he was miserable. He'd wanted to take her again. Wanted to wind her up and make her come apart, but she needed the opposite. She was tense. Rigid and stressed. Tonight she needed reverence and admiration.

It hadn't taken long for her to fall asleep once he began to show her what she needed. Now, hours later, he lay tucked into the bedroll next to her, wide awake, and all he could do was watch her sleep, and cursed his self-sacrificing honor.

She wiggled in her sleep. He smoothed back her hair and kissed her temple. "Time to get up. We need to get you to your railcar before anyone realizes we were gone."

"It's morning already?" she asked in a sensually husky voice.

"Yep." He managed to say through his dry throat when she smiled up at him seductively. He was falling for her. Hard and fast. He may already have crossed the barbed-wired fence of danger when it came to the woman tucked halfway beneath him.

How was he going to get her to fall for him once she found out about his family? Because if he were to be completely honest with himself, he'd lost his soul completely last night as he watched her sleep.

He had to have her.

Forever.

But when she found out that his father, and by proxy Wall himself, provided most of the funding for Nichols's agriculture campaign, she'd never talk to him again. Especially since it was this same campaign that had threatened to shut her out of the mountain.

He hadn't told her the other night, and thankfully Nichols had enough sense to keep his mouth shut, seeing as Wall had shown up with Victoria.

He didn't know it then, but when the woman—gloriously naked in the firelight next to him—had tiptoed her way across the stockyards, Wall had completely lost his heart. Now he had to choose between Victoria and his family.

Speak of the viper herself, the woman reached up and twined her arms around his neck, pulling him down. "We have time, don't we?"

She kissed him like the brazen, sensual woman she was growing to be.

He kissed her, taking his time to pay homage to her mouth and he roamed her body with his hands. He wanted to, but truth was they didn't have time. He'd already waited until the last minute to wake her. Any longer and the men would be in the trees by the time they came off the mountain. He gave her one last peck, and backed away. "I would love to spend the entire day exploring the way your body moves against mine, but we've got to get you back before the fallers find their way to The Grove."

She slouched into the bed, and her lip jutted out in the most adorable pout. "I suppose you're right."

By the time Victoria had dressed, Wall had pulled on his clothes, doused the embers in the fireplace, and tidied the cabin. He grabbed her hand, and towed her outside, securing the door tight behind him.

The sun wasn't quite over the mountains to the east, but there was enough light in the pre-dawn morning to make his way to the trail. Victoria clutched his hand with both of hers, but followed without question.

After a while, the sun began to brighten the forest around them, and Victoria's tense shoulders dropped to sport her normal prim posture. "I'll be leaving tomorrow with the men."

"What do you plan to do once you get back? Have they mentioned anything to you?"

"No." Victoria eased around a large rock in which she'd had difficulties traversing the year before, and Wall smiled. While she may not know it herself, she was growing into a mountain dweller like the rest of them. "I don't think I'll know anything until my father comes home. If we can locate him."

"Have you sent a man to search for him?"

"Yes. Paul took a train out to Seattle to fetch him the day I came up here with the men. I only hope he can bring him home."

"At least you'll get answers, and support." Wall helped her down a slippery section of the trail, but studied the trees around them. They grew closer to The Grove, and the morning sun was getting brighter.

"Everything will be fine once he returns."

Wall suspected she said the last more to herself than him. He hoped so, but one thing he knew was every family had their secrets, and sometimes those secrets could destroy the family. He only hoped this wasn't one of them.

The Grove came into view, but to his relief no loggers dotted the trees. He picked up the speed, and moved off the trail, to skirt the meadow where Garrett's train stood waiting to be loaded.

After a while, Victoria's own train came into view and he hurried her to the railcar where she'd planned to stay.

She turned to step onboard, but he spun her around, and kissed her one last time. "Take care today up at The Grove."

She nodded. "I will."

At that, he left her and headed toward the loader. Both relieved to finally work with his hands, and irritated that all he could focus on was where she was in the forest.

But he needed to get the loader fixed, and today.

Once there, he stuck his head in, and began to work. He remained this way until the muscles from his stomach to shins began to ache. The only sounds filtering in through the thin metal sheeting surrounding the loader was the nearby chop of a logger on a tree, and more closely his wrench against the blasted gear. He tightened one last bolt.

Satisfied, and needing a good stretch, he stepped back and away to study the machine as he tilted his head to one side, and then the other.

"Wall." Victoria's sweet voice sounded from his right. Next to her, the city men walked silently. One with a hungry gleam in his eye. "Mr. Churchill wanted to know if you could accompany us up to The Grove."

Wall wiped the grease from his hands onto his pants. "I'm about finished here anyway."

"Splendid," Churchill said, and stepped next to him to follow as they began to make their way to The Grove.

Wall took the lead, being as he was the only one in the group with experience navigating the hazards of the forest. They climbed the hills and he motioned toward where the debris had once littered the ground. "As you can see, gentlemen, Miz Victoria keeps a clean operation."

Victoria stepped near Wall and remained close as they hiked the hills. Showing various points of operation along the way.

"This land is quite impressive," Smith said as the sun began to wane toward late afternoon. The group headed downhill. A man who up until now had not uttered a word in Wall's presence. "Although, is this the area where the men are working under permit? According to my calculations, it is not." He pointed up the hill to where the new Grove was barely visible through the trees as they hiked away from the operation.

"I assure you, sir, everything here is in legal order. That section was given to my father during the Timber and Stone Act of 1878. The old Grove—" She pointed ahead of them on the trail to where the widowmakers dotted the trees above. "On the other hand, was permitted. Once the permit expired, we moved to Great Mountain land."

Crack!

Wall knew the sound all too well. He spun around and yanked Victoria under his protective embrace as the widowmaker fell with a crush of vegetation beneath it, a hundred yards from where they stood.

The scent of Victoria's hair drifted from under his chin and he knew she was safe.

The men beside them searched their surroundings in a white-faced panic, but to Wall's relief all were whole. Alive. His chest eased from the tight pain of fear, and he released her. She stepped back and peered up into his eyes.

"What a fright!" Churchill exclaimed, but the man sounded a bit too enthusiastic to have been so close to death, or at the very least excruciating pain. Wall suspected he was up here for the thrill of the logging-camp experience rather than simply work. The other two, however, he hadn't gained a reading on.

Mr. Smith's face darkened and a deep crease formed between his eyes. "And is this where Brewer died?"

"What?" Victoria clutched her ever-present necklace to rub the stone, but squared her shoulders.

"Our man Brewer." Smith waved toward the expanse of the old Grove. "Is this where he died?"

Wall's heart must have rivaled hers because her breathing heaved like it did whenever she got excited. His heartbeat was for a different reason, however. Part from the moment they'd had, and part because he thought she knew the men were from Helena. It was only a matter of time before the topic of the dead man came up. But by her reaction, she hadn't known. He should have warned her.

It took a split-second for Victoria to gain her composure, and luckily she did or else he'd have to interfere, and he knew how much she hated when he stepped in before her in matters of business.

"Mr. Brewer met an unfortunate accident over there. You brought the report to me yourself when you arrived. His death was deemed an accident." She pointed to the edge of the trail where they'd found the body. "Had I known he was going to be up at my camp, I could have had an escort for him to ensure something like this didn't happen."

"Would an escort have been able to stop the widowmaker from falling?" Smith made a show of peering at the top of the trees. "These are littered with death traps. If a herd of cattle were to wander into these trees the rancher would lose almost an entire herd. Not to mention the dangers for people finding their way into this part of the forest."

"It's a good thing then that we are here instead of a rancher," Victoria responded with her usual bite. Wall smiled at her fight. "As per the permits directions, this section was selectively logged. We took only every other tree, and left quite a few behind. The permit we logged a few years back was a clear cut. That left no widowmakers, and we both benefited handsomely. If the government wants to force my company to use this sort of technique, then they have only themselves to blame for the widowmakers."

Smith, with his ever-present lack of communication skills, answered with a simple humph, and began to walk down the trail. All the while keeping one eye in the treetops above. Peters followed in much the same way.

Wall motioned for Victoria to walk in front of him. With a tense smile, she obeyed. If any of the time he'd spent with her over the last few months taught him anything, it was in reading her smiles. That one was her irritated grin. Tense and short.

Churchill followed carefully but with a much jauntier bounce to his walk. The man did not seem to be there with the same purpose as the other two. Perhaps Churchill was the man Wall needed to talk to. Get answers from him. He suspected the way to do that was through the lake.

* * * *

"Churchill," Wall called out as the men meandered toward the train. The man in question noticeably downtrodden as he followed his two coworkers. Their time at the camp was about to end, but he'd yet to get the man alone, and he had just enough time to take the man out to the fishing hole.

The previous night, Wall had wanted to take Victoria back up to Mother Goose's Cottage, but the dry lightning crashing off the mountainside prevented any outings of the clandestine sort. Gentleman his mother raised him to be, he'd escorted her to her railcar instead.

Today, she and the men had done one last round of the lake and camps, and prepared for the trip back down the mountain.

But first, fishing.

Not that Wall was a big fisherman himself, but the man now walking toward him from the group of stuffy dandies appeared to be more than an enthusiast when it came to the rod-and-reel sport.

"Did you get a chance to check the lake for your brown trout?"

He shook his head, his face cast down. "No. Those two Helena boys have kept me busy until sundown every day."

"Are you busy now?"

"Just waiting for the train to head down."

"Victoria says it'll be another hour before you head out." He motioned to where he stowed a couple of poles against a log near the path to the lake. "I've borrowed a few poles from the Bonner cook's boy. Wanna have a look and see if your browns have made it to Seeley?"

"Let me just tell Smith and Peters." Churchill disappeared down the tracks following the other men. In a few minutes, he returned with a smile, and a small black satchel. "Shall we?"

Wall waved down the path, and Churchill took the lead. Wall scooped up the poles as they walked by the log. After a few quiet minutes, they drew near the lake. Wall handed Churchill one of the poles, and pointed to another path off to the side. "I know a good spot at the mouth of the river. It's up the path a few minutes."

The man's smile stretched across his face even more, and he juggled his pole in his hand and headed in the direction Wall indicated.

"Where we're going is the best fishing hole on the lake." At least that's what the Bonner cook's boy told him. In his experience, out in the middle in a bateau was a good choice in fishing spot, but when faced with the rare dilemma of no boat, he'd had to make do with the boy's advice.

"Excellent. The mouth of the river is the perfect spot to see any coming and going as well."

Wall rounded the familiar bend in the river where they'd tied the raft the year before to keep it away from a saboteur hell-bent on destroying the river drive, and headed toward a large boulder situated near the bank.

"You seem different from your colleagues out there. If you don't mind me saying so. A bit more easygoing." He set down his gear and began to prep it as Churchill did the same.

"We're from different worlds, to be certain." The man gave the sort of nod that showed the silly chaos running through his brain, and then pulled out a pen and paper from his satchel and began to write on the top page. Sort of like a pinecone bobbing in the middle of the lake. Wall smiled. Whatever the other two's intentions, this man was anything but malicious. Too bad he had to use him for information. It felt sinful to deceive such a happy soul.

"So how'd you join up with the likes of those two?"

"Oh…I…I…was in the office when the judge came in to ask us who wanted to go up and do a survey of the logging operation." Churchill set down his paper and pencil, picked up the rod, and then flicked his wrist. The line flew into the water to land with a plop far out into the deepest spot within distance to them. "I've been wanting to get up here to check out the progression of the fish. Catching a ride on Miss Harrison's railcar was an even better way to get up the mountain than I'd hoped. We even had lunch served to us."

Wall half chuckled at the comment and tossed his line into the water. He sat back against the boulder to wait. Of course, Victoria would have wooed them on the train. In all the years Wall had ridden to the logging camp, he'd spent his trip on the cold, hard floor of a box car. Crammed in next to other loggers and equipment. His only meal during the long ride up the mountain had been whatever he'd brought with him, and men never thought to bring food on trips of that length. "Miss Victoria is quite a woman. Never had a boss like her."

Churchill answered with a nod.

Wall continued, "It's a shame she's only found out she had a brother."

Churchill answered with a shake of his head and tsk, and he concentrated on adjusting his line in the water.

Well, this is turning out to be a waste of time.

"Have you ever met her brother?" Wall asked, hoping a question would motivate the conversation.

"Me? No," Churchill said, without taking his eyes off the water. "But I hear he's got some sort of deal with the mayor for a school or something."

"What do you mean?" Wall reeled in the line the slightest of bit, and then let it come to rest at the bottom once more.

"This thing with Montana becoming a state has the agencies all busy." Churchill chanced a look at him, away from his coveted pole. "It's going to happen, you know. Montana's finally going to become a state. Those of us on the inside are certain of these things." He turned his focus to the line once more. "I figure it wouldn't hurt to tell you since you're up here and away from people. Anyway, the local government is gearing up to make some changes. We're going to be making schools and such, and we'll need timber for that. They plan to run their own mills to get the wood. Rumor has it this Luther guy is going to oversee the mill operation for Missoula schools."

"Luther?" Wall couldn't help but let his voice show his shock. This was news to him, but would explain why he was trying to get control over the mill. The sidewinder didn't want to connect with family, or have a stake in the 'family' business. It was about the mill, and possibly revenge.

Churchill must have caught the subtle hint, because he glanced his way. "Yes. He had an excellent resume. Luther had timber training, and his father once owned a mill somewhere. They had some legal battle over the grounds or something, and he lost it to his partner. So they are trying to get it back."

"Yeah, except it isn't theirs to get back," Wall said under his breath.

Churchill frowned. "Are you certain? Luther is Miss Victoria's brother, and the judge said he's entitled to half the land at least."

"The judge told you that before you even came up here?"

Churchill turned a deep red. "Blast! I probably shouldn't have said that. The court proceeding is still going on from what I hear."

"Do you work for the judge?"

"Oh no, no. I just work for the cities assessor's office. Not the judge himself."

"Then how do you know all of this?"

Churchill tugged on his line and his attention jerked to the water as he began to reel in a catch. "We're in the same building as the judge. People say all kinds of things around me thinking I ain't there. I overheard Luther and the older guy talking to the judge after Miss Victoria left with her men."

"And you didn't think to mention this to her earlier?"

Churchill shrugged, and eased the hook out of the mouth of a bull trout, only to release it back into the water. "My business is to get the value of the property, and I can't afford to find myself on the bad side of the judge, so I keep to myself."

"But you told me."

"I figure you can help the lady out in whatever way you can. If you had the proper information." He set his hook again, and threw it in the water.

"Were you going to tell me if we hadn't had this time to talk?"

"I'd planned to leave an anonymous note, but I ain't no martyr. With these two hounds following me, I couldn't take the risk. Not with this brown program we've got going on."

"You don't trust the other two?" Wall tried to make the question sound subtle, but in all honesty, he didn't think there was any way he could have.

"They aren't here to assess the land. From what I understand, the man they spoke of...the one who died, he was an assessor like me. They aren't. I can tell by the way they are looking at the land. They aren't numbers and value."

"No?"

"Nope. More like faults and follies."

"Great Mountain follies?" Wall frowned. Victoria ran a clean operation and in all his years working for her father they'd prided themselves in the way their operation outshined their competition in all ways. Including its impact in the forest around them.

"They were talking about the widowmakers up there like you climbed up a pine and hung them yourself. Can't imagine why. It ain't like they could have been prevented, the way I understand it."

"No, they couldn't. Those are made by falling nearby trees."

"You didn't hear this from me, but do you see that ridge over there?" Churchill pointed to a hill on the other side of the valley.

"Yes."

"Peters and Smith said the territorial office in Helena plans to scoop that up and make it into range land for some of these local homesteads. The land will come right up to Luther's lumber mill land." Churchill rubbed his chin. "Come to think of it, I'd venture to guess that's why they gave Great Mountain some clear-cut permits and some not. They were making meadows."

"Makes me wonder why they'd give her selective permits for this last one, then."

Churchill rubbed the side of his face and frowned. "Beats me. Maybe to force her out with this court case?"

Wall let the topic drop, and sat silent. What the fisherman next to him didn't realize was he'd given more information than he'd intended.

The land Nichols planned to turn into agriculture land was the large chunk of land right smack in the middle of the Great Mountain lumber camp, and the edge of the Lazy Heart property line. After all, his father had expanded the property size by at least forty-thousand acres since Wall had been alive. The two faces of Wall's life were separated by only the valley where Seeley Lake lay; logging on one side, and his family's cattle ranch on the other. Although most at Great Mountain knew he was a cowboy, they didn't know where it was he came from.

Seeley Lake was a hypothetical fence for Wall. On one side was Victoria and the riverman job that he loved, and the other was his family and cowboy life, which he adored.

And in the center Nichols's attention had been drawn—a man placed firmly in his father's pocket. There was no doubt in Wall's mind who put the territorial office's focus to the valley and mill land.

Chapter 10

Victoria watched her corset burn in her bedroom fireplace. She was sick of the thing. Why did women's fashion always force one to sacrifice comfort for beauty? Well, she was done. From now on she planned to wear only what she could bend over in without having to stretch her leg out to balance.

Once satisfied the blasted fabric was well on its way to a fiery death, she dusted her hands and turned toward her door. Somewhere in her house, a stack of mail waited to be sorted from her time up in the mountains, and she suspected she had more at the mill.

The blessed silence of nothing but her movements echoed off her walls as she made her way through her house, and to her desk. She sat and began to sort through the mail left by her servant, only to stop when she got to a wire sent the day before yesterday.

She ripped it open, and immediately began to panic as tears threatened to fall.

"Ms. Bates! Ms. Bates!" Victoria screamed as she scrambled around her desk. By the time she reached the door, her maid opened it. "Did you read this when you put it in my office?"

"No, miss. It ain't none of my business."

"It's from Paul. Father's missing on a mountain called Hurricane Ridge over past Seattle."

"What? Where is your mother?"

"I don't know." Victoria began to pace. "All I know is this." She handed her maid the short wire she'd received from Paul upon getting to Seattle. "It simply says father is missing on Hurricane Ridge. Wait for further information."

"Oh, dear. That's out near Port Angeles. On the peninsula." The older maid plopped down in a nearby seat and batted at her chest. "I do hope your dear mother isn't with him. Why would he go up there? What were they doing?"

"I haven't a clue, but we need answers." Victoria struggled to keep her emotions in check, which she'd learned to do in finishing school in London, but ever since taking over the mill this year, she'd found controlling the tears burning behind her eyes had become increasingly difficult. "I'm going to make certain there isn't anything at the mill that needs my attention, and then run into town and send a wire to Paul. If I'm lucky he'll respond right away. Could you have the boys in the stables bring my buggy around front?"

"Yes, ma'am. And I'll keep an eye on the post for any more letters." Ms. Bates blinked rapidly, and stood to bustle out of the room.

Victoria set her teeth and strode out of the house toward the mill office. She had only a few steps between her front door, and the door to the office, but it was enough to give her a jolt of mountain-fresh air wafting down from the nearby hillside across the river.

Since spending time up at the camp, she'd grown to love the effects the atmosphere up there had on her. The freedom it provided. She could exist up there the way she wanted with no one to tell her how to dress or who to be. She could *almost* make love to a man in a cabin in the middle of nowhere surrounded by nothing but trees, and no one would know but she and Wall.

She needed that again. Needed Wall again. The way he made her feel with his expert touch. How he took away all the problems that existed in her life and made them disappear. Even in her office it hadn't been the way it was at Mother Goose's Cottage, and he hadn't even made love to her. She'd wanted him too. Even more now than before.

With each moment she spent with the filthy cowboy turned riverman, she grew more and more lost to the ways of his world. Ways so new to her. Ones she'd grown up believing were beneath her. Were somehow for the less fortunate, but Wall was different.

The pile of mail on her desk rivaled the one from home, so she plucked it up and examined the letters. With nothing of importance, she pivoted, and hurried outside.

The ride to Missoula was long enough to set her imagination rolling with each bump in the road as to where her father might be. Had he fallen from a cliff, or been eaten by a mountain lion? And why in Hades name was he in Port Angeles to begin with? They'd gone to Seattle to visit her mother's ailing sister, and not to traipse around the mountain side.

Now, she wasn't so certain. Her father always had something up his sleeve. What was it, and where was he? He certainly wasn't dead. She'd feel it in her soul if he were. Wouldn't she?

By the time she'd come to the conclusion that her father had some backwards scheme planned and had disappeared according to his own machinations, she rolled up to the telegraph station and parked.

As Paul had done before, she stepped assuredly into the building, head held high.

"Anything for Great Mountain?" she announced as she entered. As though they should know who she was.

"Yes, miss." The clerk scrambled. "Came in this morning, in fact."

He rummaged through a stack of papers, and held it out to her. "You are Miss Victoria Harrison, are you not?"

She looked at him as if he were daft, but truth be told, she'd only seen the young man once, so she couldn't fault him. "Of course."

She grabbed the paper, and read it, but the news hadn't changed with the exception of her mother. Her father was still missing, and Paul was still searching, but he did state that her mother was with her sister in Seattle.

"Can you send a message to Paul Clark at 1800 Hill Street in Seattle?"

"What would you like it to say?" The clerk took a blank transcript paper off the stack and began to write.

"Send Mother home."

The clerk typed it out and nodded.

"Thank you," she said, and gave him a coin from the wrist bag she kept around her arm whenever she went to town.

She'd planned to stop by her parents' house to check on the situation with their servants and see if they'd heard any chatter before heading back to the mill.

It took her less than a quarter of an hour to traverse the streets to her parents' house. She leapt from the buggy just as someone from her father's barn came out to greet her.

"I won't be long," she said as he took the reins and she leapt from the seat. "In and out."

Without another word to the servant, she ran into the house and searched the rooms. In the sitting rooms, the small maid her mother had hired recently cleaned underneath the desk.

"Miss," she said to get the girls attention. "Has there been any news about my parents?"

"No, ma'am," the girl answered.

Victoria checked the mail, but finding nothing of importance, she turned to leave when a knock on the door sounded.

"I'll answer it," she told the maid.

In a few steps, she opened the door to reveal Luther, standing with a smug grin plastered on his greasy face.

"Dearest sister," he said the words more as a jeer than an endearment, and it made Victoria want to forget all the years of refinement she'd been taught and punch him square in the jaw.

She shifted weight onto her right foot. "What do you want?"

He opened his hands as if to show he was innocent, but he was far from it. "Can't a guy want to get to know his sister?"

"How did you know I was here? I don't even live here anymore. I live at father's Bonner home."

"I got my ways."

"You've been following me?"

"Nah." He gave a one-shouldered shrug. "I just happened to be passing by and saw you pull up is all. I wanted to come and have a friendly chat with you. Brother to sister." He leaned against the doorjamb.

"Don't call us that. I still don't believe it's true. Just because you claim a birthright, doesn't mean it happened."

"I got the certificate that says it did." He stood up from the doorjamb.

"And I suppose you happen to have it on your person so you can prove it on a spur of the moment occasion such as this."

"Nah. Don't need to. Get me next to a picture of *dearest mother* and you'll see the resemblance."

"Oh, I saw plenty of resemblance to the man who paid off people to sabotage Great Mountain Lumber Mill last year."

Luther sighed and shook his head. "Yeah, my pa, he doesn't like losing. Always trying to find ways to get back at people for things done wrong to him."

"Like what?" She crossed her arms over her chest and began to tap her toe. She didn't miss the insinuation he gave that her father had done Sanchez wrong in some way.

"Let me in and I'll tell you."

Victoria took a second to consider the ramifications of letting a man like Luther into her father's home, but when it came down to it, he was her brother. And there were a million questions rolling around in her mind regarding the fact. Like why did he take a job at the mill instead of letting them know he was family? Why hide the relation at first?

She opened up the door wide enough to let him through, and directed him to her father's study. She shut the door, and followed him. He walked through to the room she'd indicated as if he owned the place, and sat in her father's chair before the fireplace without even being invited to sit.

"Let's start with why didn't you tell us who you were when you first came to Great Mountain?"

Luther adjusted in his seat. "That's easy. I wanted a job. Wanted to get close to the family who abandoned me."

"We didn't abandon you. We didn't even know you existed." She glared. He could accuse her all he wanted of protecting what was hers, but she wouldn't stand for false accusations. "At least I didn't."

"Not important." He waved off her comment.

"So you came for revenge, is that it?" She sat in the chair before him, mimicking his pose the way she'd seen her father do to other men when in meetings.

"Sort of."

"What do you mean sort of?"

"I've lived here my whole life. I only found out about who my birth mother was recently." Before or after your father tried to destroy Great Mountain?

"Before, but I didn't know he was doing that until your father banned me for life with him," Luther scoffed. "As if a businessman could banish someone like a king from a storybook."

"What do you want?"

"I want what was denied me."

"A family?"

To her surprise, Luther shook his head. "Nope. I had a family. I was raised by my grandmother. *We* were a family." Luther scooted to the edge of his seat. "I want my half of the company."

"Yes, you're already trying to steal that from me in court. The problem I'm having is that Great Mountain doesn't belong to my mother. It belongs to my father, and you aren't my father's child."

"No. I want my father's half of the company. See, your father took it away from him when he found out about your mother's affair. Beat him half to death, and tossed me out with him. I've come to get my father's half of the company, and when I do that you're going to sell me your half and I will own all of it."

Victoria glared, but inside her head reeled. None of this could be true. Not her father. The teddy bear of a man who sat before her daily and read the paper like and old man needing his slippers. He was a shrewd businessman to be certain, but not the type to beat a man to a bloody pulp, and toss a newborn baby out in the cold.

"You lie."

Before she could even react, the chair beneath Luther scraped against the wood floor and he grabbed her by the neck and hauled her to her feet.

She struggled under his hands to pull away. "I don't lie. I will have all of Great Mountain and you will sell it to me or I will take it. By force if I have to. But it will be mine eventually."

Victoria slammed her fists against his arm, but it did nothing to loosen his grip on her neck. She kicked out, but missed his legs. She tried to suck in air, and as she tried a second time, he finally let go.

She gasped and clutched her neck where he'd held her as he left. The damn man wasn't a brother, he was the devil's servant. Sent to Victoria to punish her for all her wickedness. Even the wickedness she didn't regret.

* * * *

Wall stood with hands on hips and studied the black plume in the sky, so different from the gray of the clouds above letting off occasional flashes of lightning. The kind of lightning that stays in the sky long enough to ignite a forest.

"It's true?" Garrett asked, coming to stand next to him, striking a similar pose as Wall.

Wall glanced in his direction and nodded, and then faced the far-off plume of smoke once more. "The mountain is on fire."

"How is it looking?"

"Like it's either going to come straight here, or turn and head up the mountain. There's no telling at this point."

"Let's hope the wind decides to blow against the flames."

"It's been a few weeks since Victoria left with the men. At least we've been able to get some loads down."

Wall inclined his head. It had been a few weeks, and with each day he spent away from the woman all he could do was dread the day she'd find out that the driving force behind the fight with the mill just might be his father. He'd half expected her to come chugging back up the mountain roaring mad and ready to fight once her father returned to Montana, and the legal battle raged on. She was bound to discover facts about the truth behind this whole mess once the next court proceeding happened. Wouldn't she?

What's happened so far down at the mill? He hadn't so much as a word from her since she'd left.

"Do you want to keep logging or get the gear loaded up onto the train in case the flames come this way?" he asked Garrett.

"Let's load what we aren't going to use, and leave the bare minimum out. I'll get the boys to get a good pile out tonight, and we'll get the bucker on the train. Since the loader is already on the car, we'll be good there. No use stopping operations if the fire goes the other way. The boys brought up the new bateau and a few supplies with the last load. We'll unload that, and get the machines you built onto the flatcar."

Wall nodded, and turned toward where the men worked in the trees. Although he was a rivermen, he'd spent many years working as a timber beast. Since his men were still down the river, he was free to work with the beasts again.

He picked up an ax lying on the ground as he neared, and joined a faller as he chopped at the base of a tree. Wall worked, chopping and sawing with the fellow faller, until his muscles strained and sweat began to bead down his face.

Around him, men did the same. Those who normally would be in various jobs around the camp trickled into The Railroad Grove after, Wall assumed, Garrett had instructed them to join in the mass fight for a last load.

They worked this way for the remainder of the day, and a second day. Shortly after breakfast on the third day they'd formed a pile large enough to take a decent load down if needed.

Wall stood back, sweat plastering his shirt to his chest as he watched the loader he'd invented pull one log, and then another onto the train. The men assigned to the train worked fast alongside the fallers to stack until the last of the trees was secured on the flatcars with chains, and the load was ready to be taken down.

Wall wanted to sink into the meadow, but more importantly wanted a hot bath and meal, but by the look of the smoke filtering its way toward the camp, he wasn't going to get that.

In long strides, he headed toward camp, searching for Garrett, but it didn't take him long to find him.

"We got it done just in time," Garrett said. "We need to get off the mountain. The fire has turned this way. It's headed straight at us, and the wind has picked up."

"Did you tell the Bonner camp?"

"Yep. And the year-round camp. They are getting their gear together now. If all goes well, we should be loaded and headed out within the hour."

"The women?" Wall knew his friend had everything under control, but he asked the question anyway, just to be certain.

"Beth is with Carrie helping to get her ready. I've told them to get in the caboose and stay there. I won't leave until I know they are onboard."

"I'll get my stuff." Wall took off toward his cabin. His fingers numbed with dread for the future of the camp. A place beloved to many. A home he adored, and one he didn't want to see charred and barren.

He made short work of getting his gear stowed in his pack, and getting it back to the train. Before long, men began to appear from various camps, all flushed with faces turned down with worry. Most ragged and dusty from a hard day's work.

Close by, Garrett stood straight and led the march toward the railcars. Wall trotted up to him. "I'm going to run and check by the lake, and Missoula camp."

"I got the cooks from each camp making certain everyone is out by the end of the hour, but with Aunt June being gone, I'd appreciate it if you'd take a look for Carrie."

Wall gave a quick salute and took off at a run. First through the cook camp toward the lake. The banks sat empty. To his left the chute sat lifeless. The serenity of the area would have been breathtaking except the smell of smoke and haze starting to choke the air lent an eerie calm.

In the distance, no eagles screeched as they frequently did on a bright summer's day. No flash of a doe across the water sneaking a drink from the lake, or skitter of a squirrel caught his attention. Instead the animals had long since disappeared. A sign they should have already noticed, except they'd been too busy chopping down trees.

Wall didn't have time to admire the difference in atmosphere, however. He needed to ensure no one remained in camp by the time the train left.

Turning, he ran toward the cabins. Once certain no one remained there, he took a quick scan of the cook camp, but Carrie had already escaped to the train.

Three horns blasted through the trees when he walked past the women as they boarded the caboose, and then reached the railcar where Garrett stood talking to the men. "All clear in the Missoula camp."

Garrett nodded and then, with a loud whistle to the conductor, gave him the thumbs up. Wall and the men boarded the train as it began to chug down the line.

Tree's swished past the open door, one by one, slowly picking up speed as the train began the journey downhill. Relief spread through his chest at the thought that they'd gotten everyone out before the fire reached the camps, and with one final load.

He only hoped it was enough to make Victoria happy with the yearly harvest. Otherwise she was going to be in an even bigger mess than she already believed herself to be in. Especially since she still has the Boilson Mine contract from the year before to meet.

With luck, the harvest, drive, plus whatever she had at the mill would be enough to meet her quota. Or, if luck was on their side, the fire would dwindle out and they could return to work.

By the looks of the smoke, however, he doubted it. A burning started in his gut when he thought of the devastation a fire like that could cause.

And what about his family? He should probably check on them. Their property sat one mountain range away from the flames, but with a hard breeze in the right direction, it could very well affect them as well. At the very least he should send a wire.

Wall forced himself to relax against the side of the railcar and wait out the ride. A few hours later, the familiar sounds of the train pulling into the mill yard filtered through the railcar doors as it inched its way to a stop.

He jumped from the train before it even had a chance to stop, and headed toward where Victoria stood scowling on the steps of the mill office building.

"I saw the smoke from here, but I'd hoped it wasn't near the camp," she said when he drew near.

The buzz of the men unloading began to fill the mill yard as he closed the distance to Victoria, and stopped in front of her. "It's headed straight toward the camp. It will take a miracle if it doesn't burn down everything."

Tears filled the corner of her eyes, and she rubbed her forehead. The sounds behind him grew to a deafening degree. Drowning out any possibility of quiet conversation.

Wall motioned toward the door behind her, gently grabbed her elbow, and nodded to urge her to go in. She obeyed.

Following the sounds of her heels on the wood floor after he shut the mill yard noise out with the door behind him, he walked into her office, and to the large window overlooking the yards below.

"It's all crashing down around me." Her voice shook with emotion.

"Is your father on his way home?"

"No." The single word portrayed so much feeling he felt it in his core. "Paul can't find him. He went over to Port Angeles to Hurricane Ridge and now he's missing."

"How is that possible?"

She shook her head a little too violently for her curls bounced around her shoulders like they were trying to shake free. "I don't know. I only found out last night. I haven't slept. And then Luther…" She choked on whatever words she had left.

He wrapped her in his arms, not caring one bit who saw them from below. She needed him now more than ever. "We'll figure it out. We'll go to Seattle together to find your father if we have to. There's nothing we can do about the fire except wait, and what about Luther?"

"He came to see me yesterday."

"Is this why you haven't sent me notes? I haven't been updated on anything since you left."

"Yes. Sorry." She stepped away and dropped into the chair behind her desk. Her hand toying with her neck. "He's planning to take over the mill completely. He offered to buy me out. Rid me of my half of the burden." She said the last with a dramatic twinge in her tear-filled voice.

"What did you say to him?"

"I told him that I would take my chances with the court proceeding because none of the company belongs to him."

Wall reached down and tugged at the curl near her hairline, and then caressed her cheek with the back of his hand. Hoping the motion would help to ease her stress, even a little.

"Let's start by getting the men situated for the duration of the fire, and then go from there."

"Yes." Victoria stood, and swiped the tears from her face. "I'll tell the Bonner boys to go home and wait for word. The Missoula boys can stay in the bunkhouse or go home if they wish. There's no telling how long this will last."

"With luck, not long."

"Yes, well, I think we've established that I am not lucky." She gave a sad smile that twisted his heart.

"When is the next court proceeding?"

"Next week." She shook her head. "Father isn't going to make it home by then. There's no way. Even if they find him, they wouldn't have time to get home. I'm hoping mother does. Luckily, she's safe. I've sent word to have her sent back. Maybe she can fix all of this. After all, it is all her fault. She's the one who had an affair and then abandoned a baby because her husband didn't want him."

"I'll be there." Not that his presence would do much in way of proving Luther's illegitimate claims to the mill, but he hoped at least it would boost her spirits.

"Thank you." She gave him a tired smile. One that didn't reach her eyes, and made him doubt she felt the same deep connection he did between them. Was he a fool in love with a woman too consumed with work to love him back? Or was she simply tired?

Chapter 11

The sun began to slip over the horizon and bring everything to life. Of course most of what Victoria could usually see was blocked out by the ever-looming fire plume. She raised her small cup of coffee to her lips and watched the mill yard from her office window as she allowed the blessed elixir to give her false hopes of a happy morning.

After Wall left her office a few evenings before, she'd felt better; only to have Aunt June enter with the news that Beth and Carrie were missing and Garrett and Simon had taken horses to go back up the mountain to find them.

So Victoria watched all day yesterday and today.

She studied the roads to the west for her father. The tracks to Seattle for her mother, and the trail leading up the mountain for her men and the two women who'd become friends to her. Perhaps the only friends she'd ever had.

Growing up, she'd maintained a brother and sisterly relationship with Garrett in London. They stuck together out of necessity, being the only Americans around. When she returned, the other women thought her too haughty to befriend, and perhaps she had been.

But last year, at the lumber camp, she'd experienced something she never had before, and then after she'd been a part of bringing Garrett and Beth together. Of course, they didn't really see one another other than the occasional social event, but that was neither here nor there. They were the only women on earth who would give Victoria even half a care when in the same room. Thus, she considered them her friends. She dreaded the moment a rider would return to tell her the men and women had died in the wretched fire.

Luckily, she didn't have to.

Only moments ago the men had returned with the women, and Garrett shuffled them off to town on the train while Simon had marched straight in here to quit. He quoted love, family, and security as his reasons, and she couldn't fault him for that.

What she wouldn't give to find that in her life. She'd found something with Wall, but she didn't know if it was love. It was real and raw, but what she felt with him was bewildering. She could never tell if he was going to let her lead or take over. She had a feeling he relented to her leadership, but wanted to be the one to take charge. And what did he want? Could she truly love a man who didn't show who he really was? His true self.

He gave her a calm she never felt. They had a connection she would never deny, and she didn't regret a single moment they shared, but she didn't love him. Not the way Simon had professed to love Carrie just now in her office.

A knock sounded and she turned as Wall entered as though she'd conjured him up with her thoughts. He was handsome, in a rugged sort of way.

"Did you hear about the fire's progress?"

"Uh, yes." She mentally shook her thoughts straight, and set her now empty cup down on the corner of her desk. "Simon said it's close to the camp."

Wall entered fully, and shut the door.

"And have you had word from your parents?"

"No, but I am at an end. The next trial date is tomorrow."

Wall took a few hesitant steps forward, and she frowned. He never hesitated. "Oh, for heaven's sakes Wall, come out with whatever is on your mind. I see it in your eyes. I think we're beyond the point of you not speaking your mind anymore. And frankly it's starting to irritate me."

He drew back, and his jaw clenched. "I beg your pardon?"

She waved toward him. "You playing the shadow constantly. It's starting to grate on my nerves."

"It's what you asked for." He said the words with a bite in his tone, and frankly she deserved it. She didn't know why she chose him to pick a fight with, or why she sometimes said things before speaking, but she did. She couldn't back down now.

"I am un-asking for it."

"Fine." He bowed his head for a split-second before stepping close to her. "Stop allowing people to walk all over you. Be the assertive woman I know you to be. The one who put me in my place the day at the stockyards, and the woman who told me off a second ago. To that end, you may find out some things that you aren't going to like tomorrow."

She crossed her arms. "Such as?"

"Such as the fact that Luther is working with the local Government, so things will not be in your favor."

"How do you know this?"

"I can't out my man, but I got word from a good source."

"How long have you known."

"A few weeks."

"Yet you waited to tell me?" She stepped away, her chest tightening with rage.

"I've been hidden in a forest, working my fingers raw to meet your deadline without so much as a word from you on the subject. This is the first I've had the opportunity to tell you."

He was right. He was in the middle of nowhere with only the train as a source of communication to her, and she'd failed to keep an open line of communication. "You could have written me."

"Next time I'm belly deep in fixing your machines so you can meet the contract with your partners, I'll stop to write you a letter."

"I take it since you were at camp when you found this out and not here it was someone up there. A logger?"

He didn't answer, so she continued to guess. "One of the men I brought up?"

"I won't divulge my sources. I've told you before."

"Fine."

He let out a hard breath, and slapped his hand against his thigh as he started to pace the floor. "You're a hard case, Victoria. You expect those around you to bend to your will, but you won't give one notice to those who do so willingly. You have no appreciation for those in your life who care for you, who love you. I was right to worry about you judging me for my family connections. You'll judge and use anyone who isn't you."

Victoria couldn't breathe as she struggled to make sense of his words. Did he mean that he loved her, or was it a slip of verbiage? And she did judge others. It had always been a fault of hers. Especially those who weren't as prevalent as she was in the Missoula social standing.

She also envied those who lived in a less-than-prosperous lifestyle as her. They were always more cheerful. She coveted them for their happiness, the way they clung to each other as they walked with one another to church on Sunday, or shopping on Saturday. The look in their eyes as they shared some private joke at a party while she talked with the mayor's harlot wife.

So she'd filled her void with Great Mountain Lumber Mill, and now it started to crumble down around her. But she refused to let Wall in on that secret in her soul. Not yet.

"And you have no faults?"

Wall paced. "I have faults. I have secrets you will more than likely despise me for once you find them out, but we are not perfect. No one in this world is."

"What are your secrets?"

"I've told you one already." Wall lifted his chin. "Luther is working with the local government. They have taken him on to the run a mill for them once Montana becomes a state. This whole trial is a sham aimed at stripping you of your mill without costing them a dime."

"Well, I thank you for warning me, and I can assure you I will be telling my lawyer."

"That's it? You're going to tell your lawyer and let him handle it? You're not going to come up with a plan beforehand?"

"What plan am I going to discover? I know nothing about legal stuff. I have to trust in my people, and in this aspect, I will trust my lawyer to save my mill from being taken over by a lowlife."

"Do you know if Luther is even your brother? What if it's all a scam?"

"I don't think it is."

"Why not?"

"I looked at a painting of my mother after he left the other night. There are similarities, and Paul confirmed the story to be true."

"Then fight some other way."

"What do you think I'm doing?"

"Damn it, princess. You have hundreds of people, and their families. Hell, a whole town out there is counting on you to win this, and by the look on your face it doesn't appear you have the fight you need to win. You have no plan other than to let your lawyer handle it."

"Be angry at me all you want, Wall, as long as you assert yourself once more. Be the man you were behind the alley again. I need him back."

Wall looked at her as if she were daft. As if she weren't listening, but she was, she simply didn't want to focus on her anymore. She knew the stakes, knew what would be lost, but in truth she didn't know what to do.

Wall yanked open the door, and stopped. "To do what? You won't let me help you. I've tried. You don't know what you want, *princess*." He gave a sarcastic chuckle, and moved his gaze around her office, stopping at her large window. "Except a tower. You already have that."

As he left, he slammed the door behind him and made her jump. The moment she was blessedly shrouded in loneliness once more, she slumped onto her couch and slid her hands over her face.

Why did she pick a fight with the one man on earth who stood behind her because he wanted to? Wall was right, she was a hard case. Even she knew as much. Life got hard, so she targeted her anger on Wall, even though he didn't deserve her ire.

Even though he'd spend his last few months doing nothing but protecting and focusing on her. A hardened, filthy river logging cowboy with a heart so tender he'd move the mountain if she so wished. And she'd ruined what she'd had with him with her spur of the moment outburst.

Perhaps Luther was right. Maybe she didn't deserve any of what she had. Maybe she shouldn't fight anymore, or maybe she should fight with someone other than Wall Adair.

* * * *

Wall slipped into the back-row pew. The trial was almost over, but he'd had to take care of something important. Something which might end up being the saving grace to Victoria, the town of Bonner and all the people within it, and may even anger his father a little. The last was a bonus. If it went through as he'd hoped.

Then again, it could very well sic the territorial office on he and Victoria. Which would be a very bad thing indeed.

He felt bad about not being here at the beginning of the trial for Victoria, but she'd made it clear her true feelings for him. She felt him weak, as he'd stayed in the background. Allowing her the liberties her position gave her, as she'd asked him to do. But if what she wanted in a man was what she'd said in her office, then by God he'd let his true colors show.

He'd suppressed who he really was for her. Because at the time, he thought she needed a silent champion. Maybe what she'd really needed was a strong hand.

The judge cleared his throat and the room grew silent.

"Since Mr. and Mrs. Harrison do not feel it important to show for the proceedings, I am forced to consider only the evidence I have been given," the judge began. "In doing so I have determined that Mr. Luther Sanchez is owed fifty percent of Great Mountain Lumber Mill."

A small rumble erupted from those in the crowd, and Wall cursed.

The judge held up his hand. "However, I am not without compassion, Miss Harrison. I will allow you to keep the mill itself, but the land, all the gear, and trees on it will go to Luther Sanchez as of today. You will have one day to evacuate your men off the mountain without the gear that is on the land or you will be found to be trespassing on Mr. Sanchez property."

Victoria toyed with her necklace and shook her head. "My men have evacuated because of the fire. There is no one up there."

"Splendid." The judge turned his attention to Luther. "Luther Sanchez, you are given the land and logging rights to everything that once belonged to Great Mountain with the exception of the mill itself." He slammed his gavel on his pulpit and stood.

The crowd did the same, and Wall tentatively approached Victoria, who stood with head bowed and talked to her lawyer.

Victoria's eyes were watery, but she didn't cry as he approached. She waved toward her lawyer. "Wall, this is Gustav."

"I was just telling her to take what she was offered and find some new land. At least she got the mill."

"Yes," Wall said, but he couldn't help but wonder how hard the lawyer fought for her. Regardless of their fight the other day, Victoria needed someone who was truly on her side, whether she'd accept help or not. She was alone.

Wall motioned for her to accompany him out of the room. "Can I take you home?"

She huffed and followed. "At least I have a home to go to."

Once outside, he offered her his arm. "Is your carriage at the livery down the road?"

On her nod, he guided her in that direction.

They walked silently until the crowd at the courthouse was no longer within earshot, and then Victoria spoke up. "I want to apologize for the way I spoke to you the other day. I shouldn't have taken my anger out on you."

Wall tilted his head to the side, but tried not to smile. He doubted more than five people in all of her life had ever heard an apology from her. "You were right. I wasn't being myself around you, but that's because you were my boss, but since there's no work to go back to I suppose I'm going to have to quit."

He sent her a teasing smile.

"Too early to poke fun at," she stated with a disapproving frown.

"Land you can buy easily. A mill would take you at least a year to rebuild unless you make it a portable mill. In my book you won, princess. You may not have taken everything, but you took what was important. You took what you needed to save the people of Bonner. We'll find a parcel of land, buy it, and start over."

"I don't have the means to buy land. I put everything I own into getting the railroad logging off the ground. I might be able to rent some logging rights somewhere."

"We'll find another way."

They entered into the livery and Wall began to ready her carriage and horses as she remained by his side throughout the process. "I suppose you're right about finding a way to recuperate the business. And with the railroad, our possibilities are expounded."

"Didn't you have a meeting with someone a while back about a new venture? When I saw you at the café?"

"Yes. You were with your brother."

"How did that go?"

She shook her head, and he motioned for her to mount the carriage. "Not well. The man is not keen on letting his trees go. He says they are too important for his livestock. He can't be bothered to even rent out his land to rid the timber for pasture."

He tied his horse to the back, stepped into the driver's seat, and took up the reins, sending the buggy in motion. "I may know some ranchers who are in need of harvesting, and I need to make a trip to bring a woman back home soon. Do you want to come along? We could swing by some ranches near my homestead, talk them into letting their trees go."

"A woman?"

Wall grinned at the shock in her words. "Jealous?"

"No. It's only, I thought—"

"You thought you could come into my life and try to steal my heart so you can leave it bleeding on the ground while you rode away on your white horse to your tower?"

"No." She snapped her gaze to the horses as he maneuvered her buggy down the road leading out of town. "That is, if you lost your heart, it's your doing, and I don't own a white horse."

Wall laughed. "Calm down, princess. It's Teddy, your chute monkey's, sister. I saw him and Simon today at the train depot as I unloaded my machines to the warehouses in town. You'll be happy to know that even though Ms. Carrie asked for a job on my father's ranch I didn't give her one. I did, however, offer it to Teddy's sister. I need to bring her to the ranch sometime this week."

"You've been busy. Is that why you didn't make it to the trial?" She grabbed on to the side of the buggy as they took a rut in the road.

"I was there."

"At the end. I saw you come in. Well, more like I felt when you entered, and then saw you."

"It's been a helluva day for business. Which is why we need to get you running this mill again because I also signed on with Simon for leather. I need it for some of my machines. If you don't run this mill, I don't run my business, and Simon loses his business."

"The added order certainly helps calm my nerves," she said dryly.

"No pressure or anything, but three companies and an entire town depend on you keeping the mill open. So how about we leave tomorrow?"

She nodded, but every muscle in her face tightened. She had some emotions to work through, and he hoped she'd come to grips with them by the time they got back to Bonner.

An hour later they rolled into the mill yard. Wall set the break, leapt off the buggy, and helped Victoria down. Her breathing had begun to get under control whenever they drew close, but a spark still flickered in her eye.

She may claim that he was nothing to her. That she wanted him to be stronger, more of a man, but she wasn't unaffected by him. Perhaps soon he could find a time to show her who he was now that the chains of master and employee were broken.

"Come in for coffee?" she said.

"I need to take care of the buggy and horses."

"After?"

He gave a single nod, and she disappeared inside the house.

Did she want something more than coffee? Did she want him? He made short work of securing the horses and buggy, and then hurried up the front steps to knock on the door.

He gave a quick scan of the mill yard, but no one was about to see him enter into her home. They'd all gone to their own homes to wait out the fire. Thankfully.

The click of her heels against the wood floor echoed through the house as she came to the door and opened it. She searched the yard as he entered. He smiled as he walked through. "Is your household staff gone?"

"Yes." She shut the door and locked it.

"Coffee?"

"There's probably cold coffee somewhere." She began to walk away from him, so he reached out and spun her around back into his arms. "I don't want it."

Not asking, not waiting for a response, he bent down and kissed her. This time hard. Commanding. Meant to show her the man he'd held back.

The passion he'd suppressed the last time he'd cradled her in his arms at Mother Goose's Cottage.

He reached up and tugged at the puffy bun in her hair as he plundered her mouth. Once satisfied he'd had enough of her intoxicating kisses, he released her lips. "Let your hair loose."

Her eyes did a thing so unique he'd only seen it once before. They sparkled in a haze, like the top of Seeley Lake just as the sun began to shine on the glassy surface while the mist still hovered over the top.

He'd remember that look in her eyes for the remainder of his years, and if he was lucky enough to have more moments like this with her after certain things came to light, he'd work to discover the look again.

For now, he wanted to watch the way her hair dusted the top of her buttocks as she walked naked to her bedroom. Her hair fell down her back, and he smiled like the wolf he felt raging within him. "Now your clothes."

She opened her mouth as if to argue, but he stopped her with a single finger over her mouth. "You said you wanted me to show you who I really am. Be the cowboy I was before, well this is what you get. Undress."

Without another word, she did as ordered. Her eyes still glazed with the perfect picture of mountain serenity.

"Where's your corset?" he asked, and let the hunger he felt for her shine in his eyes as he watched her perfect curves.

"I burnt it when I came back from the mountain."

He growled his approval, and swooped her up into his arms to crush her in a kiss that heated his core. To hell with her bedroom. He began to walk through the hall, not knowing where he went, and then turned into the first room he found.

He set her down with her back to an overly stuffed chair of the drawing room. To his right, the curtains stood open to the mill yard, and in five steps, he closed them, and pivoted to stalk toward her once more.

"Turn around."

Chapter 12

Victoria had no control over anything. Not her breathing, not her heart, and certainly not her body as it obeyed Wall's commands without question. Typically, in a man, she hated assertiveness. Loved to be the one to command a situation, but with Wall it was different. She'd tried taking the reins in her relationship with him, and he'd allowed her to as she'd requested, but the dynamic felt wrong.

In this realm, he'd never let her lead. His expert hands shaped her body into something it had never been before with each caress. His undeniable ability to bring her joy in something she'd always heard talked about in whispers behind gloved fingers, and with condemning eyes behind a preacher's pulpit. Something as sinful as this shouldn't feel as though the world flattened for her every time Wall began to kiss her. His loving shouldn't feel right.

Only it did.

More right than anything ever did in this world. More than when she'd finally become mistress of Great Mountain Lumber Company. More right than when she'd finally returned home to Montana from school in London. More right than when Garrett had broken off their engagement the year before.

She and Wall may not be made out of the same material at the draper's, but they were certainly made to be together in matters of the romantic kind.

Wall urged her to lean over the chair with gentle pressure between her shoulder blades, and she obeyed. She didn't know why, but her heart sped up at what might become of such a vulnerable position.

She could focus on nothing but the way his fingers felt against her skin as he slid them down her spine, stopping where her hips met her waist.

They roamed her body without care to where they went. She couldn't think of anything else. Could barely get more than half a breath in before she'd need another. The anticipation within her tightened. Grew. Thanks to the time in her office she knew what was to come, and she wanted it. Wanted more.

She was greedy.

Victoria started to stand upright to turn and tell him as much, but he pushed her down with gentle pressure on her back. "No, princess, stay as you are."

"I don't want to wait any longer."

"I'm afraid you don't have a choice in the matter." With his words, he bent and began to forge kisses down her spine. She closed her eyes and gripped the tight fabric of the chair arms as the back of the chair pressed into her midsection.

She thought his kisses near her shoulders wicked, but when he began to trail them down to the sensitive skin just above her buttocks, stars flashed across her vision. She tensed as lightning seemed to shoot to every fiber of her core, focusing solely on her most secret of places.

And then he reached down and slid a finger into her heat where the lightning centered and the muscles in her stomach began to spasm. "You have to stop."

"No." He nudged the inside of her feet with his toes. "Open."

Another command she obeyed without question.

She stepped wide, opening herself to him as she bent over the chair, her backside propped high for him to view if he so wished.

"God, you're beautiful," he said mere seconds before releasing her from his fingers, and pressing his manhood inside her.

She gasped at the sweet intrusion.

With each thrust, another noise arose from her core, and she couldn't hold it back. Not if she wanted to. She felt him all the way into her stomach, pounding against her womb as he thrust in and out. As if she were one of his mechanisms and he the master, the creator, twining, twisting until she could either break or bend to his will.

She wanted to do both.

Her fingernails bit into the fabric on the chair until she thought they might break, but perhaps the pain might help ease the tension shooting out from every point of her body.

If he could read her thoughts she wouldn't be surprised, for he reached up and wrapped her hair around one of his hands. Tugging, and playing with the long strands. The sensation, while normally would irritate and hurt, instead forced her to the breaking point. She wanted more.

He slammed into her harder, and she shattered around him, causing him to groan in pleasure. A wave of peace slid over her body from head to toe, but he didn't stop as she'd thought but kept going.

She glanced back at him. Every line on his face was drawn up, and his jaw tense. His pupils so large they made the sky blue in his eyes into nothing but an outline. Something shimmered in their depths she didn't see before. Lust, yes, happiness, of course, but there was something deeper. Adoration perhaps?

"You're mine," he told her, but she wasn't certain if it was more of a statement, or a claim. Truth be told, she liked both. She turned her head and smiled to herself as he picked up the rhythm again.

And she once more grew desperate.

She wanted the peace back, but to her fear and delight, the sensual pulley began to work. Heaving and twining until even her arms screamed out for release from where they strained to ground her to the chair.

He kept going until he brought her to the highest peak again, and once more blessed peace erupted throughout her body. On her wave, he released himself deep inside her, and slumped over her, balancing on his arms as he hovered over her back. "Do you have staff coming tonight to help you?"

"No." She inwardly laughed at how her voice muffled into the chair. Wall must have heard the ridiculousness, and pulled out and backed away, leaving her to right herself.

She stood and turned to face him. Only then aware of how naked she was before a man who wasn't her husband.

"Is anyone working tomorrow?"

"No. I've given the workers an extended weekend because of the fire. The mill workers will return on Monday so we can hopefully make the contracts we already have."

"Good. I'm staying." He didn't ask. Commanded. But she wanted him to. After everything that's happened to her today, how could she not? She needed Wall and the comfort he provided her.

"Fine, but we draw the curtains throughout the entire house, and you're gone before the sun. I can't have Ms. Bates or one of my workers catching you in here, and ruining me forever." She ambled toward the hall where she'd left her dress. "I've done a good enough job at that on my own."

She bent to pick up her dress, but Wall plucked the garment from her fingers. She stood and spun around as he tucked it under her arms. The blasted man had already dressed in his trousers before she even had a chance to grab up her garments. He took a single step closer. "Where's your bedroom?"

"Upstairs. Second door to the right."

He motioned for her to show him the way, so she did. All the while she felt his eyes following the sway of her hips. The wicked sensation only lent to the sensual pull of the evening.

After today she didn't know how her life would turn out. If she'd lose all she'd worked for, but she wouldn't regret any of the times she'd spent with Wall. Not when they were the only times in her life when she felt at peace.

She began to walk up the steps and his hand brushed the hair aside at the small of her back, but he touched her in no other way. She shivered, and led the way into her overly large room.

She waved at the ornate furnishing. "You're right about one thing when you call me princess. I like my comfort. When it comes to sleeping, anyway."

He raised both eyebrows and cocked one side of his mouth back in a smile when he spotted her feather-stuffed bed. He slid her an approving grin, and she responded in kind.

"Out before the sun," she reminded, but nudged his arm with her elbow in a good-natured motion.

"Maybe I'll never leave."

"You'll give Ms. Bates heart problems. Shock her to death if she walks into my room to find a naked man. She still thinks I'm running around in bloomers."

"Hhmm." He tossed her dress on the floor near her chair. Only then did she notice he'd grabbed his shirt and boots as well as her clothes. He began to walk around the room as if assessing the furnishing. "This will do."

"Do for what?" She bent and picked up the clothes, folding them to lay them gently on the arm of the chair.

He turned a seductive smile on her. "For the rest of the night."

"Oh," she said as he stalked toward her and wrapped her in his arms again.

Victoria leaned into his chest and let him take over. Forgetting the mill, the obligations in town, her missing father. With him, she simply existed. What she wouldn't give to exist forever as she did that moment. With him. To simply live.

* * * *

The banging continued in Wall's head until he woke with a jerk, searching the darkness for the source of the noise. In his arms, Victoria lay snuggled, deep in sleep.

Bang, Bang, Bang.

He picked out the deep reverberation of a fist on a door somewhere in the house, and shook Victoria. She moaned and rolled her head. "Someone's here. I'd go down myself, but I don't think you want us discovered."

Although, at this point, what did it matter? He hadn't been lying last night when he'd laid claim to her. She was his, and sometime in the past few weeks of strife, she'd laid claim to his heart as well.

Now all he had to do was get her past his family. His father. The opposition not only to his life, but he suspected Victoria's business venture as well.

Victoria grumbled as she scrambled out of bed and into a frilly dressing gown from her wardrobe. She really was the most adorable sleeper, and most grumpy of morning people. Of course, judging by the lack of sun, it was quite early.

By the time Victoria tiptoed across the room and reached out to turn the knob, a knock sounded on the bedroom door itself. Wall smiled as she cracked it open only enough for whoever was on the other side to see her, and whatever they could of the wall beside her.

She mumbled something, took a candle from whoever was in the hallway, and then shut the door again. With the room now illuminated, she turned to him. "We're wanted downstairs."

At the words, his heartbeat kicked up.

"Both of us?" He'd done it. He'd rode the log of life too fast and fallen off into the churning waters, taking Victoria down with him. How did anyone even know he was here?

"Yes. My mother has come from Seattle. She would like to speak with us."

"Who knows I'm here?" He stood and began to dress, as she picked something more suitable from her wardrobe.

"I don't know." Her voice shook, and only then did he realize she held back tears. Come to think of it, he didn't think he'd ever truly seen her cry. He'd seen emotion, maybe watery eyes, but she'd never let them go like women were apt to do. Well, town women anyway. Most of his sisters never cried. Except for his sister Bethany. She'd cried when the boy she'd fallen for headed for the Klondike to find his fortune. The boy claimed he'd be back wealthy enough to buy even the Lazy Heart for her, but she knew she'd never see him again.

Wall finished dressing and wrapped her in his arms when he was certain she was ready as well. "We'll get through this. We'll even marry if we must. I'm not the sort of man to be discovered with a woman like you and then abandon her."

She glared. "Don't worry yourself over me, Wall Adair. I'm perfectly situated without a man."

Wall set his teeth. What sort of woman refused an offer of marriage after being discovered in a compromising situation? What about marrying him was so repulsive to her? Probably being forced to stoop so low as to be a cowboy's wife.

He wanted to say something, but in all honesty, he didn't know how to respond to her. He let her go and stepped back, opening the door. She didn't want him the same way he did her, that much was clear.

Victoria brushed past him, and led the way down the stairs and to her father's study where a prim woman sat with a straight back and dark, high-necked dress. She turned her head their way when they entered, but didn't stand.

"Beatrice Harrison. And who are you, young man?" she asked in a regal voice—the source of Victoria's haughty disposition apparent to him now.

"Wallace Adair, ma'am." He nodded and stood with his heels together and hands clasped at his back.

"Adair? Hhmm." She turned to Victoria. "What have you to say for yourself, young lady?"

"Only that I am a woman of means, and can do as I choose. How's Father? Have you found him?"

At the question, Beatrice's shoulders dropped the slightest of bit. "He is not lost except in his own mind."

"I don't understand. I went through an entire trial for ownership over the mill on my own because I received word that he was lost at Hurricane Ridge."

"He was discovering the trees over there, and may have gotten a little lost. He'll be found soon. I've no doubt he can find his way back whole and well since he's done this before up here in the Montana mountains."

"The trees?" The disbelief in Victoria's voice echoed through the room. "He abandoned me in my time of need for trees?"

"Giant trees as big as this room apparently."

"I lost the land to Luther Sanchez."

Curious as to her response, Wall studied Beatrice as she smoothed a fold in her skirt, concentrating on the fabric for longer than needed before raising her chin once more. "And what was the outcome?"

"I lost the land."

"But the mill is safe?"

"Yes."

Beatrice gave a single nod, but her face remained in a blank, unaffected stare. "Excellent. We will rebuild. What sort of tactics did his lawyer use?"

"Shouldn't you be asking; is my son well? Is he handsome? Prosperous? Wait, you already know these things because he's been working here for the past few years. No doubt at your urging. Did you persuade father to hire him on because of your guilty conscience, Mother?"

Victoria moved to stand next to the fireplace, and Wall adjusted his stance and stepped slightly behind her to lend what comfort he could with his heat. At least he hoped it would help her.

"You know."

"The whole town does. Luther was given half of the operation during the proceeding."

"As is his right. We're lucky he only got the land. It's easy to find more trees. Harder to rebuild a mill."

"How is it his right to take away Father's company?"

"There's a lot more to the story than you know, and now isn't the time to talk about it." She flicked a glance at him.

Victoria must have understood because she lifted her chin. "He's been the only one who's supported me through this entire ordeal, and I'm more than likely to tell him later anyway. He already knows everything. You may as well tell us now."

Partly hidden from Beatrice, Wall lifted his hand and caressed the small of Victoria's back with his knuckles. She leaned into his touch a fraction of an inch as if taking strength from him. She was a scrapper. A verbal pugilist, and a woman any man would be proud to have stand by his side in times of trouble.

Beatrice squared her shoulders. "All right then. Sanchez was your father's friend and business partner when this whole Great Mountain venture was barely a dream. They'd planned to open it together. Even purchased a parcel of land at the time."

"Business partner?" Victoria asked, stunned. "You had an affair with your husband's partner?"

Wall wanted to step closer, tug her back into his embrace, but to do so would be unthinkable. He dropped his hand to his side, and remained still to listen. Quiet and invisible as this family aired their skeletons before him.

"He was devilish and handsome, and after you were born your father cared for nothing but making the mill thrive. When Sanchez began to notice me, I was alone. Lonely if you will. In need of someone to care, and one night after a party I made a mistake while your father stayed back and hobnobbed with whomever." Beatrice waved as if to shoo away the memory. "Months later I realized I was pregnant with Luther, but by then it was too late. Your father hadn't touched me in over a year so there was no hiding it."

"So you allowed him to toss your child out on the street with your lover when he was born?"

"It wasn't as violent as that. Your father is not a monster."

"That's what Luther believes. Has probably been raised to believe."

"No. I loved him, and your father was fine with forgetting my indiscretions and making it right, but Sanchez wanted Luther. His mother wanted to raise him in their home."

Victoria crossed her arms across her chest. "So you just let her have him?"

"No. We didn't. Not until they began to blackmail us for him. They threatened to take our secrets to the newspaper. Ruin us forever, and by then the mill was a success. No one would sign on to buy wood from your father if my secret had come out. Not with our reputation. So we agreed as long as Sanchez allowed us to buy his half of the mill outright. Luther grew up in a very substantial household out in Florence."

"So why is it his right to come and take the mill from me now?"

"Because he didn't live in poverty, but he didn't live in excess either. And our choices, our indiscretions have stripped him of his true family."

"Is that why you had Father take him on when he came for a job?"

"Your father didn't need convincing. He's a good man. Has stayed with me despite everything. Worked toward pleasing me ever since. He knows what I sacrificed as a mother, letting my child go for him, and even before then when I kept his house silently and alone."

"Why didn't I know this? Why don't I remember this as a child? Or even you being with child."

At those words, Beatrice gave a relieved chuckle. "I was afraid you did notice. Understand. But you were very young and had a nanny back then. You probably remember only her, and shortly after we sent you to the finishing school in London to protect you from the truth."

Victoria didn't respond. She began to sway slightly so Wall took her arm, and guided her to the chair to sit. He took a stance behind her as Beatrice turned her piercing stare on him.

"Now, young man. I know who you are, and I can see by everything here tonight that my daughter has at least taken a fancy to you. I expect you to treat her better than I was treated at the beginning of my marriage, and I also expect you to be out of my house before anyone notices you were here this late into the night."

"Yes, ma'am." Wall gave her a single nod. In truth, and especially after tonight, he'd hoped taking her to his father's ranch would open up something new inside of her. Show her who he was, and grow on her enough to make her love him.

"Mother," Victoria chided. "Mr. Adair is well aware of the need to be gone before the sun, and furthermore we will not be forced into anything. Even by you, and how did you even know he was here?"

"Ms. Bates, of course. She misses nothing. You'd be smart to remember that in the future." Beatrice lifted one condemning eyebrow at her daughter. "And I would think you'd have more sense than to succumb to lust before love. I assumed you'd already had an agreement."

"There is no such thing, and I will not be bullied into it by you. I'm well set up here for my future, and in no need of a husband."

Beatrice stood. "Providing for her well-being is not the only reason a woman needs a husband. I will expect you to allow me to announce the engagement within the next few months. When the time is right. In the meantime, young man, you can sleep in your own home or out in the loggers' bunkhouse from now on."

Like the queen of Great Mountain, she swished out of the room, leaving Wall alone with Victoria.

"I'm sorry about her," she said, and stood to pace the room.

"The apologies are mine. I should not have stayed."

She stopped, and spun around to face him. "Don't worry about what she said. You are not obligated to bind yourself to me. I knew what I was doing when we started this affair."

His heart twisted. Did she truly mean what she said? Did she not care for him as much as he was growing to care for her? He'd entered the arrangement not knowing what to expect from her, hell, from himself. But as the months grew, he'd discovered a need to be with her. Forever. Allowing her to dismiss what they had would never do.

Chapter 13

Wall and Victoria waited outside the boarding house as the early morning summer sun melted the dew from the grass on the other side of the white picket fence. Wall tried not to smile at the way Victoria held herself all stiff at the sight of the woman. Whether from years of training to act in such a way, or something more personal, he wasn't certain. Either way it made him inwardly laugh.

She'd proven she could ride the river, but now they were about to enter cowboy country. How would she react then? And once she met his sisters.

Teddy's sister, and her little two-year-old tow-headed son, clambered into the backseat of the rented buckboard as Wall jumped down to heave their single trunk into the back and close the tailgate.

"We appreciate the opportunity," the woman said, her voice small and tired.

"It's our pleasure, miss. Teddy says you can cook like you were taught by an angel. The old cook at the ranch has been getting on in years for a while now, and my pa has been talking about finding her some help." Wall smiled reassuringly at the woman, and climbed in the driver's seat, twisting around to view the company in the backseat.

"I'm Wall, and this is Victoria." He motioned toward the silent and stiff woman warming his right side.

"Rose," the woman said, "and this is Benjamin. Ben."

The boy next to her buried his head into his mother's side.

"Hello, Ben," he said. "You must be, what, three?"

"Next month," Rose responded.

Wall smiled at the mother, and focused on the boy again. "Once we get there, you'll have to let my brother Jax and I show you the chicken who likes to swing."

"What?" Victoria asked, her voice more curious than anything else, as the boy smiled but hugged his mother closer.

Wall turned and winked at Victoria as he took up the reins to snap them and send the wagon rolling.

"Is she nice?" The woman's voice seemed to bounce down the road with the wagon.

"The cook or the chicken?" Wall tossed over his shoulder. "The cook is very nice, but the chicken will peck your hand if you try to take her swing, and your arm if she wants you to push her on it."

Somewhere in the middle of the wagon noise, Wall heard the boy giggle. He shared a glance with Victoria who must have heard the small noise, and had also formed a smile of her own. Maybe the country would do Victoria some good after all.

"I'm certain Ben was thinking of the chicken, but I was talking about the cook."

"Rose is such a pretty name," Victoria said.

"Thank you. I was named after my grandmother."

"I was named after my mother's favorite queen."

Wall chuckled. "Of course you were."

Victoria gave him a glare that would shut up any man. "Which is why she had said she sent me to learn in England... Of course I learned differently as of late, but that's not important. Mother said she saw the brilliance coming out of the country during the queen's reign. Truly even you can admire that much at least, Wall."

"There is a lot of expansion and industry coming out of England—and America as well, but I wouldn't trade my childhood on the ranch for all the summers learning machines. What I do is all self-taught. I tinker."

"Your tinkering is going to save my company." Victoria leaned closer to him until her heat penetrated through his shirt sleeve. "I can now target areas where I don't need a river leading to the mill."

"Pardon me," Rose interrupted. "Is it a long ride to the ranch?"

"Another two hours."

"Would you mind if we climbed in the back and took a nap. We haven't had much sleep lately. The boarding house was overbooked, and we had to share a bed with another woman."

"Do you need me to stop?"

"No. We should be able to manage, as long as we don't hit any big ruts in the road."

"I'll try my best." Wall studied the road to keep a steady roll as the noise of Rose and her son settling in the back rustled around them until they quieted so nothing but the wheels on the ground could be heard.

Wall glanced back, but the ranch's new cook's and her son's chests rose and fell with signs of a deep sleep.

"I thought we might start with some of the smaller ranches that I know need some trees cleared. Maybe get a start there, and then go after the places with major timberland up high in the mountains. I've also made an offer on the side of the mountain opposite where the Great Mountain Lumber camp used to be. As long as it's not burnt up by the fire, we'll be set for wood."

"You did?"

"I was going to wait until I heard something back before I told you, but I figured I should probably tell you since it will be for Great Mountain use. A partnership of sorts."

"What?"

He couldn't tell if she was happy or angry. "It's not final. I put in a bid, but I'm waiting to hear back to see if it went through."

He left out the part where Nichols was rumored to have designs on the same land. If he got the bid, though, it wouldn't matter.

"You bought land for me?"

"Well, for us. If Great Mountain goes under then I don't have a job to go to in the spring and summer." He tossed her a playful grin. "What would I do for fun if you lost the mill?"

"Logging is fun to you? And I thought you quit."

"Yes, ma'am, and I'd never quit on you. I'm the kind of man who likes to use his body. Isn't afraid of hard work. The kind who can handle a woman like you. Not many men can, and that's not an insult." Wall winked to ensure she didn't mistake his intent.

"Whether or not you intended that as an insult, I take it as such. I'm not a hard person to love."

"I didn't say you were. That's not what I was referring to."

"Sshh." Victoria snuck a peek at the sleeping guests in the back. "You're a wicked flirt, Mr. Adair."

"All the good men are."

She gave another one of her genuine grins. Meant only for him. Once he talked to his father, straightened out the whole ordeal with Great Mountain and the governor, then perhaps he would be able to persuade Victoria to marry him. When nothing would be in place to stand in their way or convince her otherwise. When she had to make a choice only for them. Because they were good together. In more ways than one.

The silence grew serene between them as she sat and swayed with the wagon while Rose and her son slept. How tired they must be from all of their troubles in life. He only hoped they could find solace in Hartland the way many people before them have.

The road to the town where his ranch lay miles on the other side of Bonner. They passed the small mill town, and the crossroad to Hartland came into view so he prepared the reins in his hands for the turn.

Victoria perked up as the wagon took the corner. "Oh, we're going through Hartland?"

"Yes," he said slowly. "Why? Do you have some business here? A friend you'd like to stop and see?"

"No, no. The man I met at the café owns a ranch around here. Well, from what father says, he owns the whole town."

Wall swallowed hard and his heartbeat kicked up. "What did you say this man's name was you met with?"

"Laughlin Hartman. He owns a large ranch and pretty much the town."

"He does, does he?" In truth, he did. Sort of. Laughlin Hartman, Wall's pappy—his mother's father—oversaw the small town, and had at one point owned and operated the Lazy Heart. Not so much the second anymore as he'd since turned it over to Wall's father, and soon Wall himself would take over the family business.

Now Pappy barked orders from the backroom, and spent his days playing Mr. Fix-it for the town gossip's problems, and on occasion acted as middle-man for a rancher or two with a beef. Which Victoria apparently hadn't learned while talking to his grandfather in the café.

"According to Father, Mr. Hartman is the man to see to get the rights for the trees around Hartland."

"But your first meeting didn't go well with him?"

Victoria frowned. "No. He shut me down. Said the trees were important for the cattle. I don't understand these cowboys like you do. Why can't they see we can equally benefit one another? There's more than enough trees to go around."

"Not all ranchers think like Laughlin Hartman. I can guarantee you as much."

"Do you really think so?" She dropped her gaze to her hands where she toyed with her gloved fingers. "I need to find trees. I went over my books before we left. I have enough to meet this year's contracts, but if I don't produce more land, more trees, Great Mountain is done for by the beginning of next season."

"We'll find something, and if luck is on our side then I'll get the bid for the land on the other side of Seeley Lake."

"Yet you don't sound confident in the plight."

He pinched his mouth tight, before responding. "There's politics involved. It's a long shot, but I'm hoping if I jumped first I can secure the land."

Victoria glared. "And by politics do you mean Luther or the territorial office?"

"I suppose they're one and the same, but in this instance I mean the territorial office."

She exhaled deeply. "Sometimes I wonder if they sat in their holes waiting for me to take over so they could pounce. Like they knew I was weaker than my father."

"You're anything but weak," he said, and then raised his chin at the row of buildings ahead. "Hartland. Unless you need to stop for anything, we'll ride through to the ranch."

"How far out of town?"

"We'll go about a mile out and then turn. It'll be another twenty-minute drive until we get to the Lazy Heart."

He waved at the town folks who recognized him as they traveled through town, garnering Victoria's playfully accusing stare. "You're quite notorious here."

"No, I'm loved here." He grabbed her hand and kissed her knuckles. His heartbeat dominated every sound around him as he waited for her reaction.

She smiled and he knew he'd won her heart, at least for the moment.

He turned the wagon down his road, and tucked her hand under his arm, keeping her near. Enjoying the silent ease in which they could now spend time. Not needing to talk, but comfortable in each other's company.

He knew she liked him enough to dally and flirt, but did her feelings extend further? Or was he alone in his regard for the woman he was bringing home to his family?

At the end of the road, the daily buzz of the Lazy Heart brought peace to his soul. His family's large white home sat proud surrounded by a barn aligned by fence. Behind the house, the chicken coop and bunkhouses dotted the field, and beyond that a large stream ran along the base of the mountain.

In front of the house, three of his sisters worked on some project of theirs, while to the right his fourth sister and mother bent over their garden.

The familiar sounds of the chickens reached his ears as he pulled the wagon up. In the barn door, his father and brother emerged, followed by a few ranch hands.

"This is your home?" Victoria said in awe.

Behind him, the sound of Rose and her son rustling around reached him as he brought the buckboard to a halt, and secured the break.

"Yes, ma'am." He faced Victoria, raising one eyebrow in a mischievous expression. "You should probably prepare yourself."

* * * *

"Prepare herself for what?" Oh goodness. Victoria hated surprises. They always ended up throwing her into a flurry of chaos, and she hated chaos.

As the initial shock of his words began to wear off, the women she'd spotted in the yard assailed the wagon, followed closely by the men from the barn. All chattering at the same time, and gathered around Wall.

Loved indeed.

The man was worshipped.

Victoria had no more than stood to struggle off the wagon when Laughlin himself stepped before her and reached out to help her down.

"Mr. Hartman," she said breathlessly. Not that he affected her ability to breathe the way Wall did whenever near, but because his presence was so unexpected.

"Miss Harrison." He tipped his hat and helped her to the ground as Wall managed to wade through the sea of women and round the wagon toward her.

She used his familiar scent to ground her to the moment. "I didn't expect to see you here, sir."

"No?" The older man gave her a grin, and then slid the same to Wall. "And here I thought you'd taken me up on my offer."

"What offer was that?" she asked.

"To stop by the ranch, of course."

"Oh." She blushed.

"Sorry, Pappy." Wall stepped closer to her. "She's come with me."

"Pappy?" she questioned, but the men ignored her.

Laughlin raised an eyebrow at Wall, who shook his head. "Business."

"It's always business with you, son."

"Pappy?" she questioned again, louder this time. Hoping one of them would get the message to answer her question.

Luckily, Laughlin did. "He didn't tell you?"

"No." She turned an accusing glare on him. This time not playful like the one she'd given him earlier. Why hadn't he told her he was Laughlin Hartman's grandson? He'd let her chatter on, struggle for logging contracts when all he had to do was speak up.

"She never asked."

"A person doesn't need to ask for you to give them important information," she chided.

"I like her," a woman said, coming up from behind. "She's spunky and doesn't put up with your bullying."

Victoria watched an older woman she assumed was Wall's mother escort Rose and the boy behind the house while four women, a young man, and a group of men gathered around them. Only in ballrooms had she been surrounded by so many people focused solely on her. Her chest tightened the slightest of bits.

"Victoria, this is my sister Willa." He pointed to the woman who'd spoken. "She's the one you need to watch out for. She'll get you in trouble."

"I will not." Willa turned her attention to Victoria, and locked arms with her. "I'm honest as the day is long. He's the one who'll go and get you caught in a snowstorm in summertime."

"Don't listen to a thing he says," another woman said, taking a stand on Victoria's other side, also locking arms with her. She let her eyes grow wide, but her heartbeat sped. She didn't fare well with people of the female gender. Never had. They generally found her unpleasant to be around, and to be honest, she didn't much care for them either. "Wall is the one who can't be trusted to tell the truth about us. Whatever he's told you, don't believe."

"I'm ashamed to say, he hasn't said a thing," she confessed.

At her words, the women all let out a roar of disapproval, and the older of the men smacked Wall on the back of the head. "You bring a woman home to this lot and don't warn her first, son. I taught you better than that."

"I warned her," he claimed.

She smiled as she spoke, unable to hide the affect the familial teasing had on her. "At the same moment you set the break."

"It counts as a warning."

He still wasn't out of the woods with her for not telling her who his family was, but it was hard to fight the effect his sisters had on her. They were quite charming in their good-natured assault against him.

"Barely."

"I like her," Willa said, and tugged on her arm. "Come on. Let's leave the men to take care of the wagon. Let's get you settled in the house."

Victoria followed the crowd of women into the house, glancing back as Wall shrugged and mouthed his apologies. She turned her attention back to the women, only then noticing that most of them were dressed down in split skirts and loose cotton shirts.

Victoria smoothed the fabric to her overly poufy dress—the neck high, and bodice tight. She'd bought the piece custom from a tailor in Missoula a few months back. She wore what was proper, what was expected, but she loved to feel the comfort of what Wall's sisters unashamedly wore today. The same clothes she'd worn while riding the rivers.

She envied these women. So happy and carefree. Full of family and love. She had a mother and father, of course, but she didn't have that camaraderie of another family member her own age. Someone to share secrets with. Get into trouble with. Forge a friendship that would last through even the roughest of times. She didn't have a brother or sister with which to bond. Not really.

"We received the letter from Wall only last night. He certainly didn't give us much time to prepare for your arrival. So I apologize if you're accommodations aren't what you're used to," the woman who looked to be the eldest said.

"I'm Bethany. I expected Wall to introduce us all, but he can be forgetful when it comes to manners."

"Really?" Victoria laughed. "He's forced me, on more than one occasion, to allow him to be a gentleman because his mother taught him manners, and he wanted to use them."

Taking the lead as they walked up a staircase to the top floor, a younger girl said, "He must like you, then, because Wall doesn't use manners around here."

"That's Georgiana." Wall's voice sounded behind her. "And she is known for telling lies." Wall's footsteps echoed off the walls. "And this quiet one is Layla. She's the sweet one who doesn't talk too much. She's my favorite."

"You're a nasty tease." Willa slapped him on the chest. She turned back to Victoria, whose face now hurt from smiling. More than she'd even done before, in perhaps her entire life. Willa waved toward the nearest door. "We've set you up in Wall's room. We figured since he couldn't give us more notice, then you could have his bed, and he can find somewhere else to sleep. Maybe in the barn where he belongs."

"Are you calling me an animal?" He lifted an eyebrow at his sister as Victoria watched the exchange.

"More specifically," Willa challenged, "a pig."

"Or a dog," Bethany supplied.

"Or a goat," Georgiana said. When everyone turned their gazes on her, she continued, "They're terribly stubborn, and sometimes like to headbutt you for no reason."

"And they'll eat everything they see," Layla said, breaking her silence. "Like Wall likes to do after he's worked the cows all day."

"Layla!" Wall grasped his heart. "You were my favorite."

She laughed, and so did Victoria. She'd never been so at ease before. Had never forgotten about her daily duties the way she did at this moment. Watching the exchange made her elated and sad all in one confusing moment. She could have had this with Luther were circumstances different. She had a family, but hers was vastly different from the one that bantered before her now.

Her family was severe and aloof. Dedicated to one another in their own way, but also proper and full of problems. This one seemed to be the exact opposite. Although, looks could be deceiving. This family had to have their secrets somewhere. Everyone did.

"If you should ever want to get away from my sisters undetected, the fourth stair squeaks so you must avoid it."

"I'll keep that in mind."

"She won't need to," Bethany said, looping arms with her once more. "We intend to make her one of us."

"You mean turn her against me," Wall clarified.

Willa shrugged. "If needed."

"You know we're always looking out for your own good," Georgiana said, and then faced her. "Now we've left some water on the dresser for you. If my brother is any kind of gentleman, he will fetch your belongings so you can freshen up."

Layla scrunched her nose. "There's nothing worse than the road grime from Missoula."

They all turned an impatient stare on their brother, who jumped to their bidding upon understanding their command. Victoria chuckled. "You've got quite an influence over him."

"Not really," Layla said. "He's just happy to see us. Give it a week or two, a hard day in the saddle, and he'll be back to being the old grump we're used to."

"You all are close, I take it?" Victoria followed the women into Wall's room.

Georgiana jumped onto Wall's bed. "You gotta be when you're crammed all into one house like this."

"Aren't you close to your brothers and sisters?" Layla asked.

"I don't have any siblings." Not really. Although Luther was now technically her brother, she'd never be able to have the sort of relationship these women so clearly had with Wall.

"I don't know if I pity or envy you for it," Bethany said.

Victoria opened her mouth to respond when Wall and his brother walked in with her trunk. "I think Miss Victoria would like a minute to decide whether or not she wants to become your bosom friend or run for the hills."

"Oh she doesn't have a choice," Willa said, but jumped up and started for the door. The other girls followed, but all paused when they reached the hallway. "We'll be out by the chutes if you get tired of my brother and want to have some fun."

Wall stepped in front of them, and shook his head. "Don't trust them. By fun they mean trying to see which one is brave enough to take on Frank."

"Who's Frank?"

At her question, Jax laughed and Wall shook his head. "You'll see soon enough. Now, where would you like your trunk?"

Victoria pointed to a spot against the wall, and sat on the edge of the bed. "Your family is large."

"And exasperating. I'm sorry."

Wall sent Jax a shared look, and the latter nodded a silent goodbye, and left. Victoria was grateful, she needed the quiet company of Wall. "They're endearing. Sweet. Fun."

"Tiresome. Troublesome."

She answered with a smile.

"About my pappy. I honestly didn't realize he was the man you talked to in town until right before we got here."

"Why didn't you tell me who you were?"

"I assumed you knew."

"Why would you assume something like that?"

"Because you are my boss."

"Yes, but I didn't hire you. My father did."

He took two steps toward her, closing the distance. "Still think I'm a filthy cowboy?"

Breathing grew difficult, but she managed a small inhale. "Maybe a little bit more clean than I imagined."

His gaze skimmed her lips a mere heartbeat before he bent and pressed his mouth to hers. Her body tingled from the inside out. Radiating toward the cause of such a sensation. She leaned toward him, needing his heat to ease the tension building.

She backed away first. "You're going to get us in trouble."

"Only if you tell." He slid his arm around her waist and tugged her to his side. "Come on. My mother and father would like to meet you."

With those simple words her stomach dropped. The elation and warmth she'd felt over the last few minutes replaced with her usual helpless dread. What would his parents think of her?

They were bound to know she'd asked to harvest their trees. Destined to know she was a single woman dedicated to running a—up until now—successful lumber company. A woman who not only took their son away from the ranch in the spring and summer, but stood for everything they disliked outside the ranch.

She was a timber maid, and Wall a cattleman.

Chapter 14

Victoria prided herself on always being the woman to charge forth beside or ahead of the men she walked with, but today she lagged behind. She wouldn't say tugging on Wall's arm as he escorted her through the house, but she'd most certainly say reluctantly.

She hadn't much time to see the house before when his sisters had brought her in, but upon second look the interior was grand. Not like her home in town where the rooms were tight and in perfect order. Arranged according to the old state style.

These were open and airy. With a sense of freedom and warmth aligning the sun-drenched walls. This house was simpler in plan, but as grand as any she'd seen in Missoula.

Wall brought her to a room with a long desk situated before huge bay windows overlooking the ranch and valley below. Along the wall a fireplace demanded the focus, and before it, two couches faced each other with small tables beside them.

To her confusion, a large wing-backed chair sat at the end of the couches, overlooking the fireplace. And more dotted around the room. She'd never seen so many furnishings gathered so close before. Then again, this was a rather large family.

"Miss Victoria." A woman, she assumed was Wall's mother, approached her with arms open, and pulled her into a familiar embrace. Touching both cheeks as if they were old friends. Victoria's tension eased the slightest bit. "Welcome to the Lazy Heart."

"My mother, Josephine," Wall said.

She gave a warm smile, and held Victoria's hands in hers. "Wall's told us a lot about Great Mountain and your family, but I must confess, very little about you. Except in what we've read in his letters over the summer."

"All good things I hope." She gave one of her social smiles. One she knew Wall recognized, but it couldn't be helped. She needed the boost of familiarity. The confidence her years of training gave her in these situations.

"Of course." The older woman motioned toward the men in the room. "This is my husband, Hamilton, and it appears as though you've met my father Laughlin."

Wall's grandfather winked, and Josephine slapped him on the arm. "You'll have to forgive my father. He's mistakenly decided he has the ability to charm people."

"I do," the older man said.

"Young lady." Wall's father stepped forward, bringing the familial conversation to a close. He held out his hand.

Victoria shook it like her father would have. Her grip firm enough to belie the nerves bundled like a nest of snakes in her stomach.

"Please," Josephine said, and motioned for everyone to sit on the couch, so Victoria obeyed.

Wall, his face happy yet not quite with a smile, sat next to her on one side of a couch, as his grandfather took a position on the other as if flanking her.

Across from them on the other couch, Wall's mother and father sat prim and proper. The first with a smile, and second with a stern, unreadable stare.

"I'm not one to cater to emotions," Hamilton said.

Wall gave a huff of agreement.

"And I'm blunt. Since you're a businesswoman, I'll give you the courtesy." He waved toward Josephine. "My wife insists on being here to ensure I'm not too blunt since you're a guest of my son's."

"I can assure you, sir, I do not enjoy being treated with frailty because of my sex, and I can take your direct approach if you'll do me the courtesy of allowing the same for me."

A sound near the wall brought focus to Rose as she eased into the room with a tray steaming with something hot. Since this was a cowboy home in a cowboy town, she assumed coffee.

And she was right.

The smells emanating from the pot proved as much. Rose set the tray on a side table, and poured a cup for each of them.

Victoria took the momentary delay to gather her gumption. Straighten her thoughts. She needed to gain the approval of, it appeared, Hamilton in order to log in Hartland. She only hoped Wall would take her side. Help her get the necessary approval she needed to do so.

"Thank you," Hamilton said as Rose finished. Once the new cook's helper disappeared, he turned back to Victoria. "I know you came to my father-in-law to ask for land rights in the mountain."

She straightened her spine. Strong posture was essential when dealing business. "Yes, sir, I did."

"I wasn't aware she'd come to see Pappy or I'd have been there for the meeting," Wall said, but his father waved off his comment.

"Unfortunately, Miss Harrison, we still can't lease you the land. We need it for cattle."

"It's my understanding that you have thousands of acres. The biggest operation in Missoula, perhaps one of the biggest in the territory."

Wall's father nodded. "True."

"With all the land, some of it even unchartered and with no history, and you can't spare enough to allow me to make you a few meadows?" She used her hands to accentuate the last, hoping the motion would help to paint the picture.

He shook his head. "I've seen the reports."

"What?" Wall interrupted. "From the territorial office?"

"Yes."

"I'd wager it talks about the widowmakers, eh?" Wall shook his head, and turned to address his next words to her. "I knew those two men from Helena were blowhards." He refocused on his father. "Those were formed by a hasty move caused by the governments interceding and demands. A clear cut would give us meadows for grass to grow high up in the mountains for the cattle. Without the danger."

Wall's father shook his head again. "It's more than the reports. If I take on Victoria's mill, then others will come knocking at the door and soon our untapped range will be overrun with logging companies stealing the trees, and destroying the summer range. We can't do it."

"What if we give her the lower section to start? It's at the edge of the valley, barely over the Lazy Heart property line."

"No."

Wall stood, and reached down to grab her hand and urge her to stand. She did.

"We're going to others in Hartland. You're not the only operation in the valley."

With Wall's words, Hamilton stood. "No, son, but I'm the biggest. You go to them, but they won't give in. Not if I haven't."

Victoria's mind reeled from the let down and information running through her brain. There would be no contract with the Lazy Heart. Wall's own father wouldn't give her a chance. The others in town may very well choose not to as well. And how had his father seen the reports on her lumber camp? She wanted to shake her head, scream, pace. Think. Instead, Wall tugged her arm, and she followed him into the hall.

Behind them, she heard a third set of boot heels. As she exited the room, she turned as Laughlin walked out and dipped his head a fraction. "Sorry about him, Wall. If I ran the ranch still I'd give you a chance, but I've long since given it over to your father."

"It's fine, Pappy."

Laughlin glanced back into the room, and then bent his head in secrecy. "Start with Old Man Jones. He's been waiting for his boy to come home from the army to clear a patch for his horses, but he ain't coming back. No one wants to tell him. Then I'd try the Widow Yancy. She's choked in trees around her house, and could use the lease money."

"Thank you." Victoria smiled at him, but this one wasn't forced. The older man reminded her a lot of Wall, only fifty years from now. Charming and polite. Not at all the dirty, unassertive man she'd called Wall in the past.

Pappy plucked a hat off a peg near the door, and tipped the brim at her. "If you find my grandson a bit too boring for your taste, miss, come find me. I'll show you where the fun is on the Lazy Heart."

"Go on, Pappy." Wall playfully shoved his grandfather out of the door, as Victoria chuckled. He turned to her when they were once again alone in the hallway. "Want to see the swinging chicken?"

"Very much."

"Stay here. I'll get you a hat."

Wall disappeared up the staircase, leaving Victoria alone in the front foyer. Finally alone, she paced the small space. She walked past the door, where inside Josephine chided Hamilton on his decorum in dealing with her, and Victoria couldn't help but inwardly praise the fierce woman. Wall's father was a force to be reckoned with, and it seemed the woman he'd chosen as a wife was the only one who could put him to task.

She meandered toward the front to get a view of the serenity of the scene outside. The dip of the valley visible to the entire ranch. Off in the distance to the right, Wall's sisters bustled around something, and farther in the fields cattle mewed about.

Victoria moved, bumping into a table below the peg with the hats. She quickly righted the furnishing, only to catch sight of a letter on a tray waiting to be mailed.

Addressed to none other than Boilson Mines. The same company she supplied wood for. The one who would suffer if she were to go under.

She couldn't help but wonder what business a large rancher had with a mining company.

The sound of Wall's boots on the stairwell made her jump as he rushed down to her. "Ready?"

She nodded, because in all honesty, if she talked, she didn't know if she'd blurt out the question burning in her mind, or even be able to get words to form in her mouth.

And did Wall know that his father not only cohorts with Nichols, but also Boilson Mines. It couldn't be a coincidence. Not when the driving force behind the governor's campaign was agriculture land, and the biggest rancher around happened to also have a son who worked for her. There was no way he was a spy for the cattleman. Was there?

No.

This wasn't a game of war and sabotage.

Except last year it was.

Could Wall have seduced her for information? To make her weak so they could get the upper hand in their fight to control the mountain?

The sound of him descending the staircase brought her focus to inside the house once more as Wall emerged.

He grabbed her hand and led her out of the house, not caring one whit over who saw. Was it a show for her sake, or simply him not caring who saw his affections toward her?

"The chicken likes to sit on the swing our father made us when we were young. It's a bit farther back in a small grove of trees behind the house."

Out in the corrals Wall's sisters wrestled with something she still couldn't quite make out. His sisters. They'd seemed genuine, and so did his mother. This was all so confusing.

Wall rounded the house and headed toward the line of trees on the outskirts of the meadow. In a few minutes, the swing appeared hanging from a tall sturdy branch jutting from an old tree, and as Wall promised a white hen sat atop the swing as if waiting to be pushed.

"Be careful or she'll peck your arm. She likes to be pushed gently, but touch the seat and she'll think you're trying to steal the swing."

Victoria tiptoed closer and pushed the chicken. The bird clucked and flapped her wings once, but remained on her perch and swayed with the motion of the swing.

"Are you all right?" Wall asked.

"Fine," she lied.

He was the only person on this earth who seemed to be able to tell her moods, what she truly thought of a situation just by the way she reacted.

How long could she keep her doubts about him a secret before she addressed them with him? Long enough to talk with Boilson Mines she hoped.

* * * *

Wall studied the way Victoria held the baby pig in her arm as he saddled three horses. Her natural gestures toward the creature. The way she warmed to the innocence. What she didn't know was the little thing would soon grow up to be as surly as Frank, but for now he'd let her have her moment.

A moment so different from the ones she experienced in town. Hell, he doubted she'd ever held a pig before today. Doubted she'd ever done a lot of things before coming to Hartland.

She still held herself back. At least she did again. Ever since the meeting with her father the day before she'd grown distant. Aloof. She warmed whenever his sisters were around, but he suspected even the devil himself couldn't withstand a group of women as strong willed and determined as the Adair sisters.

"Ready? Pappy says Widow Yancy has tea at the church every third Tuesday of the month."

"At the church?"

Wall nodded, recalling the traditional gathering of clucking hens, as his father so lovingly called the Hartland Women's society. "There's a meeting there of sorts. If we get there in time you could join them. Maybe feel her out."

"You won't be there with me?"

Wall shook his head. Not only were men strictly not allowed at the church at that time, but he wanted to check the post for news about the land purchase. "I've got some things to do in town."

She seemed satisfied at his answer. Happy even. Which made the bottom muscles of his mouth want to turn down. Why the sudden air toward him? Was it his father? Was he no good to her now that the refusal for logging rights was renewed?

The gentle roll of the wagon wheels on the ground sounded outside the barn, and Victoria stood to dust the straw from her backside, beautifully bedecked in her split skirts once more. The way she'd been on the river.

He slid an appreciative eye from her perfect hair, to the mud on the toe of her boots—which, it seemed, she'd yet to notice. In only a few short months the woman before him had transitioned from the London schooled socialite she'd been trained to be, to the earthy goddess who stood before him now.

He might have to stop calling her "princess" if she kept up the way she did. Then again, he liked teasing her with the moniker.

Wall and Victoria emerged from the barn as Jax pulled the wagon to a stop, and his sisters all began to climb onboard.

"Everyone is going?" Victoria asked.

"I'm fairly confident my sisters started the event. Although I can't be certain. The whole thing is dreadfully secret, and a bit frightening to us men of the valley."

He hadn't seen a genuine smile from her since the meeting with her father, but that little tidbit elicited one. At least his sisters' antics could make Victoria happy. Perhaps she had a mischievous streak in her veins she'd never been able to satisfy before. If so, she'd fit right in with his family.

First, he needed to find out what was bothering her.

Victoria climbed onboard as Wall tied the spare horses to the back, and then took the driver's seat next to her. He directed his next words at his sisters, "There will be no sneaking off today. For any reason. Willa. And I'll expect everyone to be back in the wagon by lunch."

"I'll have you know I had a very important appointment to keep that day, and as you can see I'm whole and well." His sister held out her arms to prove her point.

"Regardless, wagon by noon."

"Oh, all right," Willa said. He decided to make the assumption that she spoke for the whole of his sisters, and Victoria. Hoped anyway.

"How do you like the Lazy Heart so far?" Layla asked Victoria.

"It's charming. I never imagined country life could be so affecting."

"It's not all filthy cowboys and rowdy drunks?" he teased.

"Oh we got plenty of them," Georgiana supplied, "but they keep to the saloon outside of town. Pappy let the cowhands have their vices as long as Hartland doesn't turn into an outlaw town."

"Where is he? Your grandfather?"

Wall turned the wagon down the main road to town. "He brought the rented buckboard in this morning. We're bringing him a horse and he's sending the buckboard back with a family who's headed out that way. Pappy's sort of the sheriff, post master, and fixer in town."

"Until Montana becomes a state and everything has to become official. Then we'll be trying to do things a bit more official."

"Trying?" Victoria asked, her face shining with humor.

"Well, up here it's just us," Wall explained. "Most of us are ranchers with business in town on the side. But were a tight community."

"I see." Victoria faced the road as the small town came into view. Square in the center, the white steeple of the church towered over the rest of the buildings with women from ranches all around bustling about.

Wall maneuvered the wagon into the field behind the church, and set the break. "Jax, take care of the wagon, will ya? I need to get the women settled."

"Sure," his brother said, and jumped down.

"When you're done meet me at the post office and we can go to the mercantile together."

His brother nodded and ran toward the front of the horses, and Wall rounded the wagon to help Victoria down, but to his disappointment she'd already leapt to the ground along with his sisters and was walking toward the row of tables set in the yard outside the church.

He caught up to her. "Widow Yancy is the one over there in the green." He pointed to the woman in question. "She never had any children, and her husband died of the fever when I was fifteen. She's survived off neighborly hospitality, grit, and a whole lotta determination since then."

"Hhmm," Victoria said, watching the widow as she spoke. "Sounds like she and I will get along splendid."

"When we're done here you and I can ride to Old Man Jones's house, and get him to sign on with Great Mountain."

"You don't have to help me, you know. I can manage my business on own. All I would need is to rent a horse from you, and directions to Old Man Jones's house."

He frowned at her sudden back step in their plight. "This is what we came for isn't it?"

"Yes, but you're not obligated to me, and I would prefer you didn't get in my way when I negotiate."

Wall stretched his neck as it began to tighten. "We're past that point in our relationship, and I'm finding your sudden change in attitude to be quite silly. Would you please decide if you want my help or not, because quite frankly, it's getting irritating to always be pushed to the back of the barn with you."

She looked at him as if he harbored a secret. "Why?"

"Why what?"

"Why do you want to help me so bad?"

"Because I swore to. Because I like my job at Great Mountain and would like to keep it."

"That all?"

He shook his head, but at the moment his sister began to clap her hand for the attention of the women. "No, but this is a discussion we'll have later."

Victoria focused on the women's meeting, and walked away without another word. What in the world was wrong with the woman who only yesterday leaned into his arms as he kissed her in his bedroom? The woman he planned to marry, if he could only figure her out.

What bug had gotten into her britches between then and now?

Wall gritted his teeth and headed toward the post office. Stretching his gate long so the strain in his leg muscles might take the focus away from the ire in his gut.

Before he even worked up a rapid breath, he took the steps and tossed open the door. Pappy snapped his gaze to him as he entered. "Scare a man like that and you're bound to get a bullet between the eyes. What's got you all worked up?"

Wall answered by yanking the mailbag off the counter and rifling through the contents.

"Ah, the woman," Pappy answered for him.

Wall still remained silent. Not wanting to talk about her. Especially not to Pappy.

"Well, a good one will twist a man up. Make him regret he ever met her, and at the same time make him hope they'll never be apart."

"How would you know? Your wife left you alone with a daughter and ran off with a card player."

"And I learned my lesson. She was all too accommodating to me. I didn't challenge her, and she didn't challenge me."

"You don't sound like you harbor any ill will toward her."

"I hurt enough for a century's worth of pain, but I had a daughter to think about so I gave her the world. Or at least a valley." He motioned toward where the expanse of the valley would be outside the building.

"I'm not certain what Victoria wants. She's always so confusing."

"All women are."

"The girls aren't. They tell it like it is."

"To you. Their brother. I'd wager to a man they fancied, they'd be a bit more reserved."

Wall chuckled. "Let's hope or else we'll never get them married off."

His pappy laughed with him as Wall dropped the bag on the counter. "Did a letter come in for me or Victoria?"

"Nope, but I'll let you know when one does."

"Thanks." Wall left as Jax walked up to the building. "Do you need Pappy for anything or can we go to the merc?"

Dawn Luedecke

"Merc," his brother answered.

With a nod toward the building, Wall led the way.

"Your boss lady seems nice, and it looks like neither one of you has seen the hoosegow."

Wall ruffled the boy's hair. "Not yet, but the summers not over."

"I know she's having some troubles. I heard Pa talking about it."

"Did you?"

"He's not happy with you choosing the mill over the family."

"I figured."

"He's got the governor doing all kinds of things to try to get you to come home."

"I figured."

Jax skidded to a stop. "Maybe you should just do it, Wall. Come home already."

Wall motioned for the boy to keep walking. "I will, but not yet. Victoria needs me."

"Haven't you stopped to think you're the reason why she's having all these troubles? If you weren't in her life she'd be fine."

Wall forced his feet to keep walking and not stop at his brother's words. He hadn't really thought about it in such a light. He'd been so consumed with helping her fix her problems, he hadn't stopped to consider he may be the main problem in the first place.

Sure he'd made the connection between the governor and his father, but not the ramifications of the plight. And knowing his father he wouldn't back down until Wall came home. He'd have the governor squeeze Great Mountain until it was gone. Not that he was a bad man, but one thing Hamilton Adair did was get what he wanted. Which at this point in life was for Wall to be home.

Now fate, and his father, were going to force him to choose. Should he let Victoria go and save her company, or keep her for himself and destroy her business, her life, and an entire town who depended on the mill?

Chapter 15

Victoria mentally shook off all of the confusion Wall and his enchanting family had on her. She needed to focus so she could secure the contract for the widow's trees, and by the looks of the hardened woman before her, it wasn't going to be easy.

Along the edge of a small gathering of chairs, two long table were set with refreshments enough for a small group. She clicked her dry tongue to the roof of her mouth, and then plucked up a small cup of tea.

Women filed in, all carrying small satchels. They tucked them under their chairs.

Careful not to spill, Victoria slid into a chair next to the widow. "I've never been to one of these. What are they all about?"

The widow pierced her with a challenging frown. "Women."

"I figured that." Victoria did her best to sound charming and innocent, but Lord above she found dealing with women difficult. They hated her. Most of them out of jealousy. Some because she harbored a broken engagement, but not one of them she cared about.

Well, most women hated her.

She watched as Wall's eldest sister, Bethany, gathered the group around and began to talk. She'd yet to be judged by them, and they'd all welcomed her with open arms and a genuine, if not mischievous, grin. Sort of like the women had formed an Adair family sister's alliance. Except she wasn't an Adair.

Bethany's one-sided conversation centered on cattle at the time, so Victoria took the opportunity to lean closer to the widow, hoping to draw her in to a sense of secrecy. "Are we against all men or just those in Hartland?"

The widow stared at her now as if she were daft. "Heavens no. We women are here to keep our sanity is all."

Victoria drew back and frowned. The widow didn't seem to want to give more than short or uninformative answers. She was missing the mark completely. Perhaps she should wait until after Wall's sisters finished their tattle.

To her amazement, the meeting continued on with more talk about the valley's happenings. Reports on the welfare of certain families, and conditions of farms after the dry summer.

Quite disappointing, really. For all the secrecy shrouded around the event, not much more than a farmer's report happened between the chairs and tables.

Not until Willa clapped.

"Now that's over, let's get to the good stuff. Missy, I believe you and Georgiana lost last month so if you would." Willa pointed toward the corners of the church, and the two women stood to run toward the edge and take a lookout position.

"What in the world is going on?" Victoria asked, more to herself than anyone else.

"The meeting," the widow said with pride, and smiled.

The women all stood, picked up their satchels, and meandered toward the table. Victoria followed.

"Five-card stud is the game of the month, ladies." Willa pulled a stack of cards from a hidden pocket in her skirts and began to take them out to shuffle.

"At a church?" Victoria had never been one for doxology works, but she'd never imagined the good women of Hartland to be secret society card players, on a Tuesday afternoon, at the chapel. "Isn't this blasphemy?"

"No. Nope." Layla held up her hand as she shook her head. "We're outside the church. Made certain of it."

"Also made certain the Good Lord's property line is over there with the chairs. All we did was talk business. The tables are on no-man's land."

Victoria rubbed her forehead as the women unbuckled their satchels and pulled out needlework, placing them on their laps, but not touching them otherwise. "Oh, Good Lord above."

The widow peered skyward. "Amen."

Seeing no other recourse, she took a seat between Bethany and the widow as Willa handed out the cards.

"So what do you do if it's raining?" Victoria picked up her cards, and looked at her hand. She'd played poker with Garrett at the lumber camp the year before. Luckily she knew enough to get her by until the end of the game. She hoped.

"The Lord may have cursed the farms with a dry summer," the widow said, "but he blessed our card game with one. We haven't had to deal with rain as of yet."

The women began to play, laying down cards, and requesting more as their turn arrived.

"So this is a fairly new meeting of yours?" She watched the faces of all the women in the group. No one seemed ashamed. No one shocked by their behavior. Their demeanor proved they banded together to have this time, and they intended to enjoy it.

"Why the secrecy about it all?"

"We work the farms and ranches with our fathers and husbands," Bethany answered. As she spoke she motioned toward various women in the group. "Keep house, cook, clean, raise children, even manage the mercantile. We want something for ourselves. Something the men can't come in and take away from us."

"So you secret away and play cards?"

"We take time to simply exist," the widow answered. "No responsibilities, no life pressures. Only fun. For two hours on the third Tuesday of the month. The losers stand lookout the next month."

"Someone's coming!" Georgiana yelled.

Like children caught in the midst of misbehavior, the women scrambled to cover the cards with the needlework from their lap. Bethany scooted Victoria's cards beneath her craftwork just as Wall walked into the clearing.

"Ladies." He tipped his hat at no one in particular.

"Wallace," the widow greeted with a slight bow to her head. "How's your mamma?"

"Doing well. The girls have no doubt told you, she sends her regrets. She couldn't make it today. Something about getting the new cook settled."

"What can we do for you, brother?" Willa said, the impatience in her tone evident behind every word. Victoria stifled a giggle. In all her dealings with the man, she'd never understood his reason behind the way he responds to women. To her. His deference for her opinion. Allowing her to take the lead…well, in most instances.

She blushed as the thought of his hands on her body cascaded through her memory like a waterfall.

At one point she'd thought him weak. That he'd allowed her to walk on him, but now she understood him better. Saw him with his sisters. His was a respect for the role women played in his life. An allowance for them to stand beside him, and not behind him.

He was exactly as he appeared to be. Pure gentleman cowboy. Clearly loved by all the women around the table. Even the widow, given the way she now batted her eyes at him.

"I've come with a message. Mrs. Yancy is to pick up a parcel at the mercantile, and when you're done with the meeting, Mrs. Harborough is needed back at the store with all haste. It seems he cannot keep up without her."

The woman who must have been Mrs. Harborough rolled her eyes and shook her head.

"Anything else?" Willa said, her tone still impatient.

"Not off the top of my head."

"Then if you wouldn't mind," Willa continued. "We still have a good half hour left of our meeting, and we need complete privacy."

"I wouldn't dream of interfering with whatever is going on here." He waved toward the table, and turned to leave, sliding a long stare at Victoria before walking away.

Even the one glance, so innocent, sent flutters to her stomach, and stole the very breath from her lungs. She was positively a ninny whenever he was around.

But she needed to get back to business. Securing a contract with Widow Yancy.

She leaned over, trying to bring them in as much secrecy as the moment would allow. "I heard you have a lot of trees on your property."

The widow glanced out of the corner of her eyes, and then back down at her card hand. "You hear odd things for someone so new to Hartland."

Victoria straightened, and pretended to care about her own cards, setting down two she hoped were bad, and trading for two she didn't quite think were much better. "I'm in the tree business."

The widow traded her cards. "That would explain your interest in my trees."

"I'd be willing to lease the rights to your trees." Victoria's heart beat faster as the sensation spread to her stomach. Hoping she didn't give away her desperation. She needed this. Her first real deal, and one made after losing all of the land she'd inherited with the mill.

"Don't think I got enough to do anyone any good."

Victoria shrugged. "It'll start me out."

The widow fell silent as one by one the players dropped out, leaving only her and the widow holding cards. The widow smiled. "Tell you what. Why don't we let the cards decide if we make a deal or not?"

"What?" Victoria didn't know what else to say. How was a game of cards any way to decide the fate of her company? Although, she supposed men have used worse tactics to make back-room deals.

"Even if Pa is against the whole thing?" Layla asked from across the table. Only then did Victoria realize the whole group listened to her conversation.

She wasn't aware Wall's sisters knew about her business dealings, or the troubles with their father. Victoria threw Layla a questioning glance, who shrugged. "We overheard Pa talking in the barn with Wall last night."

"Arguing more like," Bethany said, and fiddled with her needlework.

"Just so you know," Willa said. "If we had any influence over my father, we'd have been right there with Wall pleading your case."

"Right." Another woman Victoria didn't even know said, "This valley could use a little trimming down. It's positively overgrown."

Victoria gave them a genuine smile. One she reserved mostly for herself, and Wall. "Thank you all."

"Well, how 'bout it?" The widow wiggled her cards.

"All right." Victoria set her cards down, unsure as to what in the world the outcome would be. In all honesty, she hadn't paid attention to her hand one whit since she'd picked up the cards.

"Well look at that," the widow said. "I win."

She laid down her cards, all neat and in a row. Victoria knew enough to know she'd lost. *Blast!*

If she were a typical woman, she'd cry. For the stress of everything she'd experienced over the spring and summer. For the loss of the first business deal she'd ever handled on her own. By herself with no one to help her out. She'd cry because she needed to.

Except she didn't cry because she was Victoria Harrison.

"I guess you can come by whenever you want to check out the trees." The widow stood, and extended her hand.

Victoria clambered to her feet in a way most unlike her, and shook her hand. Confusion did not begin to describe what she felt.

The widow chuckled at what Victoria's expression must have looked like. "I bet you thought you had to win, eh? Nah, the way I see it, you're giving me the money and clearing my land so I can finally use it. I'm the one who's winning. I go to church on Sundays, and here when we have our meetings, but other than that you can find me at my homestead."

"I'll be by sometime this week." Victoria glanced around the table to the other women's smiling faces as they gathered their possessions, stowed them in their bags, and then began to clean up the table and chairs.

Victoria helped, reeling with the thoughts and emotions of the last two hours. The sheer freedom she felt hiding away behind the church with a group of women, playing cards in secret. The sense of belonging and acceptance the women of Hartland gave her without even so much as a question.

Here she existed as a guest as though she were a part of the community. She felt at peace. As though here, in Hartland Montana, she belonged.

* * * *

Wall held Victoria's horse still as she mounted, and then swung up into his own saddle. She'd went to the Women's Society meeting looking slightly nervous, and a bit unsure. Now, she shined. Hell, even the lighter strands of her dark hair picked up the sunrays with a golden sheen. Although it may be she'd spent more time outside on his father's ranch than her normal routine allowed, but he liked to think her body responded to her happiness at his home. "How'd you fare with Widow Yancy?"

"Secured the trees. Like I said I would."

"I had no doubt." He raised his chin to show his approval. She seemed to need the extra encouragement whenever possible. She wasn't unsure about her ability to lead, but she needed the support of those around her. And since Paul left to find her father, she had only him.

They began to ride down the road toward Old Man Jones's homestead. He waited until they were out of earshot from anyone traveling around town, and then caught her attention with his eyes. "How much land do you need to cover your contract for next year?"

Victoria searched the sky as if the clouds would drop down the answer. "For a year? And with the new contracts? I would say what we harvested at the old Grove."

"We were there for two years."

"Yes, but we only had river logging, so we only had half the contracts we do now. With your inventions, and Garrett's trains, we've doubled the needed harvest."

Wall mentally ran through the ranches in the area, and shook his head. Even if they got every farmer at the base of the mountain to agree, they'd barely be able to cover one season. They needed his father's thousands of densely forested, mountainous acres in order to have a solid foundation to reinvent the mill. Or for the bid he'd placed on the land next to Seeley Lake to go through.

God willing.

The day Victoria fought Luther in court and lost her land, he'd visited the land office and offered every penny he had. He'd told her about it while they drove to Hartland. Had needed to confide in her, but didn't tell her that every dollar he'd saved while working for her, he'd placed in the bank. His money. Not his father's or the Lazy Heart's, but his hard-earned cash to do with as he would.

And he wanted to buy her land to rebuild the mill. Land his father's pocket politician planned to mark for cattle use. Which was another way of saying he wanted the land so he could force out the lumber companies not controlled by him.

Wall suspected his father wasn't the mastermind behind the scheme, but simply supplied him with a well-placed parcel of land that would aid Hamilton in getting Wall to come home for good.

"I checked the post, but I haven't heard anything about the land yet."

"We'll have to take it one year at a time, I suppose. Until we get a solid stance on a section of land."

"If only your father would fold."

She spoke the words even he was thinking. He couldn't fault her for saying them. "My father is stubborn as hell. Which is probably where my sister's get it from."

"They're charming. Wish I could have grown with a family like yours. Stubborn or not."

Wall's stomach dropped as he realized she still hadn't heard from her father.

Old Man Jones's road came into view, and he motioned toward the copse of trees up near the base of the mountain. "That's where we're going." He turned his horse down the road, and she followed.

"How are you doing with your father's situation?"

She shook off his words. "I have to leave it up to mother to worry about. If I don't keep the mill alive, he won't have anything to come home to once he's discovered."

Wall didn't react. In all honesty, didn't know how to. She coped the best way she knew how, and with her it was diving into work apparently. "Let's hope he gets home sooner rather than later."

"He will." She kicked her horse to lope down the long road that ended at the small ranch where they were headed.

His horse panted hard between his knees by the time he caught up with her as she skidded her mount to a stop in Old Man Jones's yard.

Like every other time in his youth when he'd visited, the scene before him felt lonely. A small cabin sat to the right of the lush clearing, and outhouse to the left. Back farther sat a small barn where chickens pecked the ground around it, and out to the side Old Man Jones's sheep milled about in a constant state of confusion.

Farther back, past the farmer's corn field, sat the grove of trees intended to be cut since before the young Jones went and joined the army. Now, not only would he benefit from Victoria's offer, but she would as well.

Hopefully.

Old Man Jones trudged from his barn, wiping his hand on his pants as he approached. His face drawn together in an unwelcome scowl until his eye met Walls.

"Young Wallace," he said, and smiled. "How's your pa doing?"

"Good as can be."

Wall dismounted, followed by Victoria. Wall waved toward her, hoping to draw focus away from his father. "This is Miss Victoria Harrison from Great Mountain Lumber Company."

"Miz Harrison." Old Man Jones bowed his head in greeting.

"I've come to make you an offer I'm hoping you'll find quite enticing," she said.

"Oh?"

"I heard you have some trees you don't need. I was hoping I might talk you into letting me lease the rights to log those trees. Take them off your hands for you."

Old Man Jones shook his head. "Did you say lease the rights?"

"Yes, sir. We offered Mrs. Yancy the same deal."

"Ah, yes." Old Man Jones firmed his chin and dropped his gaze to the ground. "Problem is Widow Yancy needs the money. Way I see it, what I need is them trees gone. I wouldn't need to be paid for you to take them away. You'd be doing me a favor."

"So you'll sign with us?" Victoria shuffled her feet and fiddled with the reins in her leather gloved hand. Wall smiled, but held back from grabbing her hand to help calm her excitement. She would be a terrible poker player.

Old Man Jones motioned toward Wall. "If young Wallace here is with you then you must have Hamilton Adair's blessing, so I don't see why not."

With those words, Victoria's shoulder dropped, and she stopped moving. "Oh…well…we don't have his blessing. That I—"

Old Man Jones slid him a questioning stare. "I don't understand. Why would you be riding with her if you aren't representing your family?"

"I represent me." Wall stood taller. Hoping his next words would help to sway the man in their favor, but his gut dropped. He didn't have the clout of his father, or even grandfather for that matter. "Miss Harrison has my approval, and I am supporting her in her endeavor."

Wall's stomach dropped even lower when Old Man Jones shook his head and frowned. "I'm sorry, son. Your pa's the one who runs the ranch, and Hartland. I can't go against him. I'd be more than happy to let you take these trees once you get your father's approval. Come back with that, and we have a deal."

"What if Pappy backed us?" Wall countered.

Old Man Jones still shook his head in response. "Can't do it."

Wall ran his thumb over his lip and studied a pebble on the ground at the old man's feet. He knew this wasn't going to be easy, but he'd honestly thought Old Man Jones's would at least be one to jump at their proposal. Being as he'd needed the trees gone for years. "His approval, huh?"

"Bring it back and we'll talk."

Wall shook the man's hand, and then turned to help an oddly quiet Victoria mount. She settled, and he did the same. They turned toward the road with a nodded goodbye.

Once clear of Old Man Jones's property, he chanced a glance at her, but to her credit she didn't cry. "It's a minor obstacle. We can stop by all of the ranches between here and the Lazy Heart on the way home and see if we can get any takers."

"And what if we don't?"

"Then we'll move on to our next plan."

"The air is already starting to turn cold in the mornings, Wall. If I don't find something more substantial than the widow's grove soon, it'll be winter before I can get something going up here. I wanted to have Garrett up here with the railroad by mid fall at the very latest."

"Did you write him already? Getting Garrett and his trains up here isn't a bad plan, even if you haven't secured the contracts. I'll talk to my father tonight. Get him on board with that much at least."

"Is there any way to get him to change his mind about supporting Great Mountain being in the valley?" She blinked several times, holding back tears now filling the bottom of her eyes, but she didn't cry. He wanted to hold her. Caress her hair, and make everything okay again.

Take her to a time when her biggest concern was what party to attend, and her father ran the mill. But if he did, they wouldn't be together, and he needed her now more than he needed the rush the white water gave him as the logs beneath his feet shuddered under the river's pressure. He needed her more than he needed the freedom being the leader of the Devil May Care boys allowed him.

He needed her like he needed the very heart she'd stolen with her fiery ways, and stubborn pride.

"There is one way."

"How?" Her face beamed with hope. He refused to be the man to take it away.

He didn't want to tell her. Not yet. First he needed to find out if he was granted the land by Seeley Lake. If so, then all his troubles, all his fears would be for naught.

"Don't worry about that. I'll talk to my father. I'll figure things out for you. I promise, you will have at least a thousand acres to harvest by winter."

Even if he had to give her up to get her the land she needed to make the mill survive, he would.

"Are you enjoying your time here?"

Victoria gave one of her smiles meant only for him. "Your family is delightful. Even if your father doesn't agree with my way of life."

"He's the only one, I assure you."

"What about your mother? She and your father seem to be close."

"They are, but they don't always have the same views on things. Have you had much time with my mother?"

"Honestly, when I'm not with you, your sisters keep me well occupied. I've not had much time to speak with her."

"I'm certain you will eventually." A bird skittered out of the trees and disappeared into the colors of the mountain peaks. Only then did he notice the non-evergreen trees were painted in yellows and orange near the peaks. "It looks like fall is going to be here soon. I'm probably going to have to leave to help my father gather cattle. Will you be okay staying alone on the ranch?"

"I won't be alone. Your family will keep me well occupied. And I've got some letters to send out."

"When I get back, I'll show you the swimming hole. Before it gets too cold down here in the valley." He moved his horse closer to hers, and bent toward her, pulling her in for a kiss.

She tensed at first, but after only a second melted into the moment.

It seemed like forever since he'd felt her warm lips beneath his in his room, and she'd drawn back since the meeting with his father. He needed to remind her, and maybe himself of what they had between them.

He straightened once more, and Victoria tipped one side of her mouth back in a smile. "You can only bring me to the swimming hole if we can go alone. Without your sisters or brother."

"Deal." The sparkle in her chocolate eyes sent heat down past his stomach and made him hard. No woman had ever made him think of nothing but her the way Victoria did. Wall was a bachelor. A cowboy. A pugilist. A Devil May Care. One of the men the Missoulian had called 'touched in the head' for what he did as a job. But he turned into a ninny whenever Victoria gave him one of her genuine smiles.

Wall was lost to Victoria.

Chapter 16

"Will you be okay with my sisters today?" Wall slid a nervous glance toward the four Adair women standing innocently next to Victoria. They were anything but innocent. Trouble followed them like a swarm of bees to a boy with a honey-covered stick.

"I'm certain she'd be better taken care of with us than following you around out there in the mountains." Willa waved toward the peaks of the range behind their homestead.

"I'll be fine," Victoria said. "Are you certain you had enough coffee this morning? I only saw you drink one pot at breakfast."

Wall chuckled at the memory of her face earlier when she'd watched him at breakfast. Clearly not impressed by his ravenous ways...at least where food and coffee were concerned. "Jax helped. We'll be home by sundown."

They planned to round up the first of the cattle to bring to lower ground before fall set in, and with it snow. They did this twice a year. The first to bring the cows up to summer range, and the second to bring them down closer to the house for the winter.

When Victoria talked the other day about the cold mornings, she hadn't realized how right she'd been. In his world, this meant a change in the ranch operation. One from haying, breeding and calving, to health checks and fighting off the fierce hand of winter.

And an early crisp meant an early snowfall. Which after last year's lack thereof, was a great reprieve from the fires and destruction a dry winter brought.

Jax mounted his horse, and his father, the Lazy Heart cowhands, and Pappy sat impatient on their own horses.

The ride to the summer range would give Wall the needed time to talk to his father. Convince him to at least give Victoria his blessing in her fight for lumber from the townsfolk.

After they left Old Man Jones's they were met with nothing but rejection. Most of which were based solely on his father's stance on the matter. When a man such as Hamilton Adair runs a town, and the people of the town are happy with the way things are going. They will do nothing to upset the balance they've created. That much Wall knew. Especially seeing as he was expected to take his father's place as overseer of Hartland once his father passed the torch on.

Wall tipped his hat at Victoria as they rode away, but his heart felt as though it stayed behind. He felt a hollowness growing the farther he rode away from her.

How was he going to do this? Let her go. He didn't want to. Wouldn't if he could find any other way.

He now knew what he needed to do to save her. To also save Great Mountain and the town of Bonner Montana, and all who depended on the mill. But a part of him wanted to be selfish and keep her for himself. To hell with the rest of the world.

He needed to leave his job as a Devil May Care boy, and retire back home as nothing but a cowboy. Send Victoria on the train home—once Garrett gets the rails to Hartland—to run her business in Bonner. What he wished she'd do is let go of everything and run to him, to the Lazy Heart. Forever.

Chances are they'd never see each other again. For aside from the occasional visit to the lumber site, once Victoria secured the trees needed to rebuild Great Mountain, she had no reason to come back to Hartland.

And in order for him to get her the needed land, all he had to do was come home.

Wall's horse adjusted his gait as he drew even with his father.

"You play a hard game, old man." Wall let one hand rest on his thigh and the other gripped the reins.

"You know what you have to do."

The cowhands, Jax, and his pappy bounded up a hill with their horses, leaving Wall and his father to talk in peace, as their own horses took the hill.

"I'm not saying I'm going to, but were I to accept your terms, would you back Victoria with the townsfolk?"

His father gave a single nod. "Yep."

"So you don't have a problem with her taking lumber in the valley?"

"What those folks do with their land is of no business of mine."

"Would you rent her two sections of the Lazy Heart to harvest?"

"No. I can't do that, son. I've already got a contract with Boilson Mines in the works. If we lend out all of our land, what's left for the cattle?"

"What sort of contract?"

"They're a mining company, aren't they?" His father looked at him as if his head were made of lead.

"Not in this valley."

"Well, they will be." His father slowed his horse, and stood in the saddle to watch as his brother and pappy drew even farther ahead. "Boilson and I have entered into a little partnership recently. I discovered some shine in Northfork Creek. Since I've already got my hands full running the ranch and Hartland, I need a partner for the gold."

"Why didn't you say anything before?"

His father gave a tense chuckle. "I wanted to make certain it was a real strike before I went and told anyone. Pappy doesn't even know."

"And now you're confident it's real?"

"Real as the land we're riding on now belongs to Lazy Heart."

"Are you going to tell the family?" Wall struggled to make sense of the information. In all his life on the ranch, his father had always grown and succeeded in everything he'd done. Which was why he was now one of the biggest cattle barons Wall knew.

But gold?

"I'll tell them when Miss Victoria is gone. No use having an outsider in on family business before the rest of the town even knows."

"Victoria isn't an outsider." His heart beat as the ramifications of his next words raced through his head. "I aim to marry her."

"Well, now, how do you expect to live with a woman like that out here? Is she going to pick up an entire mill and move it out to the middle of nowhere like some traveling merchant?" His father's face turned gray, and he frowned. "Or do you intend to defy the family. Betray everything you've been taught. Have been forged to be, and move to the city?"

"Bonner is hardly a city, and I don't even know if she'll have me yet."

"Get the idea out of your head, son. Give up and come home, and I'll back your woman with the townsfolk. I'll even ride to their farms with her, but I won't give her any Lazy Heart land."

"What about north of Lazy Heart?"

"That's unchartered. Wild. And already claimed by the government."

"What's your aim there?"

"What do you mean?" A heifer came into view, and his father turned his horse toward the animal.

Wall waited to speak. Helping as they rounded the frightened animal up and began to push her with their horses the way they wanted her to go.

Once settled at a slow enough pace, Wall caught his father's eyes once more. "Nichols. What's your hold on him? What do you stand to win from leading him like a green gelding?"

"Representative Nichols is a friend of mine who I happen to enjoy a good cigar with every now and then when he's in town. If he happens to want to help me out on suggestions I have during our social time, that's on him."

"Like forcing me home by destroying the mill?" Wall said. Ahead of him, his brother and pappy wrangled a few other head of cattle and guided them into the growing herd.

"Oh, now, son." His father waggled his finger like Wall was a boy again. "I did no such thing. All I did was play a little politics. That business I hear about the sabotage and whatnot wasn't me."

"No. A man named Luther and his father did that to gain a footing with the local politicians so they could control the local government timber contracts. You are broadening your horizons to include the entire territory of Montana."

"Only the area that is of interest to me."

"I'll come home when I'm ready. Whether you force me to or not."

His father leaned over as their horses kept walking, and slapped him on the shoulder. "Well, it's time to be ready, son. Pappy's got the town, I'll be working the mining partnership, and I need you to take over the ranch. I can give you until spring. After which, we can't do without you."

Wall inclined his head, but the muscles between his eyes ached. He didn't have a choice, but at least he had some time. "What do you think about bringing the railroad to Hartland?"

"Hartland isn't important enough for the railroad. I've been trying to get a line out ever since they brought the tracks into Montana. If you can get an engine to run through here, you're a better man than I am."

"Not me. Victoria." Wall grasped the reins tight in his gloved hand, waiting for his father's response. He wasn't quite certain whether his father disliked Victoria for who she was, or what she stood for.

To his amazement his father simply huffed. "I suppose you're expecting me to argue?"

"It had crossed my mind."

"You don't know me at all, son. I'm not one to put my pride above progress for Hartland. If Miz Victoria has success where others have failed, then I applaud her gumption."

"But you don't think she can do it?"

His father shrugged. "All I know is I haven't been able to get the rails to Hartland in all the years I've been running this town."

His horse skittered to the side and neighed, jerking his attention away from the topic. To his left, his father's did the same as the few cattle they'd collected began to fight to run in the opposite direction.

"What is it?" he called to his family as they struggled to keep the cattle under control.

Pappy motioned into the trees. "Grizzly!"

Wall turned as the muscles in the giant bear's shoulders dipped and shuddered as he swiped at something on the ground. His growl reverberated through the trees as the shrieking screech of the weak creature beneath his massive body cried out.

"Let's go!" his father ordered. "Get the cattle to a safer meadow, and check for more higher up the hillside."

Wall took one last look at the powerful beast, and followed his family, pushing the cattle as he went. He'd seen bears before. What man, or woman, living in Montana hadn't?

But this one was ferocious. Starving, and late at getting his winter's worth of fat stores. A place like this wasn't meant for a woman. Wasn't meant for Victoria, and he lived barely on the outskirts of the mountain. Still well within this grizzly's territorial range. He could have just as easily come down to the homestead to find a meal to keep him through the hard winter ahead.

Did he really want to ask a woman like Victoria to live in a place like this? Especially when she was used to having the safety of her mill yard cocoon her like the butterfly she was.

At least he had a few more weeks to figure out what to do. Right now, he needed to concentrate on the cattle, and the safety of his family and their livestock.

* * * *

Victoria slipped on the tough leather gloves Willa had lent her the first day she'd gone out and about on the ranch, and listened to Wall's sisters bicker over which one would be first to enter the pen. She had no clue what they were about to do, but Willa promised it would be exciting.

By Georgiana's sunken posture, and Bethany's triumphant smile, the elder sister had won the squabble.

"Okay." Willa grabbed Victoria's hand and towed her to a spot along the fence. "When I yank up the divider you get ready to use this board to shove Frank left. He won't want to go. He'll want to go right with all of the others, but he can't. Got it?"

"I think so." Victoria took the wide planked board. She still wasn't certain who exactly Frank was, or why she was shoving him to the left. She gathered he was an animal of sorts, but the line of fence where they stood lead to the barn. And in the barn housed the horses, some milk cows, a few pigs, a goat, and some very entertaining chickens. Frank could belong to any of them.

"Frank's a mean one, and he's tough," Willa said. "You gotta get wide and low and use the board to shove him over. Don't let him knock you down or he'll run right over you."

"I'll be behind you if you need me," Layla offered, and ducked through the wood fence to take up a spot.

Victoria steeled herself and followed Layla through, taking a spot at the fence junction, and adjusted her board in her hands to angle it toward the other opening.

"Don't duck away!" Bethany trudged past her into the line of corral where they'd intended Frank to go.

"Where's Georgiana?"

"She's at the end to secure the gate."

"Oh." Victoria jumped as Frank thumped behind the long wooden divider where he waited.

"Ready?" Willa shouted?

Victoria nodded as the other's shouted out their response.

To her dismay, Willa didn't even bother to count before she lifted the divider, and the biggest pig she'd ever seen came charging out from his holding.

"Get low!" She heard one of the girls shout.

She obeyed, and held her board tight, hoping it would make her look stronger to the pig. The beast had to be up toward six hundred pounds. Frank charged straight toward her, not the least bit deterred by her board.

"Shout at him!" another sister suggested.

"Pig!" Victoria shouted, not knowing what else to say. "Go away!"

Somewhere in the distance of her focus, she half heard Wall's sisters laugh, and she couldn't help but laugh at herself as well. Even with the adrenaline coursing through her fingertips as she gripped the board.

As if he noticed a weakness in her, Frank's black, beady eyes met with hers, and he charged. Her whole body went numb the closer he got.

"Go away!" she yelled so hard her throat scratched.

Her mind screamed for her to duck out of his way, but Willa shouted. "Shove him!"

Victoria bent down to use her shoulder behind the board when Frank jammed his snout straight into her exposed thigh, causing instant pain to erupt up her leg and hips. At the same time, she shoved. He staggered a bit, but butted against her again.

She wasn't down. Hadn't lost to the pig so she pushed again and again. Fighting with the animal until she inched him toward the open length of corral where they'd intended him to go.

Seeing the opening, the animal gave up and ran toward Bethany.

Once Frank was well away from her, Victoria stood straight to watch his progress, only to see Bethany step to the side as Frank drew close to her.

Like a cowboy in one of those rodeos she'd seen at the county fair, Bethany swung her leg over the top of Frank's back, and rode the beast down the length of the corral until she reached Georgiana. Once there, she leapt off and into the mud as Georgiana slammed the gate shut to the corral where Frank would stay for the time being.

"What in blue hell?" Victoria never swore, but the moment warranted the words. She wouldn't call Wall's sisters ladies of the first water, but they were certainly ladies. What she experienced just now with them was perhaps the most dirty and exhilarating moment of her life. And it involved a giant pig named Frank.

If she wasn't careful, she might start to turn into a filthy cowboy. If she hadn't already, because frankly these last few weeks at Wall's home were perhaps the best ones she'd ever experienced in her entire life.

"You can have next turn," Layla said as she brushed by and headed toward her sisters.

"I think I'd rather not." Victoria rushed to catch up, dragging the board along as she went.

"Suit yourself. It's quite fun. Even I enjoy a good ride on old Frank, and I'm the one who hates to work the animals with the men." Layla stopped next to her sisters, and then dipped down to step out of the corral. "Now we get to help Ma."

"Why'd we have to move Frank?" Victoria asked, following Layla's path through the fence as the other girls found their way out as well.

Bethany dusted the mud off her split skirt, a grin still stretched across her face. "When the men are gone it's up to us to take care of the chores around here. Frank's a bully. He broke through his holding pen and into the main pig pen. He started tearing up some of the other pigs so we had to put him in the bigger one until Pa comes home to fix it."

"And now we get to go do more appropriate work for us females." Layla turned and headed toward the garden.

"Layla's the prissy one." Willa rolled her eyes, and followed. So Victoria and the rest of the sisters did the same.

"More conservative," Layla corrected when she caught up with the sisters. "Proper."

"Less apt to get into trouble," Georgiana supplied.

Victoria followed and chuckled at their repartee. Which she seemed to do a lot since she'd been here. Between bouts of self-pity for what she failed to have as a child. She wanted this. Wanted the sibling rivalry. The good-natured bickering followed by intense fun with each other. But she'd never have such a thing. Not with Luther.

Her sibling rivalry extended way beyond the good-natured and straight to vicious and conniving.

The thought of her brother brought to mind the letter to Garrett. She needed him to agree to come to Hartland. Needed this boon in her company. Needed to hear word about her father. Needed her life to get back in order.

Needed to once again feel like she could breathe.

They entered the garden as Wall's mother stood straight from where she plucked carrots from the ground, and tossed them into a nearby basket. "Ah, good. Did you get Frank settled?"

"Yes," Bethany answered, took up a row, and started to harvest the crops.

"Splendid. Grab a basket, take any row, and start plucking." Wall's mother tossed another carrot into her basket.

Victoria picked her way across the vegetable garden, following Wall's sisters, and copied what they were doing. A bubble of laughter caught in her chest, but she stopped it before letting it go. She'd never harvested crops before. In all of her years growing up in such a wild state, she'd never had to forage for her own food.

Sure she'd gone out and picked huckleberries with her parents on occasion, but that was more for sport. Like hunting, only for delicious purple fruit. This was the life line for this family.

It didn't look too hard.

The girls scattered along the large planted rows, but Victoria stayed close. She ran the pad of her thumb across the smooth curve of the weave in the basket, and bent down to yank a small carrot free. Dirt flung off the roots as she swung it from the ground and into her basket.

"Oh, no, dear. Just the bigger ones." Wall's mother, Josephine, held up the carrot she'd just plucked. "The smaller ones we'll save and then get them right before the frost. I hope you don't mind helping us out for a week or two while the men gather the cattle."

"Not at all." Victoria searched her row for the perfect-sized target. Once found, she began to fill her basket. "I do need to send a letter. When is the next time anyone is going into town?"

"If you run in and place your letter by the front door then when our neighbor swings by, he will take it on his way to fill in for Pappy at the post office."

"Would you mind?" Victoria motioned toward the basket of vegetables.

Wall's mother nodded. "Of course."

Victoria made short work of getting the letter set with the pile of mail near the front door. With a peek down the hall toward the kitchen where Rose and the older cook worked, she took a quick look to see if there were any more notes to Boilson Mines.

Perhaps she should visit Mr. Boilson himself. See if she can't draw out any information on why Wall's father would need to involve him in his affairs.

The thought that she might be sticking her nose where it didn't belong crossed her mind, but throughout the last few months she'd been burned one too many times. She couldn't let her guard down. Not now.

But the fact that it was Wall's family caused butterflies to fight a fierce battle in her stomach. He was as honest and true as they came, and she suspected at least most of his family was the same. She wasn't certain about his father.

Before anyone threw suspicion her way, she ran outside, and back to her task. As she walked, she studied the knees to her split skirt, now caked-in mud and something a bit darker. Some stain she didn't want to think too hard about.

"All set?" Josephine asked as she took her place once more?

She smiled and nodded at Wall's mother.

At the start of the season, she'd criticized Wall for his filthy clothes, yet here she knelt in the mud, her fingernails black with dirt—and not hating it.

Not that she loved fighting giant, overly fed pigs, or plucking carrots from the ground, but the task was somehow satisfying. She'd been wrong to judge Wall and his kind for all those years.

"I would like to apologize for not being more attentive to you over the last few days." Josephine gave a quick glance, but continued to work. "I've been getting Rose and her son settled. I'm glad to see Wall and the girls were able to keep you occupied, though."

"You've all been very hospitable. I appreciate you taking me in on such short notice."

"It's our pleasure." The older woman's eyes twinkled with the same secretive flare she'd seen in her mother's eyes the night she and Wall were discovered alone in her house. "Any friend of Wallace is always welcome here."

"Does he bring many friends home from town?"

"Some of the Devil May Cares have visited on their way through for the winter, but other than that, you're the first."

"I hope they behaved themselves. They tend to be a rowdy bunch of hellions at the camps, but men like that make the best lumberjacks."

Josephine chuckled. "Men of Wall's ilk are wild by nature, but most have good hearts." After a brief moment, she continued. "I hope you'll forgive Hamilton for his old ways. He's a businessman first. He doesn't always show compassion in the way he deals with things."

"Please don't fret over my sensibilities. I'm used to dealing with men like your husband. I can handle the rough ways of a hard deal."

"Wall tells me that your father is missing. Have you heard any news?"

Victoria sat back on her heels to ease the growing ache in her lower back from her position bent over the row of vegetables, and sighed. "No."

"Well, I'll continue to pray for his safe return, and we'll just have to keep an eye out for news."

"Thank you."

In fact, she'd written Garrett, begging for both news of her father, and to get him to bring a rail line to Hartland. Knowing him, he'd agree. He knew a good venture when he saw one, and this part of Montana was virtually untapped when it came to timber harvesting. She had no doubt he'd agree, but she did dread the news he'd bring regarding her father.

While her mother managed things at the mill, all she had to do in Hartland was work to secure more contracts, and wait. Being with Wall and his family made her part of the task all the more enticing.

Chapter 17

"Have you seen Victoria?" Wall asked his sisters. They all sat frowning in the parlor as his mother instructed them on the proper technique for needlepoint, a hobby they'd all taken up within the last year. Layla, of course, excelled at the task, while the other three struggled, but managed. Barely.

"She's gone to see the chicken at the swing," his mother answered.

"Thank you." Wall pivoted and headed out. He'd spent the last week rounding up cattle with his father, and had barely spent any time with Victoria. Sans nights when he'd been able to come home and sit with her in the parlor with the rest of the family, but then it was only a few hours before the girls would shuffle her off to bed.

What he wanted to do was get her alone. Maybe steal a kiss. Touch her. Find the balance he only seemed to have in his life when she was around.

He took long strides across the clearing to the copse of trees where the chicken loved to sit, only to skid to a stop at the sight of Victoria sitting on the swing with the chicken on her lap. "She's never let anyone sit beside her on the swing, let alone pick her up."

"She likes me." Victoria flashed her white teeth in triumph.

"She's not the only one." He motioned toward the house. "You seemed to have charmed my entire family."

She set the chicken down, and stood, dusting her hands. "Or they've charmed me. I've never felt so at ease before just existing."

"Hartland has the ability to make a man forget the rest of the world exists."

"It's quite enchanting."

"Regarding the rest of the world. Father says to go ahead and try for the rail line. Apparently, he has failed miserably for years to get them up here. Something about Hartland being too small and unimportant for the railroad."

"Well, that's about to change. I received word today from Garrett. He will be here within the week to begin drafting the plan for the line."

"How does it feel to succeed where others have failed?" He stalked toward her, letting the smile stretching across his face show his intentions. "My only regret is what the rail line will do to us."

He pulled her into his arms before she could speak, and tugged at his favorite curl.

"What do you mean?"

"My father will back you with the townsfolk. You are free to go get as many contracts for trees as you wish." His heart sank at the memory of the conversation he'd had with his father.

She didn't smile like he'd expected. "Why do you look so melancholy if you came to deliver me good news?"

"I will have to make a deal with the devil." He laughed sardonically. "So much for being the leader of the Devil May Cares. Seems I do care after all."

"What deal?"

"I can't come back to work at the mill. I have to stay on the ranch."

"You'll have to give up your job with me for your father's support?"

Wall dropped his forehead against hers. "I'd give up anything for you."

To his surprise, Victoria stepped back and shook her head. She began to pace like she did whenever she thought through her troubles. "No. I'm sorry. I know how much you love your job on the river crew."

"Not more than I love my family. Or you."

On his words, she spun around. "What did you say?"

"I love you." The words came out as a desperate whisper. Desperate for her to understand. Desperate for what they couldn't have.

Victoria's mouth opened as though she wanted to speak, but she didn't. His heart beat with the words that didn't come. Did she not feel the same? As he'd feared.

"We are on two different paths. Once you get the contracts you need, there's nothing to keep you here. In fact, you can't stay and keep the mill running. And in order for you to get those contracts, I can't go back with you."

As if finally released from whatever held her back, she said, "I love you. I've only realized the truth of it while sitting here with this silly chicken on my lap." Her chin began to quiver. "I don't want to leave your side. I don't want to leave here."

He scooped her into his arms once more, and kissed her. Hard.

Once he'd gotten his fill of her luscious mouth, he drew back. "But you don't have a choice."

"No." The tears she'd held back fell down her cheeks. "If I fold without having my father to take over the mill again, dozens of families, a town will be destroyed."

"And you can't run it from here."

Again she shook her head, and dipped her face low to her chest.

He reached up and, with his index finger, lifted her chin to make her look at him. "Then let's live for today, and hope the land purchase goes through."

"If it does, what then?"

Wall shrugged. "We have a respite from me being forced to come home. At least for now."

"We can figure the rest out later." She snuggled her face into his chest, and entwined her arms around his waist. "Let's pray they take the bid."

He kissed the top of her head, and caressed her hair. Silent as they stood. His thoughts running through more options, but none that would work to give him any more time with her.

What they needed was a distraction, and he knew the perfect way to escape from reality.

"Come with me." He grabbed her hand, and tugged her down the path behind the swinging chicken.

"Where are we going?"

Wall took a quick glance at the clouds, but he knew the weather planned to hold steady with a warm front. At least for another few weeks. The changing leaves had yet to reach midway down the mountain, but the valley where the homestead was remained warm enough for a last dip.

"Do you remember when you bathed in the river?"

From behind him he heard Victoria giggle. "How can I forget something like losing my clothes down a river?"

"We're going to do something like that. Only together."

Victoria skidded to a stop and her hand slipped from his. He spun around. "Don't get shy now. I've already admired every inch of your body."

"What about the others? And isn't it a bit cold to be swimming?"

"Don't tell me you're afraid of a little cold. And what others? You mean my family?"

"Your cowhands. The cooks."

"Scared?" He took his finger and traced the collar of her shirt.

"Frightened beyond belief." Her chest began to heave the way it did whenever her resistance began to deplete.

"The cooks and hands are busy with Pa and Jax. Ma and my sisters are sewing, and Pappy is at the post office today. There's no one out here but you and me."

"That's what we thought about my house," she said, but began to walk hesitantly toward the creek as he guided her once more.

"We can get caught a thousand times, but it doesn't change the fact that someday we will find a way to be man and wife." He stopped at the edge of the best water hole he'd ever found, and slowly began to pull her shirt from the waistband of her skirt.

"Someday," she repeated.

"You're not wearing your split skirt today." He didn't know why he commented, but he noticed. Something so inane, but on her it was important.

"We weren't chasing pigs or pulling helpless vegetables from the ground."

"Or riding rivers. Or traipsing around a logging camp," he included. "I think you're a lot more adventurous than you give yourself credit for, princess."

"Like making love to a man in a river for all the world to see."

"Not all the world. Just anyone at Lazy Heart." He let her know he joked with his smile, and finished stripping them both of their clothes. "And not a river, a swimming hole."

She wrapped her arms around him, merging both of their heat as he picked her up and brought her into the water until they sat chest deep.

She gasped as the water hit her. At the same time, he pushed into her, causing her to take in another desperate breath, infused with a passionate desperation.

Victoria withdrew her mouth from his and leaned her head back, exposing her neck to him, so he paid homage to the delicate skin within his reach as she used the water to help her move over him in a rhythm designed to drive him to the edge. Fast.

"Slow down," he ordered.

He didn't want to finally have her only to complete the task before he got a chance to take pleasure in the woman who'd stolen his heart with her commanding ways.

She shook her head as if she intended to disobey him, so he pulled out of her and pushed her away in the water. She dropped her feet from around his waist and frowned.

"Hold on, princess, I'm not done with you, but I'm not going to let you make this a fast loving, either." He cocked one side of his mouth back in a wolfish smile and started to stalk toward her, eliciting a little coquettish squeal from her as she tried to swim away. Taking his cue.

He herded her back into the little cove where he'd tied the rope swing when he was young. There, a large tree, bent and extending over the river only to curve upward back toward the sky, would give him the perfect advantage to torture Victoria the way she'd done him mere seconds earlier.

Reaching out, he scooped one of her perfectly rounded buttocks in one hand, and the other he palmed the small of her back as he tugged her close again.

"I'm assuming you use that for something other than heaving logs onto a train." She waved toward the rope.

Wall slid his hand down to caress the sensitive skin between her thighs as he let a deep groan out at the idea she conjured with her statement. "Let me show you."

* * * *

An absolutely wicked sensation slid over Victoria with each water droplet cascading down her body as she emerged from the water following Wall. He led her up the bank. Stark naked.

She'd lived her life pin straight and so narrow there was no room for error. Now she wanted to follow the leader of The Devil May Cares onto a large tree trunk thick enough for them both to sit on, but one bent ever-so temptingly over the swimming hole.

She followed Wall close, half to keep warm and half to hide what she could from anyone who might happen to walk by and see them. Victoria glanced around the well-hidden haven. Well, if anyone could see them.

"Step past me." Wall's voice was deep and husky, the way it got whenever he spoke to her in his lover's drawl. She loved it. The timbre sent instant heat between her thighs and made her melt at even the slightest of commands from her river logging cowboy.

Hers.

She hadn't lied when she told him she realized her love while sitting there with the chicken. He was the reason she'd gone out to think. She'd gotten the letter from Garrett and knew her time at the Lazy Heart was drawing to an end.

She didn't want to go.

She wanted to stay there with him. Forever. She would give up everything for him if she were the only one who would be affected, but he was right. At least a hundred people depended on her success, if not more. Were she the only one involved, she'd cut her losses and stay in Hartland.

"Victoria," he urged, and she shook off her lover's reverie, and stepped past. As she did, his calloused hands began to roam the fair skin of her stomach and breasts.

Her breath caught when he moved them lower and, as he did before, dipped one finger deep within her heat as she stood before him with her back facing his front.

His manhood hard against the small of her back, she focused on the small pulse she felt from him. He wanted her. Loved her as much as she did him.

"Grab the rope," he commanded.

She obeyed.

The knot along the course rope helped keep her steady regardless of the sway of the makeshift swing and Wall pressed her back with his warm palm. She leaned over like she did the night at her house, and pressed her backside out toward him at the same time he entered her.

She sucked in a sharp breath at the sensation of his welcome intrusion. "Yes."

On her single word, he grabbed her hips in both of his hands as they balanced on the log over the swimming hole. He pushed deep inside her, and then out. Repeating the motion until she felt as though she would yank the rope straight from the sturdy branch where it was tied.

Cool air replaced one side of her hips and she almost cried out in rejection of the movement when he reached up and tugged at her shoulder, and he slammed even harder into her.

She couldn't take it anymore.

Not the intense pressure of him deep within her womb, not the scratch of her bare feet on the bark, not the burning in her legs. She wanted to show him how she felt about him. Prove to him that what he'd done to her meant more to her than anything else in her life. "Stop," she pleaded.

"Oh, princess, you're killing me," he said, but obeyed, although deep inside her.

She moved to stand upright, and he pulled out.

She searched the tree trunk, and seeing the perfect, wide spot next to a branch in which Wall could lean against, she pointed. "Sit there."

Hesitantly, and with great care, he sat naked and leaned against the branch.

She began to step tentatively to straddle his hips, and he moved down enough for her to crouch over him. As she did, he slid into her. So hard and deep, she felt him all the way into her stomach. She placed her hand over her lower abdomen and felt the pressure from him. Yet somehow she wanted more.

She grabbed the branch above his head to help her move as she began to ride him, mimicking the rhythms she'd come to love so much.

The lines of his face grew sharp and his eyes pierced her like the shards of ice from the glacier just north of her now lost logging camp. He was pure, rugged male. More handsome than any man she'd ever met before, and all hers.

She wanted to rake her fingernails sensually over his chest for the rest of her life. Kiss him in the morning before he got up to wrangle cattle, or ride the river—whichever job he chose. She wanted him.

Her knees began to ache the harder she rode, but she didn't care. The pain somehow added to the ecstasy of the moment. A moment she would have to cherish and take with her when she left.

He grabbed on to her sides and helped guide her until the hold she had on her control snapped. She yanked on the small protruding branch above Wall's head and it snapped. At the same time, in the distance of her mind, she heard him groan, and his body relaxed beneath her.

Only then did she realize she'd broken the tree limb that she'd used as leverage. She pinched her lips together to stop from laughing and showed him. With a lopsided smile, he grabbed the stick and tossed it down to the ground. "Perhaps you're not a princess anymore. Maybe I should call you wildcat instead."

"I think I've long since lost my princess status." She moved so she could sit on his lap until the lover's high ebbed. He wrapped his arms around her hips, cocooning her in his protection and warmth.

"How do we get down from here?" A giggle erupted from deep within her chest.

"Do you want to?" He leaned over and nibbled on the peak of her breast.

"Not particularly. We can stay this way forever if you swear no one will ever discover us."

"I can rope the moon and give it to you, but I cannot promise you no one will find us. My brother is very fond of the swimming hole."

Victoria gave a dramatic sigh. "Then I suppose we should at least get back in the water since we are perched in a tree for all to see like two love birds."

All Wall did in response was kiss her shoulder and grunt his agreement.

"Wall." She nudged his shoulder.

"What?"

"I really don't want to get caught naked. It's been a fear of mine since my clothes went down the river."

"Then I suppose you'd better stand so we can get down." He said the words, but at the same time he tightened his arms around her waist.

"Wallace Adair," she warned.

"Oh, all right." He let her go, but frowned.

She took a few steps toward the bottom of the tree, but it looked more difficult going down than it did coming up. Her heart began to beat faster. "How do we get off?"

Wall chuckled as he stood, and reached out to get the rope where mere moments ago she'd grabbed on to for balance. "Swing out and once you're over the water, let go and drop down."

"You've got to be joking."

"No, ma'am."

Victoria reached up to fiddle with her favorite necklace and stared at the water. "Is it safe?"

"It's been tested hundreds of times without incident."

She dropped her necklace, and reached out to grab the rope from Wall, running her hands as high as she could up the line of knots. She'd wrestled pigs and swung with chickens. Why not? "Are you certain?"

"Just aim for the middle where it's the deepest, and then make certain to let go when you're at the peak of the swing."

Victoria took a deep, courage-boosting breath, and pushed off with her feet. The air cooled her passion-heated skin as she swung out. As she reached the peak, she heard Wall call out, "Let go!"

She loosened her grip, and her body dropped, along with her stomach. She wanted to giggle and cry out in fear as she plummeted.

The rush of water slid up her body and covered her head and she kicked and began to swim to the top. She crested and opened her eyes in time to see Wall catch the rope.

He readied it. "Swim over a bit."

She side stroked, and after she'd gained a few feet, he swung out and dropped in beside her, splashing as he fell.

He crested the top and turned to her.

"That was exhilarating," she said, as she followed him while he swam toward their clothes.

"I love to see the delight you get in the things I've experienced my entire life. I only wish I were there to see you wrangle Frank."

Victoria laughed. One of her deep belly laughs she rarely gave. "You heard about Frank and me?"

Water droplets cascaded down Wall's body as he emerged onto the bank, and Victoria followed. Admiring how regal he looked with nothing on. Like a conqueror. Her conqueror.

"I would have loved to see you push him around." Wall slipped on his trousers, and yanked his shirt over his head.

Victoria, too, began to dress. "He's quite the stubborn one."

"You fit in really well on the Lazy Heart." By now Wall yanked on his last boot as Victoria struggled to button her blouse. He stepped toward her and started to play with her curls as she finished dressing.

She dropped her hands once the only thing left for her to do to be completely dressed was to pull on her socks and boots. "How are we going to overcome this? I don't want to lose you now. If I move to Bonner, and you stay here, we'll never see one another."

"Nonsense. I'll come and visit whenever I'm out your way."

"Stolen nights is not what I had in mind for the man I fell in love with."

"Just pray the bid comes through. I should have heard something by now, so I suspect I'll be hearing something soon."

"Not soon enough."

"Come on." He plucked her boots off the ground and handed them to her. "Tonight is a shindig at one of the neighboring farms. We should probably get back to the house."

"And you expect I'll dance with you?" She slipped on her boots.

"I had counted on it."

"I suppose I can give you one dance. If Pappy doesn't take all of my time."

Wall sucked air in between his teeth. "He's a slick one. Been charming the ladies for decades from what I hear."

Victoria entwined her arms around Wall's waist and peered up at him. "Well, you're the only cowboy who can charm me."

"Then we'd better live for tonight, and figure out tomorrow with the sunrise."

Victoria let go of his waist, looped her arm through his, and followed him toward the Lazy Heart. In truth, if she had the opportunity, she'd follow him anywhere. If her life were her own to do with as she would. If her father were discovered and returned to them. If life were different, she would give up everything if she had to and simply exist with Wall Adair.

Chapter 18

Wall studied his reflection in the mirror hanging in his mother's foyer, and buttoned the top button of his best flannel shirt, and then plucked his hat off the peg near the door. He'd wiped off a month's worth of dirt from the brim earlier, but it didn't seem to get it clean enough.

He spit on the stain, and rubbed hard at the spot until the rumbled of his sisters feet sounded on the ceiling above him.

His father and brother emerged from the room to his right. "I swear those girls are as subtle as a thousand-cattle stampede."

"And just as dangerous," Jax supplied, rubbing what Wall could only assume was some wound one of his sisters had given the poor boy.

"If you end up marrying that girl, Wallace...have boys."

Wall chuckled. "Will do, sir."

Victoria, his mother, and sisters all rumbled down the stairs as quiet as they were in the rooms above him, and Wall turned to extend his arm to Victoria—who shone bright in a frail, peach gown he'd seen her in before, but one he'd never thought looked as radiant on her the way it did as she stood beaming at him. "Shall we?"

As though she'd never been happier in her life, she slid her hand on his arm and walked beside him with perfect poise. Even if she were to ever live the simple life in Hartland, which he doubted would ever happen, she'd always carry herself the way he saw her. With a regal air. A princess.

He escorted her to the awaiting wagon, and she glanced around as she climbed aboard. "Where's Pappy? I wanted to save him a dance."

"He had to meet the mail carrier, so he'll catch up with us later." Wall helped his sisters climb aboard the wagon, and then mounted his horse.

Next to him, his brother did the same on his own mount, as his father took up the reins to the wagon, and Victoria and his sisters filled the inside seats with their pretty smiles and poufy dresses.

Victoria adjusted her skirt, and leaned over in secrecy to hear something Willa said to her, and then burst out in laughter, and Wall's heart broke.

She was his. Meant to be with him in every way. Even his family loved her, and she them. His only hope was for the land purchase to go through to buy them more time.

The wagon began to roll, and Wall kicked his mount to a walk next to Jax and his horse.

"Are you going to leave us again?" Jax asked in a voice only he could hear.

"Why would you ask such a thing?"

"I see the way you look at her, but Pa says she can't stay. When you look at her, you have the same wild look in your eye you get right before you leave for the logging season. Like you're gone from the Lazy Heart already."

Wall pinched his lips tight. He didn't know what to say to the boy. If his deal went through, he would be leaving the ranch for a time, but if it didn't, he'd be swearing himself to a life of misery running the Lazy Heart alone. Like Pappy did.

"Even if I leave again, I'll always come back. The Lazy Heart is my home."

"One of these days you're going to go away from Hartland, and never return."

"Well, you could always help me convince Pa to lease a section or two of the Lazy Heart to Victoria. Then even if I did go logging, I'd still be on our property."

"That's true." Jax moved his lips to the side like he always did when thinking. After a moment, he nodded. "I'll talk to him."

If they were closer, Wall would have ruffled the kid's hair. Whatever path Wall was supposed to take, he knew would be the right one. His family did need him as much as Victoria, but the thought of not having either in his life made his chest burn like someone took a branding iron out of the fire and jabbed it straight into his heart.

He was doomed to misery either way.

After a few minutes, his father turned the wagon down the neighbor's road, and Wall rode ahead to help secure a spot for his father's wagon.

He entered the field where buggies were already lined up, and found a spot to secure his horse. Jax tied up his gelding next to him, and they waited.

Somewhere, off in the distance, the general mayhem of the gathering echoed through the homestead, mixed with the rhythmic thud of the wagon wheels crushing the grass as his father pulled to a stop and set the break.

Wall began to help the women down, one by one, until he reached Victoria. He may have held her a little too close for etiquette as he set her on the ground, but he didn't care. Not tonight.

"What happens first here?" she asked, as they turned to follow his family toward the gathering crowd near the outside of the barn.

"Well, we all get in our best bib and tucker, we dance, we eat." Wall stopped and searched to make certain his parents weren't within earshot, and then bent so only Victoria could hear. "And when we're really soaked the men go out back and knock fists."

"For fun?"

"Of course. That's how I became a pugilist."

"I heard the Devil May Cares call you that, but never knew exactly why."

"We get a good row whenever there's a social event. It's no third-Tuesday-of-the-month-poker game, but it works for us."

Victoria snapped her gaze to meet his eyes. "You know about the gambling?"

Wall tipped half his mouth back in a quirky grin. "Every man in the valley knows. We just pretend we don't so we can get away with our little secrets."

"And here they thought *they* were getting away with something quite naughty."

Wall focused on the party ahead. "Don't go telling them we know. Let them have their delusions. We love them even more for it."

"Your secret is my secret."

He winked at her, and then led her into the mayhem where they were instantly swept up by his sisters as their father took the platform and commanded the attention of the crowd to kick off the party.

"The dancing is about to start," Bethany said when their father finished.

"And of course, you must dance with me." Layla blushed, and slid an apologetic smile at Victoria. "After Victoria, of course."

"You know very well you're all going to dance with me at least once." He tugged Victoria closer to his side. "But you're right. She's first. And I expect while I'm busy with you four, Jax will watch over her and not let anyone else steal her away."

"Like Micah Jacobs?" Georgiana sneered toward the man in question.

"Yes," Wall said. "And anyone else."

"I'd be happy with you and Pappy."

"What about me?" Jax asked.

Victoria beamed down at him. "You too, if you'll be so kind."

"I'd be more than happy to watch over you while my brother is busy."

"Much obliged." She nodded at his brother, and pride swelled in his chest. She was truly a treasure.

The band began with their usual waltz, and he swept Victoria out on the dirt dance floor as other couples began to take their places.

"It's lucky this is the first song." She leaned into him as they danced.

"Luck hasn't nothing to do with it. The band always plays this first. It's sort of their warm up to the faster songs."

"Oh, so you knew."

"Of course."

She fell silent, and her gaze spread out over the crowd. Wall, too, surveyed his surroundings. Off in the distance, the unwed men who hadn't attracted a partner stood with heads together. No doubt planning the inevitable brawl later in the evening. An event which happened every party since he'd become old enough to care for anything other than toys and horses.

Directly across from the oblivious men, whatever women who hadn't garnered the attention of a man before the dance sat with their mammas, or somewhere off in the distance, they helped with the food. Farther out, his father and the ranchers gathered, as usual, to talk trade and business, while the children ran around like chickens in a hen yard.

A scene so familiar to him, yet tonight the sense of home somehow imprinted so firm into his mind he didn't want it to end. Especially with Victoria in his arms.

But alas, the band played the last chord of the dance, and she stepped back, smiling up at him as if he'd given her a gift she'd never forget.

He wanted to kiss her right there in the middle of the dance floor for all to see, but he wouldn't.

Instead, he turned and began to usher her back to his sisters when he heard his pa call his name.

"Layla, you're next, but I need to see Pa."

"And I believe Jax has the next dance with me." Victoria sent his brother a questioning glance, and he blushed and nodded.

This time Wall did ruffle the boy's hair as he walked by toward their father. "Thank you."

In a few steps, he tipped his hat back to better view his pa.

"Pappy brought this for you." His father held out a letter.

Wall searched the crowd only to see his pappy disappear toward the food table. Wall took the letter, and his heart beat sped up when he read the scrawl on the front.

"It's about the land I want to buy."

"I know."

His father's words gave him pause. He wasn't certain if he'd told him his plans, but even if he did, the certainty behind the two words went down like he'd swallowed a live fish.

He opened the letter and read it as fast as he could. "Rejected?"

He glanced up at his father, who stared emotionless at him.

He flicked the letter toward him. "What did you do?"

"I may have had a friend in the land office tell me of your application."

"So what? *You* bought it?"

His father shook his head. "Nope."

"Then what?"

"I just let Nichols know that land he wanted for the project was being bought up before he could get it is all."

Red slid before Wall's vision, and his hands tingled. He fought hard to control the rage boiling inside his core. He wrapped one palm over his other fist to keep himself from slamming it into his father's face. Which he so desperately wanted to do.

"You can't win, Wallace." His father's words penetrated his fog, and he stepped forward to administer the blow, when a small warm hand pressed gently on his arm.

He glanced down at the now familiar site of Victoria's small hand as she stepped into his vision, pulling him from the rage he'd felt mere seconds ago.

"Ah, Miss Victoria." His father pulled his pipe from his pocket and smacked the end to empty any old ash. "Wallace here was telling me that I can announce the good news."

"What good news, sir?" she asked, looping her arms through Wall's. He laid his hand over her arm, needing the extra contact to help ground him.

"Of my support of your plan to help my neighbors harvest their trees, of course."

Wall clenched his teeth, and clutched her arm. She opened her mouth to speak, but he knew what she was going to say. She was going to sacrifice herself, the town of Bonner, for his pride. He couldn't allow such a thing.

"Announce it," he bit out, and then all but yanked her as he turned and marched past the crowd of dancers, past the table of food, and out toward the horses.

Victoria all but running beside him. "Why did you do that?"

"For you."

"Not for me. We agreed we would come up with another way."

"There is no other way!" He skidded to a stop and spun around, searching their surroundings for anyone who may have overheard. "He's won, Victoria. Go home. Go get your trains and your timber beasts, and send them back up this way, but I can't be a part of your life, or Great Mountain anymore."

"You may have settled for this, but I have not. I'll find a way out."

Wall gave a sarcastic chuckle, as a flash of color caught his attention. He watched as a group of men headed into the forest, and he knew why.

He let a smile stretch across his face to match his mood. Only one thing could help, but he doubted Victoria would understand.

At this point, he didn't care.

"Come on." He grabbed her hand again, and urged her to follow without the slightest of explanations. She'd understand soon enough.

* * * *

Her shoes weren't made for running through stick-covered vegetation, but she followed Wall anyway. She'd never seen him in such a state, and she didn't like it. She wasn't scared of him, but she didn't like to see him hurt.

They could find another way to save the mill without him having to sacrifice his freedom. He didn't have to do this.

"Where are we going?"

"To work off some of the fight my father put in me."

"Now is hardly the time," she said, glancing around to see if anyone followed. They didn't.

He chuckled. "As much as I would love to work off anything with you like that, I had something different in mind."

"Oh," she said, and then fell silent as she followed, hoping to catch a glimpse of anything which might help her figure out his intent.

Finally, after what seemed an eternity of walking, the deep rumble of men shouting echoed through the trees, and she realized where they were headed.

"Boxing?"

"I like to call it pugilism, or fisticuffs. Boxing sounds so harsh."

"But you've been doing it forever as you mentioned."

He nodded as he fought his way to the front of the crowd, ushering her behind. "Since I was little. Even toured the West a little after school. Before I joined on with Great Mountain. Went as far as Reno before I came home."

"You mean before you got your head knocked off."

He gave a lopsided grin, but didn't answer. Instead he turned and shouted encouragement at the man who was down. His voice caught the attention of a few onlookers who focused on Wall, and then her. She moved closer to him, clutching his hand and pressing herself closer to him as she watched the men fight.

"Don't be shy," Wall yelled over his shoulder. "You've seen this at your lumber camps."

"Yes, but I wasn't an outsider then."

Just then a loud cheer erupted from the men and the victor leapt from the fallen loser with hands raised in victory.

As the volume of cheers died down, someone from the crowd cried out, "Wall's here! Who wants to take him on?"

She clutched his hand tighter, but he stepped forward, so she let him go. She grasped her necklace, watching the huddle as the men determine who would fight Wall. After a minute, Wall rushed back to her, and yanked his shirt free of his waistband to hand it to her. "If I win you get to log Caleb's homestead farther down the valley."

"I don't want a contract this way."

To her surprise, he kissed her hard and fast, not caring who saw. Her heartbeat sped up, both in shock and slight giddiness. He smiled. "You don't have a choice."

"Wall," she called, but he'd turned to rush into the make-shift ring.

"Best let him go when he gets like this." A familiar female voice sounded beside her. She turned as three of Wall's sister shoved their way beside her.

"Oh, thank God. I thought I was going to have to experience this alone."

"Are you kidding?" Georgiana asked, surprising Victoria with her presence seeing as she was quite young herself. Barely older than Jax, who couldn't be more than fifteen. "We don't miss Wall's fights."

Jax took up a position on her other side, and stood with arms crossed. He didn't say a word, but she watched the way he interacted with the men nearby. He'd taken his role as her protector in Wall's absence seriously, and she adored him for it. She'd never had a brother who cared for her the way Wall's did. Luther wasn't a brother, no matter how much she wished circumstances to be different.

"We saw the group of men sneak off and waited five minutes. That's how you do it with the mammas around. Layla stays behind to cover for us. She doesn't like the blood."

A third man stood between Wall and his bare-chested opponent, and on his mark, they began to circle one another. Throwing occasional jabs, but not yet connecting with flesh.

Willa shook her head. "Wall's beatin' the devil around the stump with this one is all. He must be in a mood."

"What do you mean?"

"Usually he likes to make it fast and as painless as possible. One or two punches and a knockout so his buddy doesn't go home hurtin', but when he doesn't, he's aiming to draw the fight out."

"Why on earth would he do that?" Victoria grasped her necklace again and ran the gem along the chain as she turned back to the fight.

"Come on, Wall!" the other fighter shouted. "What's your game?"

At the man's words, Wall snapped a quick jab forward, and the man's head jerked back with the punch. But he wasn't out. The man righted himself, and smiled as he swiped at the blood now trickling down his face. "Better."

With that, the man attacked, and the fight began.

The first blow the man threw, Wall ducked, but he followed it in quick succession by a second that landed straight on Wall's face. Victoria stepped forward. Her natural instinct drawing her to run to his side to tend to his wounds.

Jax held her back with a hand on her arm, and she stopped. "You're right. Sorry."

Victoria forced herself to stay put as Wall continued to fight the man until finally he knocked him out with a punch hard enough to send the man flying across the ground.

Wall tripped toward her as Jax finally released her arm.

"Wallace Adair," she scolded, and grabbed him, supporting him as he approached. "No more fisticuffs."

"Sorry, princess. I've got three more fights lined up for tonight. Seems I've got a few people anxious to give up their trees to you in exchange for a go around with me."

"Don't you dare," she scolded. "I won't take these contracts, especially if you get them this way."

"Don't listen to him, Victoria," Willa said, and held out a piece of paper to her. "Father's already gone and told the town you have his support. Mother, Bethany, and I got a list of farmers who need their logs cleared. No need for paying them either."

"Except the Widow Yancy, of course," Jax clarified. "She still needs the lease."

Victoria took the paper, and waved off his concern. Touched that even the youngest of Adair's cared for the welfare of the people under their family's leadership. She turned to Wall. "I will not allow you to bloody yourself for me."

He pulled her close, without a care to anyone nearby. "I did that for me, but I would die for you."

"Oh, Wall." She didn't know what else to say as her heart sank to her stomach. Out of the corner of her eye she watched his family move away, leaving them in what relative privacy they could. "You don't have to. Don't do this to yourself. You're one of the greatest inventors I've ever met. For hell's sake, you made machines to revolutionize Montana logging. We will figure out how to overcome this obstacle, even if we have to spend some time apart. We'll make certain it isn't forever."

He ran the back of his hand down her cheek. "You're a rare woman. Strong and determined."

"The sort of woman a filthy cowboy like you needs." She nudged him with the shirt he had yet to put on, and he took it. "Even if I have to go home, I'll come back whenever I can. I won't stay away forever. Just promise you won't go falling for some Hartland girl before we figure out how to be together."

"There's no one else for me. You're safe there." He slipped his shirt on, and jammed the hem down his waist band, eliciting a shouted objection from a group of men down by the fighting ring.

Wall faced them and held out his arms in surrender. "Consider this a forfeit. You win...for now."

"So you've had your fill of getting punched in the face?"

Wall shuffled his feet toward the path out of the trees. "I suppose."

"Then we should probably clean you up a bit before you go back."

She held on to him as they met up with his sisters and brother, and began to make their way toward the trail, stopping to let Wall clean up enough to make himself presentable.

They meandered together back to the homestead where the band struck up a fast country dance when a new face in the crowd caught her attention. She tugged on Wall's arm and motioned to where Garrett stood waiting.

He noticed them at the same time, and hurried over. Raising his head in greeting as he approached. "I've come to fetch Victoria."

"Why?" An ache started between her brows as she frowned, and dread spread to her stomach at his tone.

"It's your father. They've found him."

Before she could open her mouth to speak, Wall's father approached. "Did you say they found Abner Harrison?"

Garrett nodded. "He should be home tonight."

"Is he hurt?"

Garrett shook his head. "I don't know. All I know is they told me he's been found, and would arrive here tonight, and to come get you with all haste."

"We'll go," Wall placed his hand on the small of her back, and she leaned into his support.

"No, I'm sorry, son. You're needed here. The snows about to settle in the valley and we got to get the rest of the cattle down before then."

"But what if he's hurt? I need to go with Victoria."

Wall's father stood straighter, as if trying to gain power from height. "You're needed at home. If we don't get those cows down, they'll freeze and we'll lose half of our years pay. Your mother and sisters will have less to eat. You have a responsibility here now. No more running off whenever you want."

Wall opened his mouth to argue, but Victoria placed her hand on his arm to stop him. As much as it pained her to lose his support, now was not the time to argue their case. "I'm confident father is okay. Mother said he'd gone exploring, and gotten lost. That's all. I'll send word as soon as we make it home and I hear more. I swear."

"Fine," Wall conceded. He directed his next words to his father. "Once she writes to me, if I find that something has happened, I will go to her, but I will come back."

"As long as there's nothing pressing on the ranch." Wall's father stuck his hand in his vest pocket, and rocked back on his heels.

Victoria turned to Garrett, did you ride or bring a wagon?

"Took the train to Bonner, and then rode from there. It's faster."

She turned to Wall, and he nodded. "I'll take you back to the house to get your stuff. You can take my horse back to the mill."

"What will you ride to go get cattle?"

"One of the stock horses." He started toward the string of horses tied up near the wagon. She followed, and he lifted her behind the saddle, and then mounted.

"How did you find us out here?" she asked Garrett when he rode up to them.

"Followed the chain of wagons headed out of town. I figured something was going on, and I'd probably find you were all the people were, knowing Wall."

Wall chuckled, and shook his head, kicking his horse into a gallop to lead the way toward his homestead.

In half the time it took them to get there, they loped into the yard she'd grown to love, and she slid to the ground before Wall even had a chance to dismount.

She wanted to stay, but knowing her father was coming home boosted her spirits. She ran upstairs to Wall's room and began to pack a bag small enough to fit over the saddle horn. Was he injured? Or had he just been on his own little holiday up there while everyone scrambled to find him?

And what would he think of what she'd done with the mill? He'd be furious with her, of course. She was angry with herself for losing the land to Luther the way she did.

The deep echo of boots along the hallway drew her attention to the door as Wall entered. "Can you have my trunk shipped to the mill?"

"You're anxious to be rid of me, eh? I've made you quite mad by fighting."

"No." She let out a deep exhale. "I'm eager to see my father."

"I'm teasing, princess." In three steps he stood before her, towering over her. She laid her head on his chest, and he kissed her head. "I'm sorry I can't come. I'll be there as soon as I can convince my father to let me go."

"I understand. I wouldn't want your father to despise me any more than he already does, and I don't want your family to suffer on my behalf because I selfishly took you away when you should have been rounding up your cattle before the snow."

"As soon as I can. I'll come to you."

"Or I'll come to you." She placed both of her hands along the side of his face. "We'll make this work. Somehow."

He bent down and kissed her last words away. A kiss she felt stamp her heart like a brand. Even if she never got to come back to the man she'd fallen in love with, she had this moment to remember him. Forever.

Chapter 19

The pads of her feet began to ache as Victoria paced before the fireplace in her father's study. He'd been in bed when she'd arrived. Well and whole, but too tired from the train ride—and she suspected whatever adventure he'd gone on—to see anyone.

So she'd waited.

And drank coffee. Lots of it. She glanced at the tray holding her empty cup with and equally empty pot of coffee. At Wall's house he would have drunk most of the pot. She smiled as the memory of his breakfast habits ran through her mind. As he did every morning before heading out to work the cattle.

Knowing her father would be awhile she'd cleaned the road dust off and changed, and then visited her office to see if there was any pressing business that had happened while she was away, but her mother had taken care of everything—opting to stay in their Bonner home, rather than return to Missoula like she'd done over months past.

The orders had gone out without issue, and now their log piles were depleted and they were on their last few trees. With everything happening, she was more than eager to speak with her father about what to do next with the mill.

Once satisfied of the mills status, she'd snuck back into the house, careful not to wake him. Now here she stood. Waiting. Pacing.

She flicked her skirts out and began to walk the room again.

Her mother eased through the door as regally as she always did. "I've already warned your father several times over the past few years about pacing right there. You both are going to wear a hole straight through the carpet."

Victoria stopped and faced her. Regardless of whatever happened in the past, whatever her faults, she loved her mother. She'd always been kind and loving. A good mother and wife. And what family didn't have their secrets.

Victoria scratched the side of her forehead. *I wonder what secrets Wall's family hides?* She was certain they had some, but alas that was for another time. Today she needed to focus on her problems.

And maybe see if her father would take over the mill again. Let her move to Hartland to be with Wall.

"Your father will be down shortly. He's getting dressed. He's anxious to see you."

Her chest dropped to her stomach. Of course he was. He needed to flay into her for ruining his mill. Victoria answered with one of her social smiles, which elicited a frown from her mother who knew her almost as well as Wall now did.

As if conjured by the conversation, her father appeared in the doorway looking as he always did. Happy and rounded, a newspaper in one hand and a fresh cup of coffee in the other.

Victoria glanced at her own cold cup and frowned. Ms. Bates must have noticed her consumption and hid the remaining pot. Unlike her father, Victoria knew she looked as tired and exhausted as she felt.

"Vickie, my little girl." Her father stepped heavily toward her and kissed her forehead. "I've missed you dearly. You'll not believe what I saw over in Washington."

"I'm assuming trees since you disappeared into a forest and gave us all a fright."

Her father laughed so hard his belly shook, and he then sat in his favorite Bonner home chair. "Yes, yes, but the biggest trees you'll ever see. It would take maybe six or eight men touching fingers to go around one."

"And you left me to lose the mill to Luther so you could discover a tree?" Her fingers began to shake, and she forced herself to control her tone as she spoke. "You made me have to struggle to keep the mill alive while you discovered a forest?"

"I didn't know you were going through all this until Paul found me out by the coastline." He waved toward where the mill office building stood outside their mill-yard home.

"You would have if you'd have checked in more than once when you got to Seattle. Told someone where you were going."

"I planned to, but your mother would have stopped me." Her father slid a nervous glance to her mother, who stood in the corner crying. "I left a note."

"I don't think she received it until after Paul got there." Victoria's hand shook now, and she didn't try to hide her tone. "You could have been killed and no one would have discovered your remains for centuries. The land over there is still wild like most of Montana."

Dawn Luedecke

"Now see here, young lady, you can't speak to your old man in such a tone." He waggled the newspaper at her.

Victoria began to pace again. "I can when he's acting like a young fool, and no one else will take him to task. You left us all helpless. We lost the mill land to Luther. Have you heard?"

"Yes. I have."

She stopped walking. "And what do you have to say about that?"

Her father raised his chin. "I say it was an inevitable occurrence."

"So you knew Sanchez planned to take half the mill and you left me? Helpless."

"I left you with Paul. How was I supposed to know he would leave you to come looking for me?" Her father slammed his newspaper down on his knee. "Or that Sanchez was back in town. Last I'd heard he'd slunk out of here like the snake he is."

"And Luther? What do you have to say about him? You deprived me of a brother for my entire life, and then hid his existence from me. Now he hates us."

"His lot in life is unfortunate, but not uncaring. He was raised in a loving household. His attitude toward us is not because of deprivation of money or family, but because of who he is as a person. His father's bitterness. He was given every opportunity to advance when he came to me for a job. He was offered a position in the mill, but chose the camp. I suspect he and his father had this plan all along, and I don't think I could have even won the legal battle. You did just fine, daughter."

Victoria crossed her arms over her chest. Her guilt eased ever so slightly. "I still haven't forgiven you for leaving me helpless."

"I don't expect you to."

Victoria stood tapping her finger against her biceps as she watched her father for a second. "Fine. Now here's what's happened since Luther took the land." She walked to the side table near the coffee where she'd placed the list of farmers who wanted land cleared, the one Willa had given her. "I've secured a list of farmers over in Hartland who need their places cleared. I've rented one lot from a widow who needs the money, but the rest of the farmers simply need the trees gone."

"Douglas fir," her father said, his voice tinged with pride.

"Yes. When Garrett brought me home, he said he could get the rails built out there by spring. I plan to send a winter crew out to cut the logs and line them up to be transported as soon as the rail line is working. We will have the fir to the mill by the springtime without needing to depend on a spring runoff."

"Good, good. How long is this going to last us? One season? What do we have beyond that?"

"I haven't figured things out that far yet, but there is prime land farther up the valley. Untouched and wild."

"But?"

"It all belongs to Hamilton Adair."

"And he is giving you problems? Do you need me to go talk to him? Convince him with a little intimidation?"

Victoria shook off her father's offer. "No. We have some time to figure things out. In fact, I thought I might talk to Mr. Boilson. I know he has some dealings up there. He might be able to help convince Mr. Adair that wood is just as important as cattle."

"We can go over there right now." Her father drank his now-cold coffee in one gulp, and stood. "You did it, my girl. Gone and got the wood for the railroad at least. The mine will back our play and we'll be set up in Hartland with the railroad logging. What a revolutionary you've become for us."

"I didn't do it. Wall Adair did."

"Ah, yes. Your mother told me you were set to be wed to the boy."

"Which is not true."

With those words, her father frowned. "And why not?"

"Because it can't work between us. He is a cowboy who is needed on the ranch in Hartland, and I am a business woman who is running a mill from Bonner."

"A dilemma for certain," her father said with a frown as he ushered her out the door and toward the stalls.

"I'll help saddle the horses," she offered, and started to slide the halter over the nose of Wall's horse.

She led the gelding out of the stall as her father brought her a saddle and blanket, and heaved it onto the horse's back. To her disappointment, she got to ride side saddle as she'd dressed in her regular wear instead of a split skirt.

Had she been on the ranch, things would have been different even with something as simple as which saddle to use. Thanks to Wall's sister's influence.

After a few minutes, she tugged tight on the cinch, and mounted as her father did the same with his horse. An hour, and one mountainous ride later, they rode into the Boilson Mine property.

She dismounted following her father, and tied her horse on the hitching post as Mr. Boilson himself came out to greet them.

"Abner," he called with a smile. He nodded toward her. "Miss Victoria."

"Mr. Boilson." She took the steps as he turned and motioned toward his office.

"What brings you to the mine?"

"I've come to inquire about your dealings in Hartland."

"Heard about that, did ya?" Mr. Boilson looked more pleased than ashamed as she thought he would if conspiring against her and Great Mountain as she'd believed. "Could go either way, but one things for certain, we're going to need more timber. Triple what we already got since we'll be starting from scratch with a new building and all."

Victoria shook her head. "I'm sorry...wha—"

"I'm not as in the loop as my daughter," her father interrupted. "Could you fill me in on your plans in Hartland?"

Mr. Boilson waved toward her father. "Of course, of course. I heard you'd gone on vacation. We signed a partnership with Hamilton Adair to mine up there. Seems he found some color on his land, and has his hands too full to bother with it by himself. We'll be doing it right. Building a whole new mine up there, way up in the mountains, building and all. So we'll need all the wood we can get."

Victoria's heart started to beat so fast she could hear the blood rushing past her ears. At least this part of her business dealings hadn't gone against her, but now she needed more wood. How was she going to provide the harvest? She clutched her necklace and stared at the table as her mind worked through possibilities. How would her grandmother have handled such a situation?

"Unfortunately, we lost the land in a family dispute so we're starting over. We can keep you supplied for this mine, but I'm afraid we can't triple the contract at present." Victoria glanced back up at Mr. Boilson, whose face dropped.

He shook his head. "Shame. That Luther fella came in here only yesterday, offering me logs, but I turned him down. Said I had a good thing going with you and didn't plan on changing my supplier, but if you can't produce the wood—"

"What if you came with us to talk to Mr. Adair?" The words flowed out of her mouth before she even had a chance to think about them.

Both men watched her with matching questioning stares.

"Mr. Adair has so many trees right there they are certain to become a fire hazard within the next few years. What if you came with us to pitch the business plan? The trees needed to run your operation can be provided from the same land you're working on. Mr. Adair takes pride in the Lazy Heart. Perhaps using the wood from his ranch to build his mine will sway him our way."

Both her father and Mr. Boilson milled through her suggestion long enough to give her butterflies. She thought the plan a good one. Hopefully others would as well.

* * * *

Wall sat on his bed and tossed his boots across the room, not caring if they made a thump loud enough to bring his entire family in to yell at him for the noise. He'd spent the last two weeks gathering cows without so much as a word from Victoria.

Was her father okay? Did she even make it back to the mill? He assumed she had or else Garrett would have sent word otherwise. Which only meant she'd moved on from him, or become consumed with her work.

"Pa wants you downstairs," Jax said as he stepped into Wall's room.

"What for? I just came in from the range and I'd like to clean up and maybe get a little shuteye." Plus, the only thing keeping him sane these days was the smell of Victoria on his pillow, and the scent had already started to fade.

He hadn't told her then, but many times during the night he'd stood outside the bunkhouse where he'd stayed with the cowhands, and watched the window to his room, hoping to catch even the slightest glimpse of her as she went about her routines. Like some thief in the night. He'd followed his mother's wishes to stay well away from her while she visited—except for the day at the swimming hole, but that was a time he'd never forget and never regret—but his promise to his mother had costed him many sleepless nights since they'd come to the ranch.

And he hadn't slept a wink since.

He was tired, cantankerous, and not at all inclined to cater to whatever demands his father had now.

Jax pivoted toward the door. "You'll see once you're downstairs, but I think you want to come quick."

Wall frowned and stood. In three steps, he plucked his boots from the floor where they fell, yanked them on, and then turned to follow.

He entered his father's office to a sight to steal the air from any man's lungs. Victoria stood near the window with his father, both of her parents, and Mr. Boilson.

His first instinct was to rush over to her and sweep her up. Carry her away to be alone, but he fought the urge. The flash in her eye showed she had similar thoughts.

"Ah, there you are," his father said, and motioned for him to join them. "Mr. Boilson and the Harrison's have come to talk business."

"Business?" He tilted his head toward Victoria.

She nodded. "I also brought your horse back."

"We have discovered a dilemma in our mining partnership," Mr. Boilson addressed his father, "and I'm hoping we can come to a logical conclusion."

"Oh?" His father frowned deep. A frown that always preceded hard business deals. "And what sort of problems have you discovered? If I'm not mistaken, we already have a signed business agreement."

Mr. Boilson nodded several times. "We do, we do. Problem is, we need lumber to support our mine, and Mr. Harrison here is my supplier, and a damn good one. I'd like to keep him on, but he's in need of more land to harvest."

"We just gave him land a few weeks ago."

"Unfortunately," Victoria's father interjected, "that will only cover our contracts for the railroad, and the lumber orders Mr. Boilson currently has contracted with us."

"We're going to need triple the supply he has now," Boilson said.

Wall caught Victoria's stare, and a smile fluttered at the corners of her mouth. His heart sped up when he realized she'd concocted the plan. Only how would this bring them together?

"We figure there's no better wood to be used for a Lazy Heart mine than from trees harvested from the land itself. Sort of like putting it back where it belongs," Victoria said, and motioned toward the back of the house, and mountain beyond.

His father's face didn't change from his business scowl, and Wall's senses centered on every flinch he might give. Trying to gauge his reaction. After a moment his father shook his head a fraction of an inch, but one side of his mouth twitched. Wall wasn't certain if he held back a snarl or a smile.

"Well played, young lady," his father said.

Victoria perked one single eye brow up. "Thank you, sir."

Wall smiled.

"What's your plan for getting the trees from ground to mine?"

Wall moved to stand beside her. Whether to be near her once more, or to give her support with his father, he didn't know, but he felt the need to radiate toward her.

As if she took strength in his movement, she squared her stance toward his father. "Garrett's rail line will be set up here by spring. We'll take the logs to the mill, prepare the boards, and ship them back. Wagons, chutes, and flumes, will take the loads between the ranches and the train."

His father shook his head. "I'm afraid I want to get the mine started before next year. We can find another supplier."

"What if we set up a mill right here in one of the fields?" Wall spit out before he'd thought through the idea.

"I'm listening." His father quirked his head toward him.

Wall took a step back, shocked at his father's reply. "A portable mill. I've heard of them being used out Wisconsin way. Luther is even said to be using one. I can get one designed and set up before the logging team even gets to Hartland."

"How would a portable mill work exactly, son?" His father's face fell back into his business scowl.

"We'll bring the logs down to the portable mill with a flume, cut the boards here, and then send the freshly cut boards up to the mine. It won't be able to handle all of the logging work, but for the Lazy Heart Boilson Mine job, it would work."

"Is that something your company could do?" His father turned the question to Abner.

"Yes, sir. I've heard of the portable mills. Never had one myself. Didn't need to, but it could work."

"And what would it cost me? You taking my wood and selling it right back to me?"

"We could cut the bill in half seeing as the logs aren't coming to the mill, but I gotta pay my workers."

"Of course." Wall's father turned as his mother bustled into the room with a tray of refreshments.

She set them on the side table, and then turned toward Victoria's mother. "Mrs. Harrison, I'm terribly sorry I've kept you so long in this room, talking business without another woman."

Victoria's mother waved off her concern. "Oh, it's fine. I'm used to waiting for Abner to finish with his business before getting to the more pleasant conversational topics."

His mother searched everyone in the room. "Are we finished? Can we have some cocoa, and sit like polite people normally would?"

Taken to task, his father extended his hand to Abner. "We have a deal. My son will start work on the portable mill as soon as all the cattle are done, and you can send your men up to start work whenever you're ready. I'll let Wall figure out the best section to start you on."

"Actually, I will be taking over the local operation," Victoria declared, and raised her chin. "Father can run the mill again. Or Paul."

"I'd be more than happy to come back to work, my dear. A vacation was all the time off I needed," her father said.

"And me." Her mother frowned at her father, and then addressed her. "But are you certain this is what you want?"

Victoria took a single step forward. "Absolutely. I want to be here. In Hartland with Wall."

Wall's heart beat faster as she stepped closer to him and entwined her arm in his.

"An unwed woman cannot stay up here alone to run a portable mill," her mother chided, and pierced him with a glare.

"She won't be." Wall grabbed her hand and kissed it. "We'll be wed as soon as you fetch the preacher if I have my way."

"You most certainly will not." Her mother insinuated herself between he and Victoria, forcing him to drop her hand.

"Mother," Victoria said. "We hardly have time for a wedding. We both have businesses to run."

"There's always time for a wedding."

"Did I heard there's going to be a wedding?" Layla's voice sounded, and Wall looked as his sister walked in with a tray of Rose's pastries.

Before anyone could say anything, she set the dessert down on the table, and the sound of her boots echoed down the hallway, no doubt going to tell his other sisters.

"Heaven above." He peeked around Victoria's mother to his intended bride. "Prepare yourself."

Her face rounded in fright, and she grasped her necklace. "Mother, please?"

"It can be soon, but you will have a wedding."

"I think this is my cue to leave," Mr. Boilson said and, with a quick goodbye to his father and Mr. Harrison, ran out of the room as if the fireplace had spit flames onto the curtains.

Before long, all four of his sisters rushed into the room and assailed upon Victoria as though she were a newborn puppy they'd been pining to see. From over their heads, she tossed him a pleading glance and all he could do was shrug. In his experience with his sisters, when they got in a mob with high pitched squeals to pierce a man's ears the way they did now, it was best a man step away.

"You're a wretched man, Wall Adair!" Victoria tossed over their heads, as they ushered her out of the room and, from the sounds of their footsteps, up to the rooms above. No doubt to begin plans of their own.

Left behind, her mother turned her attention to him. "Wallace, I expect you will take care of her."

"Yes, ma'am."

"You know my expectations."

"Yes, ma'am. She will come before anything else in my life. I promise."

"It seems she will have plenty to occupy her out here on the Lazy Heart," Beatrice said, and cast her eye to where the chatter picked up volume ever so slightly.

"My sisters adore her."

"So do I," his mother said from her position near the couches. She motioned for Victoria's mother to join her, and she obeyed. "If you'd like, we can start planning the more sensible aspects of the wedding while the girls titter about whatever frivolous things young women tend to focus on."

"Sensible." Beatrice raised her eyebrow with a smile, and joined his mother, leaving him alone once more.

To his right, his father stood with Abner, and through the few words he caught the gentle mumble of a small political debate. Nothing to interest him. Taking his only chance, he slipped from the room and out the front door.

Relief spread through his chest and eased the knot tied since she'd left. He stepped from the front porch and searched the windows where the chatter filtered through the pane, but he couldn't see the girls, so he headed to the barn to wait until Victoria was once again available.

Plus, he needed to talk to his brother, and he knew just wear to find him.

He walked into the barn and found him mucking stalls. "Victoria and I are going to be married."

"I heard."

"Are you upset with me?"

Jax stopped and faced him, leaning on the pitchfork. "Are you going to leave again? I was under the impression it was either us or her."

"Not this time." Wall ruffled his hair. "Victoria's staying here on the Lazy Heart. I might build her a house, but I'll be here."

He squinted one eye. "Promise?"

"Yep."

With a single nod, Jax went back to work, so Wall picked up the second pitchfork, and opened the next stall. The tension he'd felt for weeks, hell years, no longer balled in his chest. He felt lighter. Happier. He could lie down and roll in the horse shit, and be happier than if he'd been given a new pair of boots.

And Victoria was the reason. His soon-to-be wife.

Chapter 20

Victoria stood motionless in her wedding dress, afraid to move as Wall's sisters hovered around her. Somewhere in the house Beth and Carrie kept warm near the fire, very pregnant and waiting to brave the outside until the very last minute. The last thing she wanted was for her nuptials to force them into labor early.

Wall's portable mill was well on its way to being complete, and her crew had already started to build the flume nearby to start work. Farther down the valley, a second crew started the work on the townsfolk's ranches as Garrett's rail line drew ever closer to the town, and with it, expansion.

Now, she stood hoping to keep from perspiring before heading outside into the cold November day to be married to the man who'd stolen her heart.

For once in her life, things worked out in her favor. As they should be. With one man she'd gotten the love she'd always wanted, and a family so full of love they couldn't seem to leave her alone. But she adored every minute of it.

"I know this isn't the time for this, but I thought you might like the distraction. Next Tuesday is our meeting, and the Widow Yancy is lookout," Georgiana said matter of factly. "You need to start your needlepoint."

Victoria responded by reaching out to grab the younger girl's hand and hold it. Georgiana squeezed hers in response.

"Ready?" her mother asked, walking into the room.

With shoulders back to help hold the heavy, but warm, material of her overly adorned wedding gown, she nodded.

Her dress wasn't what it would have been a year ago. It didn't define the latest wedding fashion in Missoula. She'd fought like the verbal pugilist Wall had once called her in order to not have to wear a veil. Mostly because she was going to be outside. What if the wedding ended up being in a snowstorm?

What woman wants to get lost in a snowstorm on their way from the house to the aisle simply because she has a white cloak over her face?

Her mother had objected, but after much discussion, and some compromise, they came to an agreement. Victoria would wear the more delicate long-sleeved satin dress with puffy shoulders and a train, which was certain to get ruined in the snow, but she would forgo the veil. At least the inside of the dress was insulated with lace and cotton to keep her warm.

And a beautiful velvet cape she insisted on would lie upon her shoulders.

She wrapped the cape around her and buttoned it at the neck, and then started down the stairs. Each woman in her life, from Wall's mother and sisters, to her mother, and finally Beth and Carrie, all flanked her. As if engulfing her in a cloak of protection as they escorted her outside to the man she loved. The only women in her life who'd ever seen beyond her outward appearance to the woman she was inside.

And Wall had been there all along to show her who she was.

"You look beautiful," Beth said as she waddled next to Carrie, who voiced her agreement.

Victoria smiled her thanks as butterflies flitted in her stomach. The cold winter air hit her face, and she couldn't be more grateful for a winter wedding.

Once in line, her father took a spot next to her and the women all disappeared to their seats as the musician's who'd played at the Hartland shindig began to play their infamous waltz.

She didn't think she could be any happier until she saw him at the end of the row of people. Waiting. For her. She urged her father to go with her arm, and felt his chest rumble with a chuckle.

In less time than it would take her to ride into Missoula from the mill, she would be Mrs. Wallace Adair. The wife of a filthy cowboy turned river logger, and she couldn't be happier.

They reached the end of the walk, and Wall took her arm. She leaned into him for both the warmth, and because the feel of him there during times of need now felt natural. She needed him like the earth needed the trees.

"You're more beautiful than the mountain peaks on an early spring morning."

"And you're more charming than a smooth-talking grizzly bear," she teased. "But the mountain peaks are beautiful on a spring morning."

"That's all I'm saying." He tweaked the curl which, she'd noticed, had become his favorite plaything. "You're prettier."

They turned their attention to Wall's father, who of course was the town justice of the peace. By the time she could steady herself, their vows had been exchanged and Wall bent her back to give her a kiss to seal them together forever.

As he brought her up, the crowd erupted, and the chill of the winter day began to seep into her dress. She pulled the hood of the cape over her hair, and smiled up at her new husband as the crowd began to mumble and mill about.

"Let's get to the barn for the party before we all freeze out here." Wall extended his arm, and she leaned heavily on it to help her pick her way across the frozen ground toward the large barn.

"I never thought I'd have my wedding in the snow, or a barn."

Wall threw back his head and laughed. "I doubt you'd ever thought you'd even set foot in a barn, let alone marry a cowboy."

"Cowboy logger," she corrected. "Don't forget, you're still one of my best fallers. I fully expect you to come help whenever you aren't busy with the Lazy Heart."

"Yes, ma'am," Wall answered with the biggest smile she'd ever seen him sport, with the exception of mere moments ago when they'd married.

"You're an odd man, Wallace Adair. You like to tinker with machines, chop town trees, and lasso cattle. I've never met such a determined man before."

"And you're an odd woman, Victoria Harrison-Adair." They entered the barn, now clean and decorated, to see their friends gathered around in various groups. "I think that's why we suit each other so well, but don't forget about fighting."

"What?" She snapped her gaze to his face where a now crooked grin played on his lips.

He waved toward the group of men she'd seen at the shindig, gathered with heads together in the corner of the barn. "I'm also a pugilist, remember, and this is a Hartland party."

"Don't you dare," she warned.

He chuckled.

"Don't fret, princess. I'm not going to. Not today. Although, I can't promise I won't fight again in the future. I'm a man after all. It's what we do." He rubbed his chin. "I wonder how the Devil May Cares would fare against the Hartland boys."

The band began to warm up their instruments. No doubt both frozen from their time outside. The plan, like any Hartland party, was dancing and food with no frills in between. Exactly as she'd always wanted her reception.

"Fine, but no more toying with your opponent." She walked into the center of the barn, and stopped as the band began to play her new favorite waltz. "Fast and hard."

Wall tipped his head low, and his eyes darkened from the color of the sky to the deepest part of a lake. "Princess, I do everything fast and hard unless you ask me otherwise."

Her heart beat to mimic the topic—fast and hard—as Wall pulled their hands between them while they danced, and ran the back of his finger over her breast. She struggled for breath at the thought of what would come later. "You, sir, are a wicked tease."

"If we were alone I would tease you up in the hay loft."

She quickly searched their surroundings to make certain none of the other dancers had overheard, but they were certain to notice her blush because her face heated something fierce.

Wall tugged her closer. "I'll stop, but we leave as soon as we can escape."

"Which will be quite difficult seeing as we are the focus of everyone here." A dancing couple from town drew near, and she gave her social smile, and greeted them.

Farther down the dance floor, Beth and Carrie danced with their new husbands, and a few of The Devil May Cares had even found partners with Hartland women—two of which were Wall's sisters. Not that he needed to see that just yet.

The song ended and they moved to the side of the room as the door to the warm barn opened up and Nichols stepped in. Strutting like a king toward Wall's father.

Victoria didn't know whether to be angry with the man, or welcome him to the party, but her social teachings told her the second.

Before she had a chance to choose, Hamilton brought him over. "Nichols, you remember my son, and this radiant thing is my new daughter-in-law, Mrs. Victoria Harrison-Adair."

"Ah, yes. We met back in the spring." He tipped his hat in greeting. "You're even lovelier now as you were back then."

"And you've gone and taken all my land, and the land Wall tried to purchase," she replied, unable to hold her tongue.

"But I see you came out on top. Like I knew you would." Nichols glanced at Wall, and then to the corner where she'd seen her father standing mere seconds ago. "You Harrison's always do."

"Yes, we do."

"I hope you don't take too much offense to being moved away from Seeley Lake and the rivers. See we had to protect the new species of fish we're introducing into the waters over there. Can't have the river logging operation killing off the money we're putting into the project."

Victoria crossed her arms over her chest as her heart began to beat at the man's flawed response. "You almost ruined Great Mountain over fish, yet you allowed Missoula to give Luther the land to log for the government?"

"He's small time. He'll be logging to provide for the local schools, and milling on site. He's not taking wood down the rivers. Your operation is the biggest in the area. Certain destruction to the brown trout we introduced. Had to steer you away from the rivers."

"So you don't mind giving us permits as long as they aren't by rivers?"

Nichols shook his head. "Not at all."

Wall ducked his head low as though to tell her a secret, but his voice rang loud enough for even the representative to hear. "Well, there goes my job and that of The Devil May Cares."

"And Wallace." Nichols focused on him. "Quite the determined businessman. You're going to make the Lazy Heart even greater than your father did. I heard you're into leather and machinery, in addition to taking over the Lazy Heart."

"Yes, sir," Wall said, but stiffened beneath her fingers as the governor addressed him. He didn't like the politician much, that much Victoria could tell.

"Victoria here is going to clear some pasture land up in the mountain and provide us with our very own wood for our mine." Hamilton puffed out his chest as he boasted.

"Yes, I heard you're partnering with Boilson." Nichols cocked his head to the side. "I also hear the railroad will be moving into Hartland. Can't wait to see this town booming under your leadership, Hamilton. I only hope you'll run for mayor once the town becomes official, and Laughlin steps down from whatever role it is you've put him in up here." The governor chuckled at his joke and took a quick look around the room. "I've come with news. Is there any way I can make an announcement?"

"Of course." Wall motioned toward the area where the band played, and Nichols started that way with his father, leaving them alone once more.

"I wonder what sort of announcement he has that's so important as to interrupt our wedding," she said.

"I suppose we're about to find out."

Wall's father drew the attention of the room and introduced the governor, who took over. "Sorry to interrupt this beautiful party. It looks as though the couple is happier than ever to have such wonderful people to celebrate with them today. Montanans, for as soon as I arrived in Missoula on the way here for the wedding I received word from Helena. As of yesterday, Montana has become a state!"

The room erupted in applause, and a low rumble of approval from all within the building. Even Victoria was proud to hear the territory of Montana would now officially be a state.

Nichols walked off the make-shift platform and into the crowd, meandering toward her father.

Next to her, the Devil May Cares approached Wall and they started talking, but her focus was on her father and his expression. The way he moved his hands, the flash of his eyes. What were they discussing?

Time ticked by with more people coming up to greet them when finally her father left the governor's side and approached her. "Seems now it's all official, the state is in need of some wood for schools and such. He's offered us a few sections up north of here. Government owned, of course, but it's work. We'll start there once we're done with Hartland."

"Are you willing to work for him?"

Her father shrugged. "I'm keeping my options open. I may end up moving over Washington way after Hartland. I can't stop thinking about those trees. Do you know what we could do with wood that big? I'd end up selling Great Mountain, of course. And you'd have to stay here with your husband. Hope you don't mind."

"Luther is determined to get complete control over the entire mill. I've no doubt he'd buy you out. Not that I want to see it go to a sniveling little wretch such as him." Victoria snuggled closer to Wall. "But whatever you choose to do with your company is fine with me, father. As long as I'm with Wall on the Lazy Heart."

"It's not certain, I might decide to stay. You'll come visit if we move to Washington?"

Victoria smiled and kissed her father on the cheek. "Only if you don't take me on a forest adventure."

Her father chuckled. "Deal."

Wall shuffled his feet beside her. "If you don't mind, sir. It's getting late, and we have a little ride up to where we're spending the night."

"We do?" She narrowed her eyes as she peered up at him. Where on earth would they be staying where they needed to ride? The mill?

"Yes, princess, we do."

"Right, you are, my boy. Best get going before dusk starts to settle in."

They made their way through the crowd, saying their thanks and goodbyes. Stopping long enough where Wall's siblings stood so she could hug each one of her new sisters, and Jax.

By the time they made it out of the barn, the sun sank deep in the afternoon sky. Wall lifted her onto the back of his horse.

"Where are we going?"

"I thought you might like to see your new portable mill."

"You must be joking."

He swung up in front of her. "Not at all."

"It is way too late to be riding up the mountain for a look at a make-shift sawmill."

"Nah. We'll hurry. Hold on tight." He kicked his horse to trudge through the ankle-deep snow, and headed up the mountain.

She wanted to argue, to insist he return home, but she would trust him. And she was a little curious. Instead, she tugged her cape up to stop the cold winter air from making her shiver.

They rode for half an hour until he crested a small hill and stopped and turned the horse. "Look, princess. That's for you."

Victoria glanced where he'd indicated. There in a small clearing stood a cabin similar to Mother Goose's Cottage. A ribbon of smoke already filtered from the chimney.

"It's not the one from the old lumber camp, but it has a feather bed, and a warm stove. We can live at the ranch, and stay here whenever we wish. The mill is over the ridge there." He pointed to a hill on the other side of where they stood.

"You made this for me?"

"Yes, ma'am."

"When?"

"I built it each night after I was done with the mill. The Devil May Cares came out and got the fire started for us." He chuckled. "Now they are probably out by the mill somewhere taking on the Hartland boys in fisticuffs."

She hugged him closer in response.

He placed his hand over hers, warming her cold fingers. "Do you think you'll be happy enough out here? It's not the city like you're used to. We don't have much, but what we will have is each other."

"I think I was meant to be wherever you are. I already feel as though I belong."

He kicked the horse toward their new mountain cabin. She held tight as they rode, and quite honestly didn't want to let go. He was warm and strong. The man who would stand beside or behind her in whatever situation she was in. The man who loved her as much as she did him. The man she would give up anything for.

She was home.

If you enjoyed *Fiery Passion*, be sure not to miss all of the books in Dawn Luedecke's Montana Mountain Romance series, including

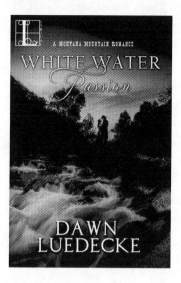

The Montana Territory is one of the last outposts of the American West—where adventure as grand as the wide-open plains is around every corner, and passion as wild as the land itself beats in every heart…

Elizabeth Sanders isn't afraid of anything, except what will happen to her beloved town if the Big Mountain Lumber Mill is destroyed. When she overhears a plot to do just that, she vows to put a stop to it, even if it means dressing as a young lumberjack to expose the saboteur. There's only one problem with her plan—her brother's handsome friend and fellow logger Garrett Jones, who arouses a desire within her soul as fierce as the river rapids.

When Garrett discovers that the odd new lad on the crew is in fact Beth, he's shocked. A logging camp is no place for a young woman—especially the spirited beauty he's admired for so long. Keeping her safe is easier said than done, however, as the attraction between them flares into true passion. As the danger mounts, Beth and Garrett must work together to survive the last log run down the wild rapids and claim any chance of saving the mill—and their chance at a future…

"**Well written, well researched. Like the river, this plot runs faster and faster. Readers won't be able to put it down.**"
—*New York Times* **bestselling author Jodi Thomas**

A Lyrical e-book on sale now.

Read on for a special excerpt!

Chapter 1

Missoula Montana, 1888

Elizabeth Sanders could vanish right now, and no one would notice. She blended in with every other woman by wearing her matching pinstriped walking skirt and blouse. Each store clerk and patron in Missoula, focused on their affairs without a care to their neighbor, would fail to notice if she walked through Higgins Street naked, let alone disappeared into thin air. They certainly wouldn't look twice when she came back this way a different person.

Hundreds of people bustled in the heat of the Montana sun doing the same old things, the same old ways, with nothing to show for their trouble but dirty shoes. If Elizabeth was going to get her shoes dirty, she preferred to have fun doing it…the Devil May Care way.

Navigating the pedestrian-riddled streets was treacherous at best. Times like this made her wish she'd taken her grandmother's buggy. At least then she wouldn't be jostled around like a dirty shirt in a churning wash bin. A deep exhale boosted her determination enough to risk a step to the side to duck around a particularly slow matriarch. The small triumph lasted only a moment before she slammed into a hard chest.

The soft fabric of a well-tailored suit skimmed her cheek a split second before warm hands reached out to steady her. The touch—firm, yet gentle—made her feel like she now balanced on the back of a high-strung and wild mustang as it fled down a hill with uncontrolled freedom. She hadn't needed the extra hand. Wasn't in danger of falling over. What sort of dullard rescues a woman in no need of liberation? She pulled away and adjusted her skirts as he let go. Her mind focused once more.

"Pardon me." She glanced up to a familiar face. One she'd seen many times in her dreams. Her breath failed as her brother's friend, Garrett Jones, peered down at her with silver-clouded eyes. Oh, how he made the world spin whenever he drew near. His handsome, yet rugged, face made her fingers ache to touch the severe lines of his jaw. The rich scent of tobacco infused with lavender and some sort of citrus drifted on the breeze. Eau de Cologne. A fragrance only the wealthiest of men in Montana could afford. A scent belying the canvas pants, spiked boots, and sturdy cotton shirt he sported every time she'd seen him on the train platform.

"Elizabeth." Did he say her name, or did she dream the word? Oh to be noticed by a man like Garrett Jones. The only man who could make butterflies flit around in her stomach and fear slide through her chest in the same confusing moment.

The hem of her dress hovered mere inches from his feet. Her face heated and heart began to pound. Try as she might, she couldn't keep her eyes off the man who led the Devil May Care boys. The man who held her future in his hands if she succeeded in becoming part of his crew at the logging camp. If things went the way she planned, she'd be staring into his amber and steel speckled eyes for the rest of the season. Did he truly recognize her after all these years of no more than a passing glance?

"Terribly sorry, sir." She shifted her bag to the other hand. "I didn't see you."

He shook his head, but remained silent. The gray in his eyes shone in a color she couldn't quite name, but it softened his jagged expression enough to make her blush once more. A slight movement in his right hand caught her attention as he tapped his leg with his index finger and shuffled his feet, but his chest remained still. After a brief, uncomfortable silence with Garrett offering no more than a fleeting glance, she chewed on her lower lip.

"I suppose I should get going." She took a half step around him, and stopped.

He nodded and gave a bow with an air so refined she paused in surprise. Throughout her years in Montana, she'd grown used to the hard and less-than-mannered ruffians who usually passed her on the street. Even those on the social circuit rarely bowed in such a stiff and crisp manner. He'd certainly never shown such niceties where she was concerned. With one last look at his emotionless face, she nodded and stepped around his broad frame. She locked eyes with him, and felt his gaze follow her while she walked by. Beth forced herself to keep a steady breath as she left.

She hugged her satchel and skirted the shadows until she rounded the corner of a residential street, and all but ran the remaining distance to her friend Carrie's house. She rapped on the large pine door, and took a quick step back as it swung wide open. Finally, she was here. Now she had to force herself to follow the plan.

"It took you long enough, Beth." Carrie grabbed her arm and yanked her into the foyer.

As the huge front door closed behind her, Carrie shoved her forward, causing her to trip quite improperly into the adjoining parlor. Swinging around, Beth flinched as Carrie peeked down the hallway and slammed the parlor door. Carrie pivoted, and shifted her weight onto one leg. "Well?"

"Well, what?" Beth dropped her satchel next to the cold fireplace, trying not to smile at her friend's trepidation, letting the emotion bring her focus back to the issue at hand. She faced Carrie as if nothing out of the ordinary were about to happen.

"Well, what did he say?"

"He?" The image of Garrett on the street took over her thoughts. His strong shoulders, the stiff way he'd bowed, and the whisper of her name on his lips. There was no way Carrie could have seen the awkward exchange, was there? Beth peeked out of the large bay windows across the room, but as she already knew, the view to where she'd bumped into Garrett was blocked by several houses and streets.

Carrie rolled her eyes. "You darned well know who I'm talking about. Your brother."

"Yes, of course." Gracious be, where was her head? Stuck back on Higgins Street and Garrett's disarming gaze. "Simon said yes." Beth raised her chin, and silently dared her friend to argue. She couldn't be swayed. "Tomorrow, I will become a logger."

Carrie dropped her shoulders in defeat, but she folded her arms and glared in a blatant show of disapproval. "Please tell me you are going to help with the cooking, or at least cut the trees like your brother."

"Nope." Beth felt the lack of air plaguing her lungs. Carrie was like a sister, and perhaps a voice of reason, so it was hugely important to get her approval for this adventure—a blessing of sorts.

Carrie frowned and the disapproving look in her eyes deepened. "Don't tell me—"

"Yep, a riverman." Her heart shouldn't run away at such a statement, but it did. To be a riverman and experience the sheer sensation of total control over Mother Nature would be the boon she needed. And in her plight, she'd save not only her brother's job, but an entire town from certain destruction by a saboteur. If she could control those logs down the river, she could easily squash a snake in the grass…or rather trees. It didn't hurt that Garrett would be there. With him at the helm—the man her brother had talked about so often over the last few years—she knew she could accomplish anything.

"Didn't you see the journal last month? They did an exposé on the Missoula rivermen. They said they're ruffians...vagabonds. The men who ride the river have a devil-may-care attitude toward life, and the social skills of a spring hog."

"My brother hasn't said such things, and I'm inclined to believe him over some two-bit reporter. I am going to be a Devil May Care boy."

"I honestly don't know why you want to do this. It is pure madness, not to mention dangerous. I can't believe Simon agreed to your foolish scheme."

"Simon's word isn't law. Please don't tell me you still have that silly schoolgirl crush on my brother."

Carrie's cheeks dusted in a pink hue. "No, but he's a voice of reason."

Beth pursed her lips to stop all the dirty secrets on how she tricked her brother from spilling out like a waterfall. The secret buggy rides where he insisted he needed to go alone to clear his mind. The midnight voices in the garden beneath her bedroom window. All of which allowed Beth this small handful of leverage over her beloved brother. "I don't want to risk making him a target for the saboteur, or losing his job if I end up being wrong. I know it's dangerous, but I have to do this. You don't know how important it is I go."

"I figured you'd say that, and when you get an idea in your head, not even a blizzard in July can stop you. Just promise you'll be careful. Perhaps you should take along someone else to help you, or let me write my godmother. She is a cook somewhere up there. You can see if there are any other positions at camp, one more suitable for a woman. You cannot traipse around like a wild woman in the mountains. It isn't proper." Carrie mimicked the look of a concerned mother.

Beth shook her head and waved off her friend's trepidation. "I want to be a riverman, not a cook. I need to have complete access to the camp, including the dangerous areas. From what Simon has told me in the past, cooks aren't always allowed up there. I can't get close enough to the action while working as a cook. I'll be fine, trust me. Simon wasn't happy about letting me tag along, but after I convinced him—quite forcefully, might I add—he had no choice." She plopped down on a chair. "He or one of his friends will watch me every second of the day. As per his direction, I'm to try to stay away from trouble."

"Everything you've ever dreamed of, a man to watch over you every second of the day." Carrie's mouth twitched in an unsuccessful attempt to hold back her 'you got what you deserved' grin.

Beth wrinkled her nose and sat back in her chair. She wasn't fool enough to think this summer would be easy, but Carrie was right. She didn't want someone watching her every move, especially when she was investigating. There were ways to get around a guard. "A little imagination could serve me well I should think."

"Are you really going down the river?"

"If I can manage it, I will. The log drive is the target, and that's where I need to be."

"You do realize the men who do that particular job are considered wild and touched in the head. Most aren't allowed in polite society."

"I can't go into the upcoming season without helping to secure a future for my brother. I'm to be presented to every eligible bachelor this year." She took a deep breath, and shook her head. "We've always been close, and I don't want to see him suffer while I go off to a life of marital bliss. He needs this job, and I need to know he's happy."

"Why would Simon need you to help? He's done fine at the lumber camp without you so far." Carrie rolled her eyes. "Really, Beth. You must think these things through."

"I have." Beth dropped her shoulders and wiggled to the edge of the seat. "There was a man. On the platform a week ago."

Carrie scooted to the edge of her own chair, and furrowed her brows. "What man? A handsome one? Are you in love already? Oh, I knew it. Just the other day I…"

Carrie's words were lost on her as the memories of the man on the platform flooded back to her.

The early spring chill had penetrated her wrap, and she'd snuggled deep into the fabric as she waited for her brother to return from his pre-season meeting at the mill. Off in the distance the train bellowed and made her sit up tall to look for the engine.

That's when she heard the man with the drawl. A voice she'd never forget. "And they are willing to pay one thousand dollars if the drive never gets to the mill. Destroy the drive, destroy Big Mountain Lumber Mill. The mill will have to pay severance, and they won't be able to recover."

The deep mumble of another man's voice sounded, but he spoke so low she couldn't make out his words. Was that a hint of a Spanish accent? She couldn't be certain.

After the man with the possible Spanish accent finished speaking, the first man continued, "I suppose the families of Bonner will be forced to find a home elsewhere?"

There was a hint of sadness in the man's words—or was it cold-hearted malice? Who were these men?

Beth's breath grew shallow. Whoever they were, they planned to destroy the mill without a care to anyone else involved. What would Simon do for work? What would the families who lived in Bonner do once the mill closed and their livelihood was torn from them? Dear Lord, she had to do something.

"Well, is it?" Carrie's voice penetrated Beth's thoughts, but the question was lost on her.

Is it what? Blast. What was the best response when faced with a question you didn't hear? "Yes."

"So the man from the platform is the man you danced with from the Mayfield's ball?"

Oh good Lord. Beth waved her had across her face. "No, no, no. I overheard two men plotting on the train platform the other day. After they finished their vile conversation, the man with the cane hobbled around the corner with a smug smile. As if he hadn't been plotting Great Mountain's downfall. A place my brother loves dearly. Not that he knew Simon works there, but that's beside the point. Someone wants to destroy the Big Mountain Lumber Mill. Imagine what would happen to all of the families if the mill were shut down. The babies would starve. The fathers would have to leave their homes and families behind to find new work, and who's to say they will? There's an evil plot afoot, and I'm the only one who can identify the culprit."

"Oh my God!" Carrie's eyes flashed in concern. "You need to tell Simon."

Beth nodded. "I will. Eventually. After I've found the man in question, I'll let Simon know. As I said before, I don't want to risk his life, or job, if I'm wrong. I'll go up and identify the culprit, and then tell him once I'm certain. My brother has done so much for me since our parents' deaths. I need to do something for him in return. If I tell him now he'll only leave me behind, and they may never find the saboteur."

Carrie slouched in a show of defeat. "Promise me you'll take care to not get into trouble. If you see the man from the platform, tell Simon. Don't go getting yourself killed."

"Of course. I'm not a fool. I have no intention of getting myself into trouble."

"But how will you pass as a man? With your curves and long hair, you're the perfect example of a woman." Carrie waved toward Beth's hair, piled high on top of her head in the latest fashion.

With a secretive smile, Beth reached into the satchel and searched through the clothing within to pull out her mother's old silver-handled scissors. She reached up to her perfect coif, a style she often worked hours on perfecting. How would she feel without the familiar weight of her hair?

Carrie eyed the sharp tool. "Please tell me you brought those to cut paper."

"Not paper." Beth forced a smile. If she was going to do this, she would do it right. Although set in her decision, she reached up to touch the silky tendrils she'd grown to love. Her best feature. She forced back the tears burning behind her eyes. The sacrifice of her hair was worth saving her brother and his job. She firmed her lips, and held the scissors out to Carrie.

"What will your nana say?" Carrie asked.

"She has taken to her bed as of late, and only leaves to visit her matron friends for tea on Tuesdays. Her maid is there with her every second of the day, so I'm of little help. I asked her if I could accompany you to visit your sister for the spring, and she agreed. I'll come home after the drive, and she'll be none the wiser. My hair will grow again, and I'll either pin it back, or I'll say your little niece Tawny cut my hair while I slept because she wanted it for her doll. Your niece is quite the troublemaker. Nana will have no trouble believing me."

"Tawny's done worse, I suppose." Carrie pinched her lips shut and stared with a calculating, but disapproving, look. Beth smiled as Carrie plucked the scissors from her hand with a sigh. She could always count on her dear friend to cave when logic and passion were at the heart of her arguments.

Two hours later, Beth sauntered down the stairs and out the door like she'd seen her brother do on many occasions. She enjoyed the feel of the trousers tight against her legs. The harsh scratch of the blue denim a vast difference from the soft cotton of her dresses—not to mention a distinct lack of a bustle strapped to her backside. The sensation of nothing but the rough work pants lent a sort of wicked freedom she could get accustomed to. The satchel swung as she walked, and she ignored the odd looks from the women passing by on their way to the shops—a few of which she recognized from the Missoula Women's Society tea three weeks past. Did they recognize her? Even if they did, she didn't care. In a few days she would be on her way to Bonner to work for the Big Mountain Lumber Mill.

Beth rushed home and snuck up the stairs leading to her room. After she made certain no one was around, she eased the door shut.

She tossed the satchel on the bed, stared into her long dressing mirror, and ruffled her short, spiky hair. Turning to her armoire, she took out an old petticoat and plopped down on the side of her bed to tear the strips of cloth that would bind her breasts. What would the gossiping ninnies of the town think of her now? Scandal followed Beth's family like a hungry dog. Not that she personally deserved the stigma, but with her parents' deaths, and Simon's debauchery whenever he was home, the town gossips painted all the Sanders in the same tainted light. An escapade like this wouldn't come as a surprise.

A knock sounded, and she scrambled to stuff the cloth under her pillow and yank on the hat from atop her dressing table. She pulled the brim over her ears. "Come in."

The door slid open, and her brother Simon peeked in.

"Hey, Lizbe. It's all set through the big bugs at the mill. I thought maybe we could go out and practice tonight. My secret's safe, right? You aren't going to tell the mayor?"

With a sigh of relief, Beth pulled her hat from her head. "It's safe for now. Practice what? And you know I hate that nickname. It makes me sound like I'm twelve."

Simon grimaced as his gaze skimmed her head. "Practice being a man. Meet me by the front door after Nana goes to bed." He studied her a moment longer, and then frowned. "Did you steal those trousers from the twelve-year-old neighbor? You look like a blacksmith's errand boy."

Beth stuck out her tongue as Simon twisted on his heels. She could hear the angry click of his boots as he disappeared down the hallway. She had no idea what he'd planned, but she wasn't about to let his reluctance or insults get in the way. Simon had no clue about the saboteur and catastrophe in the making. Eventually he'd appreciate what she'd sacrificed, after she saved his job, the lumber camp, and the entire town.

About the Author

A country girl born and bred, **Dawn Luedecke** has spent most of her life surrounded by horses, country folk, and the wild terrain of Nevada, Idaho and Montana. She enjoys writing historical and contemporary romance and spends as much time as she can working on her current manuscript. For more information visit www.dawnluedeckebooks.com.

One of the last outposts of the American West, the Montana Territory is filled with promise and adventure for those with brave souls—and open hearts...

Leader of the Timberbeasts, logger Simon Sanders's biggest problem a year ago was deciding which willing woman to seduce. But since being mauled by a cougar he's become a pariah in Missoula's social circuit—and to himself. All he wants is to hide his scarred face and disappear into the bottom of a whisky bottle. His plan is going well—until his sister's best friend, Carrie Kerr, kidnaps him and forces him to deal with his demons. If he didn't know better, Simon would swear the bossy beauty is a demon herself...

Carrie doesn't like to use the word kidnap. Unknowingly transport, perhaps. In any case, she can no longer watch Simon destroy himself in self-pity. Not since she lost her heart to him as she nursed him back to health. Now, whatever happens between them, she's determined to bring him back to the one place he swore he'd never return to, the place she's sure will reignite his spirit. But if things go awry, will she will she lose all hope for him to win back his life—much less share it with her?

Printed in the United States
by Baker & Taylor Publisher Services